Playing for Paradise

Rachel Fitzjames

ISBN: 978-1-967700-09-7 (Paperback)
ISBN: 978-1-967700-08-0 (Ebook)

Library of Congress Control Number: 2025923663

The story, all names, characters, and incidents portrayed in this production are fictitious. No identification with actual persons (living or deceased), places, buildings, and products is intended or should be inferred.

Book Cover by Maldo Designs

Editing by Melissa Rotert – Wordplay Copy & Line Edits

A note to readers

Each book in the Spruce Hill series features on-page, open-door steamy scenes, along with swearing and some degree of suspense. There may be a limited amount of on-page physical violence as well as the threat of peril facing one or more characters. Specific content in this story that might be of concern to readers includes religious trauma (historical), religious fanaticism, vandalism, and arson. As a general reassurance, no animals or children are ever harmed in my books.

For more details, please visit my website at or use the QR code below.

To the nerds, the gamers,
and everyone who marches
to their own drum.

Contents

Chapter One

MILO

THE FIRST THING I noticed about the woman was the way sunshine from the wall of windows gilded her hair with red and gold. It was a shade of dark brown that might've been unremarkable from across the ballroom if not for the way it gleamed in the light. Her head was all I could see at that moment, since the rest of her was blocked by a shifting sea of bodies.

The second thing I noticed was that she looked completely removed from everything going on around her.

Utterly alone.

Her gaze was focused downward at something in her hands, either her phone or the brightly colored paper displaying the Comic Con schedule—I'd caught glimpses of both as the crowd seethed between us, cosplayers and regular attendees interrupting my inspection with every passing second. A big pink flower held a twist of hair back from her face, with the rest tumbling in loose curls over her shoulders.

"Milo, for the love of Valhalla, just go talk to her."

My head jerked back toward my friend Olivia, who stood behind her table of fan art paintings and prints with her hands on her hips. Even though my comic shop, Dueling Dragons, was decorated with her artwork, I made it a point to purchase something at retail price when she was vending at an event.

It was the least I could do to support my best friend.

She finished cashing out a customer, then scowled as she pointed a purple-tipped finger in my direction and said, "Go. I appreciate your help during the rush, but now it's time for you to go enjoy yourself, especially if it involves scoring with the rockabilly goddess you've been staring at for the past ten minutes."

Goddess was the perfect word for the woman shimmering in the sunlight across the room.

Olivia and I had similar tastes in partners, so we'd each played wingman for the other more times than I could count—though usually I was the one running assistance and she was the one to score.

"Liv, I appreciate that, but I'm not here to pick up women."

Her scathing expression was the only sign she'd heard me over the din echoing across the hall, but before she could reply, my phone vibrated in my hand and I glanced down to see an email from my landlord, Jim.

Sorry, Milo, but a bid for the space next to DD came in just before yours. If anything changes, I'll let you know. One came in after, too, but you're second in line.

I swore under my breath, fighting down a wave of disappointment.

Dueling Dragons wasn't going to make me a millionaire, but business was steady. From comics to collectibles, board games to dice sets, the store carried something for everyone, especially as traditionally nerdy pastimes experienced a renaissance among younger generations. Online shopping bit into my margins, since I'd been too preoccupied with the actual store to get my website ready for ordering, but the residents of Spruce Hill were nothing if not loyal to our little town. If they could patronize a local shop instead of a big corporation, they usually did.

I had just enough space to run some very small event nights in the store, but after my nephew asked to have a birthday party there last summer, I'd started thinking about what I could do with an extra room or two.

The storefront next to Dueling Dragons was vacant for months thanks to some hidden damage from the previous tenant. It had been home to a cat cafe for just over a year before the owner abruptly moved to Boston. Apparently, one of the feline residents spent a good deal of time using a particular corner as a litter box. The resulting smell was bad enough that I waited—too long, unfortunately—before telling my landlord I'd take it.

I allowed myself a moment of perverse pleasure thinking about my new neighbor scrubbing the odor of ammonia from the carpet before realizing Olivia was talking to me.

"—then send her my way, got it?"

"Find your own goddess," I muttered, but I lifted my hand in a wave as I turned to seek out the woman across the room.

She was gone.

A FEW HOURS LATER, I sat at a crowded bar in the hotel lobby, swirling the dregs of a Jack and Coke while I considered all the ways my weekend trip to Comic Con could possibly get worse.

It seemed to have hit rock bottom, but I wanted to brace myself just in case.

Loving the subject matter of the event never quite translated into appreciating the crush of bodies around me for so many hours a day. I considered attending at least one convention a year to be a necessity for my business, but the thought of another day of this made me want to leave right then, even if it meant driving an hour back to Spruce Hill in the darkness of a December night.

I sat there, nursing my drink and wondering if I could get my store website launched soon enough to make up for losing the added square footage, when the soft swish of fabric alerted me to someone by my side.

"Is this seat taken?"

At the soft words, I turned and almost choked on my drink. The woman—my rockabilly goddess—regarded me with huge hazel eyes from mere inches away.

"No," I replied, more forcefully than intended. When her lips parted in surprise, I continued quickly, "No, I mean, it's all yours."

For fuck's sake. What was wrong with me?

Fortunately, she accepted the coverup with a tiny smile as she slid onto the stool beside me. Up close, details I couldn't make out across the crowd were thrown into sharp relief—the dark pink daisy clipped into her hair, the black dress with a swishy skirt boasting a dinosaur in a jeweled pink collar, a tiny floral tattoo peeking out from the neckline along her collarbone. I forced my gaze upward to the big, loose curls in her hair, the dark lashes framing her eyes, and lastly, that wide, lush mouth, as rose-tinted as the flower in her hair.

Goddess indeed. There was something ethereal about her, a certain air of self-possession, like she knew exactly who she was and would remain unapologetically true to herself, no matter what.

It was sexy as fuck.

When the bartender appeared in front of us, the woman smiled brightly at him and asked, "Could I get a glass of champagne?"

"Celebrating something?" I asked as he turned to pour it for her.

"Just a lifelong dream finally coming to fruition. Will you let me buy you a drink so you can toast with me?" She swiveled her stool toward me as she voiced the question.

I opened my mouth to politely decline, then wondered why I would ever consider refusing this beautiful woman. My weekend might be going to shit, but that didn't mean I couldn't enjoy a tiny portion of it.

"Sure."

Her lips curved upward, but it was the delight in her unusual eyes, a swirling mix of browns and golds reminding me of constellations, that captured my attention. In fact, I was so distracted I almost didn't see that she had offered me her hand. When I finally noticed it, her fingers curled slightly before straightening again as I wrapped mine around them.

"I'm Eden," she murmured.

Eden. Paradise.

I barely stopped myself from repeating it back to her just so I could savor the sound of the word on my tongue.

"This is usually the part where you'd tell me your name."

I was still holding her hand in mine, still staring at her like a buffoon. Despite my silence, she didn't laugh or make fun of me, just waited with that tiny smile on her lips. A hot flush crept up my neck.

"Milo. My name is Milo."

"Nice to meet you, Milo," Eden said as the bartender set a fresh drink in front of me. She lifted her glass and I raised mine in return. "Cheers."

"To dreams coming true."

Our glasses touched with a barely audible clink, then I watched her close her eyes and sip her champagne before I took a drink from my glass.

Her smile fell a little when she set her flute down. "You looked unhappy when I walked up. I'm sorry to rub your nose in my good mood."

"No, no, I'm fine. Just a small hiccup in my plans. Nothing a little celebration won't soothe," I assured her.

"If you're sure…"

"I'm sure, really. Is this your first Comic Con?" I asked, afraid I'd put my foot in my mouth to say something like *you're exquisite* or *spend the night with me.*

She nodded slowly. "Yes, it is. I didn't realize how big these events are, but I enjoyed wandering through the vendors."

"Find anything good?"

"I bought this flower clip," she said, touching the daisy in her hair. "I couldn't resist, since it matched my dress."

"It suits you."

Her eyes went wide. "It does? Why?"

Afraid I was going to blow it entirely, I let out a breath and said, "It's beautiful and delicate, but bold. Sweet, but it draws the eye and captures your attention."

Those rosy lips parted in surprise. "I'm not bold."

"You walked up to a stranger in a crowded bar, Eden." The shape of her name on my tongue felt sinful and so very right. "I'd say that's pretty bold."

"I guess I did," she agreed, one corner of her mouth tugging upward.

It was like watching her bloom with fresh confidence, as though I'd gifted her with something precious by giving a completely deserved compliment.

We drank, falling into silence side by side, until Eden swiveled toward me again. Her gaze dropped to the champagne bubbling in her flute, then lifted to me as she smiled. Something flashed through her eyes, a hint of vulnerability behind the renewed boldness of her expression, a crashing wave that disappeared before I could identify it.

"Are you staying here?" she asked.

I blinked. "At the bar?"

"At the hotel."

Heat washed over my face. I closed my eyes against the flare of embarrassment and muttered, "Right. The hotel. Yes, I have a room for the weekend."

Her fingers tapped at her glass for a moment, then I watched as one fingertip stroked along the stem. I swallowed a groan. No matter what Olivia hoped I might gain from an acquaintance with the woman at my side, this was probably nothing more than a friendly drink.

At just over six feet tall with a shaggy, russet kind of vibe—a full beard I kept trimmed short and curly auburn hair just a bit too long because I never had time for a haircut—I was what most women seemed to consider as a harmless big brother type. Even at a convention full of nerds, it made sense for a woman alone to seek out a friendly presence rather than braving a bar full of annoying dude bros on the prowl.

I could do that. I could be a shelter for her, a shield while she celebrated her mysterious success and then went on her way.

In fact, I was so committed to not being a dick that when Eden's hand settled on my knee, I almost choked on a sip of my drink. It wasn't aggressive, not even suggestive, not yet—just warm and tentative.

"I've never done this before," she said softly, "but Milo...I wondered if you might like to continue celebrating with me. In your room. Tonight."

Shock zipped through me, followed by lust so potent I couldn't breathe. For one brief, embarrassing second, I wondered if I was being pranked, but another flare of vulnerability appeared in her eyes as she waited for my response.

Maybe I should say no. Maybe it'd be better to enjoy the evening in the safety of this public space and then tuck her into a cab.

But if her vision of celebration could double as my consolation, was I really going to deny either of us?

"Yes, Eden," I replied, my voice low. "I'd like that very much."

The smile that split her face was radiant, but it was the way her fingers tensed on my knee that swept the breath straight out of my lungs. I set my hand over hers and she rotated her palm, twining her fingers with mine.

"Do you want to finish your drink?" she whispered.

"Not really," I whispered back, grinning.

Eden released my hand for a moment to grab some bills from her purse and laid them on the bar, then she caught my fingers again and pulled me toward the lobby.

Thinking that maybe my luck had finally turned around, I followed her to the elevators. The doors closed behind us and her lips parted for one breathless second as we stared at one another, then she moved.

Straight into me.

I caught her at the waist just as her arms went around my neck, caught her mouth as it lifted to mine. She tasted like strawberries and champagne and all my darkest fantasies. With my fingers tangled in her thick locks, I kissed her until I forgot where we were.

The elevator dinged when we reached my floor, breaking through the haze. We stepped apart, those few inches clearing my brain just enough to realize we needed to move before the doors closed again, then I led her to my room.

We paused just inside the door when she tangled her fingers in my hair and dragged me down for another searing kiss. It consumed me like I wanted to consume her—every taste, every sound, every touch—then she took my hand and led me toward the bed.

"Eden," I breathed against the soft skin of her throat. "You're sure about this?"

"Yes."

Her response was beautiful in its simplicity, forceful in the confidence behind the word, and I wanted to drop to my knees and thank my lucky stars for sending this siren into my path.

"I only have one condom," I said, though I was more than willing to make it count.

"I have plenty," she replied, scraping her nails gently up my ribs as she shoved my shirt upward until I yanked it over my head. "My cousin sneaks them into my purse every time I see her."

"Tell her I said thank you."

Her laugh turned into a gasp as I trailed my lips along the neckline of her dress, making my way around her body until I stood behind her. She sighed, swaying slightly, as I kissed the nape of her neck.

"You said you'd never done this before. You're not a—"

"No. No, I meant propositioning a stranger," she replied, tilting her head so I could run my lips up the side of her throat.

"Right." Her pulse leapt under my caress, so I said, "It's my first time doing something like this, too."

I felt her muscles ease, just the faintest release of tension, and she turned her head to smile at me over one shoulder. I'd never had a one-night stand, never slept with someone I hadn't known for virtually my whole life—the wonders of living in a small town—and knowing that we were in this together emboldened me further.

"Now, Eden, I'd like to undress you."

"About time," she teased, but a blush crept along her cheekbone before she turned to face away again.

I lowered the zipper of her dress with excruciating slowness, dragging my knuckles along the ridges of her spine before pushing it off her shoulders to reveal a frilly pink petticoat and a black strapless corset thing. The sight of them destroyed my commitment to drawing this out until she was ready to combust.

"Holy shit," I breathed. "What is this called?"

"A bustier?"

"Bustier," I repeated, committing it to memory—both the word and the sight.

"You like it?" she asked.

"It's going to haunt my fantasies for the rest of my life."

Her hazel eyes danced at my awestruck reaction when she turned around and shoved the fluffy petticoat down over her hips, revealing black satin panties that matched the top. I coasted my hands over the sleek fabric, teasing her nipples through the layers until she gasped, then she spun around again.

"There's another zipper."

This time, my patience was shot. I slid it quickly down and peeled back the sides of the garment, letting it fall to the floor as I stepped up behind her and let my hands wander across her bare skin until she turned to unzip my jeans and shoved them down. With each article of clothing we shed, I forgot more and more about the disappointing text from my landlord.

Christ, she was a gift.

"Please, Milo."

"Please what?" I asked, experimenting with varying pressure on her nipples, listening for the hitch in her breath as she arched into my touch.

"Take me to bed."

We were only a few feet from it, but I swept her into my arms and laid her against the pillows. She reached up to unclip the daisy from her hair, tossing it to the pile of clothes on the floor.

I explored her tattoos, both the flowers along her collarbone and a shooting star on one side of her ribs, tucked right under the curve of her breast. She trailed her fingertips over my beard, murmuring her approval of its softness, then through the hair on my chest and over the stomach that would never house a six-pack.

Given the way she dragged her nails over the skin there, the way she purred deep in her throat as her hand moved lower, Eden didn't seem to mind.

We spent what felt like years exploring each other. Decades, centuries, I had no way of knowing how much time passed as I teased her, tasted her, sought out every hot spot of pleasure she possessed until she begged me to fuck her.

As if I had the ability to refuse.

When I finally sank into her, one word reverberated inside my head like the strike of a gong.

Paradise.

Each gasp, each moan, each purr from her throat echoed around us like music. She was lush and round, soft as silk under my hands and lips. That vulnerability from earlier didn't convert to shyness—she knew what she wanted and didn't hesitate to ask for it.

And that chemistry between us led to the most intense orgasms I'd ever had.

As though the hotel room surrounded us in a bubble, separate from the outside world, we didn't talk about anything personal between rounds. No last names, no hometowns, no careers. It was like a dream, a fantasy where nothing existed outside of touch and taste and overwhelming sensation.

Eventually, after we used up the row of condoms she had in her purse, she fell asleep sprawled across my chest. I drew mindless shapes over her hip, nuzzling the wild mess of curls haloing her face, until I drifted off, too.

After the best night of my life, I opened my eyes to glaring sunlight that highlighted the generic decor of my hotel room. The only proof it wasn't a dream were my clothes scattered across the floor, and there, tangled with my crumpled tee, a bright pink daisy.

This time, I was the one left utterly alone.

Chapter Two

EDEN

I WOULD NEVER LOOK at a cat the same way again, not after spending three weeks trying every natural and chemical odor removal on the market in an attempt to get the smell of cat pee out of the back corner of my new store.

Ringing in the new year with cleaning products was not how I'd imagined life in my thirties.

"Why me?" I asked aloud, throwing a rag soaked with enzyme spray down on the stained carpet. "I have always been a friend to feline-kind. My dream is finally coming true, and now customers will be hit with this god-awful smell while they shop for lingerie. Perfect."

"Are you talking to yourself again?"

I leveled a glare at my cousin, Adelaide, though it melted away when I saw her brother standing behind her. A toolbelt hung low on his hips and he tossed a measuring tape up and down with one hand like it was a baseball.

"Rob! Please tell me you're here to work your construction magic on this freaking floor."

He winked at me as he playfully bumped Adelaide aside. "That's exactly why I'm here. It's going to get loud, so I suggest you ladies go get some lunch while I work. Bring me back a roast beef sub, would you?"

"Get rid of that smell and I'll provide a year's worth of subs. You're a lifesaver," I yelled over my shoulder as Addie tugged me out the back door of my new shop.

It wasn't much to look at just yet. We'd papered over the picture windows at the front to stave off curious passers-by. The clothing racks were still empty and crammed into one of the back rooms, and my stock covered every available surface in the other one. The cat pee had taken more time and attention than anticipated, much to my dismay, and I needed to see what miracles my cousin could work before Addie and I started on the decor.

There was a chance the shop would be an epic failure. I warned myself of that fact every seven minutes or so since I'd first secured the location in a cute-but-slightly-rundown plaza with street parking only. Spruce Hill was a bustling small town, but I knew some of the residents wouldn't be particularly happy about a lingerie store popping up out of nowhere.

My own parents were among those who'd hate the store's existence, if they'd known about it.

Fortunately, I was an adult. I no longer needed their permission or their approval, and they didn't live near Spruce Hill, so they'd probably never find out what I was doing. After washing their hands of me years ago, I wasn't even sure they'd care about my shame *or* salvation anymore. As far as they—and their church—were concerned, I'd been a lost cause for a long time before I left home.

I'd spent the last ten years working a variety of jobs, scrimping and saving and researching and planning for this moment—ever since getting the hell out of Dodge the minute I heard my parents discussing potential husbands to throw me at after high school. I'd thought my years of rebellion up to that point would convince them to let me go my own way, but in that moment, I realized I was wrong. They spent my entire childhood telling me I was sinful, trying to shape me into the kind of woman my mother had become, and I wasn't about to let some stranger from their church step in to "guide" me the way they wanted.

So I left home immediately after graduation, took a bus to seek out my cousins in Spruce Hill, and moved on with my life—without any contact with my parents. They might see a lingerie store as further proof I was destined for damnation, but as for me? I was ecstatic about finally opening Garden of Delights.

The shop would be more than just a retailer for size-inclusive lingerie, it would be a haven for those who needed it.

Addie and I left town together for college, rooming together in the dorms and then sharing an apartment for over a decade in the city, but she'd recently moved back to Spruce Hill to work for a rape crisis center. When I followed her here to bring this dream to life, she offered to help me out part-time with the store as well as hosting weekly support groups for survivors of sexual assault in one of the back rooms. Her friend and coworker, Monique, would be offering sex ed classes—and the occasional sex toy party, since she was a sales rep for Pleasure Players, a company that sold all kinds of fun accessories that went well with the shop's theme.

"Once Rob is done, I'll draft up the layout we talked about," Addie said as she pulled me down the sidewalk.

I'd scored a prime parking spot just in front of the shop, so we bundled up and walked down Main Street to get lunch. Parallel parking was not my forte, but hopefully my parking luck would continue. That was the only downside to this particular location—no parking lot.

However, it was also a big factor in the significantly lower rent than the other places I'd scoped out further into town.

"Do you think we'll need to replace the whole carpet?"

The calculations running through my head were not promising if that was the case. Not only would that cut into my budget for getting the store up and running, it might mean weeks more in delays.

The rent was low, but not *that* low. Every day I spent waiting would cut into my savings—every dollar I wasn't earning

with the shop was one that might mean the difference between affording my own place and having to accept Adelaide's offer to share the loft above her parents' garage, which
she'd moved into when she returned to town.

We'd lived together long enough for me to value my new
one-bedroom apartment in Spruce Hill, even if it was on the
dumpy side. Finally moving forward meant I did *not* want to
take a step back.

"Nope," Addie replied brightly. "I've got it all sorted,
don't worry. We'll position the counter so it hides that corner. Rob found a scrap of that same carpeting anyway. It'll
be totally disguised."

I adored my cousin, and one of my favorite things about
her was the way she spoke about anything she was invested
in. Her voice was as effervescent as her personality, like the
embodiment of pink bubblegum. With pale blonde hair
to my dark brown and her extra four inches in height, we
didn't look related at first glance, but she was the one who'd
introduced me to pin-up style makeup and retro dresses. We
were as close as siblings, without the bickering.

Or, in the case of my actual brother, without the shared
religious trauma that made communication pretty much
impossible.

"My mom has been talking up the store to all of her friends,"
Addie continued. "You're probably going to be swamped with
middle-aged housewives right off the bat. I told her she doesn't

get commission for those sales, but she doesn't care. She's like a one-woman ad campaign."

A fond smile tugged at my lips. "I hope she knows how much I appreciate her support. And yours."

Addie winked and formed a heart with her hands. "Love you, babe."

Growing up, Addie and Rob had been my best friends and greatest champions, even though I didn't move to Spruce Hill for good until six months ago. My cousins and their parents, Aunt Jocelyn and Uncle Mike, kept me from floundering through tumultuous times at home when I was a kid. Even now, with the store, they were my biggest cheerleaders, always ready to come to the rescue.

Someday, I hoped to return the favor.

We ordered our sandwiches and sat at a little table in the front corner to eat them, mostly because I couldn't stomach the thought of taking them back to the store until Rob had proven successful in his endeavors. The ammonia smell was enough to put me off food completely.

After my first bite, my gaze caught on a woman standing on the sidewalk across the street, staring at the cafe like she could see straight into my soul. She was dressed like my mother—a long denim skirt paired with a blouse that covered every inch of skin from neck to wrist—and her expression an all-too-familiar mix of righteous hellfire and condemnation.

I froze, my heart plummeting into my now-queasy stomach, until my cousin's voice broke my concentration. When I glanced outside again, the woman was gone. Maybe she'd just been a figment of my imagination.

Just thinking about my parents had me jumping at shadows.

"So, two weeks until the grand opening?" Addie asked around a mouthful of tuna salad.

Shaking off the weird moment, I very pointedly finished chewing before responding. "If all goes well, yes. Is that enough time to get the word out?"

"Absolutely. Eden, you're going to knock this out of the park. I feel it in my bones. Monique's already got two parties booked, I have at least a handful of ladies signed up for my first group meeting date on the calendar, and you know everybody who walks through that door is going to buy something. I've seen the stuff you ordered, it's all *hot.*"

I knew all of that, but it was much more convincing hearing it out of my cousin's mouth. "You're right. It'll be great."

"And you'll still be able to get to badass class?"

Choking on my bite of sandwich when a laugh burst out of me, I nodded. I'd started taking Brazilian Jiu-Jitsu several months ago, partly because a friend of ours had been mugged during a girls' weekend trip to the city and partly because I needed an outlet while my dream of opening the store was still up in the air, ephemeral and just out of reach.

I'd enjoyed the four-week session so much that I kept at it, even when I had to trade working shifts at their front desk in order to afford classes.

"Yeah, but I'm taking some time off before and after we open, just until we get into a good flow. I still think you should join me at class when I go back. You'd like it."

"I do like the idea of being as badass as you," she mused.

For the next fifteen minutes, I let Adelaide's chatter drift over me, knocking concerns like peed-upon carpets and profit margins straight out of my head. This was my dream, and it was finally coming true.

"How should we celebrate?" Addie asked.

My brain short-circuited as memories of that night at Comic Con flashed through my mind, image after tantalizing image, reminders of the last time I celebrated my success.

Milo's hands on my body, his mouth against my skin, the thread of command woven through his deep voice as he drove us both to new heights the minute I gave myself completely over to him.

Then my idiotic decision to run away instead of facing the fact that I'd finally done something impetuous by approaching a stranger for a hookup—and the immediate regret that followed when the door clicked shut behind me. I'd panicked and snuck out, fighting the shame my parents had fought so hard to instill in me.

Maybe they hadn't failed as badly as they'd thought, because the flush of reproach that coated my skin when I woke up in his arms sent nausea crawling up my throat, choking me with years of reminders that I was worth nothing in their eyes, behaving as I had.

No matter how many years I'd spent embracing my sexuality, fighting against their bullshit, it still managed to sneak past my defenses at times.

And every time, it strengthened my resolve to fight even harder in the future.

"Hello? Eden?"

With a jerk, my gaze focused on my cousin, whose expression had grown soft. "Sorry. Lost my train of thought."

Addie's blonde brows lifted high on her forehead. "Did you? Or were you thinking about your Viking?"

We never kept secrets from one another, not for longer than a day or two—I regretted revealing this particular secret, however. Did my cousin really need to know that I'd made the first and possibly *only* wild, impulsive decision of my life the night I stumbled upon a comic book convention? Should I maybe have limited the details about the tall, auburn-haired man who'd provided more orgasms than I'd ever had in one night?

"Too late," Addie muttered.

I glared. "Are you reading my mind now?"

"When you're clearly questioning life choices that brought you immeasurable pleasure? Yes."

"I'm not questioning that choice," I countered. "I'm regretting telling you about it because I can sense that you are never ever going to let me live it down."

"Live it down? Eden, I've spent all of our lives wishing for you to find true happiness. I'm not teasing you for your nerd-boy hookup, I'm just baffled that you didn't at least get his phone number. Or last name. Or literally any identifying information so you could hook up with him again in the future!"

I sighed, trying not to let my too-astute cousin hear the echo of heartbreak in the sound. "Well, I didn't, and it's too late. Yes, he was sweet and attentive and funny, but I'll probably never see him again."

Her big brown eyes locked on my face, but she reached over and took my hand without speaking. I returned her squeeze and forced off the melancholy before it could settle too firmly about my shoulders.

"Celebration. Right. My place, cupcakes from that food truck lady, wine from the place we toured in Geneva, and at least a hundred of those red pepper feta cups you brought to Christmas Eve at your parents' place last year?"

"Oof, you like labor-intensive celebrations, huh? What if we set that aside for a bit and go for drinks at The Mermaid to celebrate your first day? I promise I'll make you more feta cups sometime soon."

I rolled my eyes, but she was right, easy would be more relaxing for us both. "Deal."

"Let's get this roast beef back to my brother and see if he managed to succeed where all of the cleaning supplies in Spruce Hill have failed," Addie suggested.

Since I appreciated her letting the subject of my Comic Con Viking go without further discussion, I flashed a grin as I grabbed the paper bag containing Rob's sub. The two of them were miracle workers in their own right. If Addie had faith in her brother's ability to save my store from the curse of cat pee, then I would, too.

It was time to set aside regrets and face the future head on.

"What did you think of the window display ideas I sent you?" I asked as we strolled back down the sidewalk toward the shop. "Good enough for a grand opening?"

"I want one of everything, so I'm going to say yes, it's perfect. I'm so proud of you, Eden. This is going to be amazing."

"Yeah," I said quietly, and she elbowed me in the ribs.

"Seriously, babe. A place where every shopper of every size and shape can find something sexy, a safe space for those who need it, an opportunity for everyone to learn and grow in their sexuality—this is big, Eden. Epic. And it's your dream, the one you've worked your ass off to accomplish. You should be proud of yourself, too."

I elbowed her back, too moved to voice my reaction to her support. This *was* big, and dammit, I was already proud of all I had accomplished.

And if I wished I had a tall, sweet Viking to help me celebrate each future success, well, I shoved that twinge of regret deep down into the recesses of my mind.

Chapter Three

MILO

"UNCLE MILO! DID YOU see the naked lady shop going in next door?"

I was reading through emails about my newest ad campaign and twirling the daisy hair clip I'd turned into a fidget toy when my nephew burst into the shop. Baffled, I blinked as he hurtled through the store to join me.

It wasn't unusual for him to make dramatic and puzzling proclamations when he arrived at Dueling Dragons after school two days a week, but this one was particularly confusing.

"The what?"

Carter tossed his backpack to the floor, spilling crumpled papers and a handful of colored pencils out onto the dingy carpet. A carbon copy of my oldest brother, Maverick, Carter was tall and lean with dark, tousled curls that never quite looked under control. He'd sprouted up in height over the summer, right around his tenth birthday, but even his gangly limbs couldn't detract from the charming grin he'd inherited straight from his dad.

Like the rest of the Davies men, Carter had also inherited eyes that could only be described as gray. In some lights, they might appear blue or green, but as Carter leveled a solemn stare in my direction, his were the shade of slate.

Carter might look like his dad, but he was a nerd through and through, just like his Uncle Milo.

In fact, Carter was the best advertisement I could get. His rave reviews about Dueling Dragons had brought in more customers in recent years than most of my promotional efforts, though I hoped my new ads would generate more traffic. Still, Carter's Dungeons & Dragons-themed birthday party was solely responsible for a dozen hefty sales and two more parties booked for the coming months.

I forced myself not to fall down the rabbit hole of lamenting the loss of the space next door, even if those parties could have held twice as many kids with just one of the back rooms over there, and focused on my nephew.

"Naked ladies. I saw them. The door was propped open," he informed me.

The new tenant had papered over the windows of the shop next door like whatever they were doing inside was a state secret. I'd heard a variety of sounds coming from the other side of the wall, starting with creative but muffled swearing, then power tools, then thumping and hammering and bursts of feminine laughter.

For a second, I wondered if my landlord had rented the place to a sex shop instead of me, but it seemed unlikely. We weren't in the best part of the major shopping drag through Spruce Hill, but this was still Main Street. Those "adult video" stores were almost always located in more remote areas outside of town—I figured there must be some kind of zoning laws at play.

But shit. Surely Jim would've mentioned it if a porn store was going in next door?

"Were the naked ladies mannequins, buddy?" I asked my nephew.

With a mouth full of the granola bar Maverick had packed for an afternoon snack, Carter shrugged and said, "Yeah, but they were wearing these...*things.*"

Jesus. *Was* it a sex shop? My mind raced with the potential items he might have seen—strap-ons? Harnesses? Maverick was going to kill me if his kid let this slip at school tomorrow.

"What kind of things, Carter? Outfits? Costumes? Uh, equipment?"

Carter's brow furrowed like I was speaking Latin. "Um. Like, lacy nightgown things, mostly. There was a shiny bathrobe, too."

"Lingerie," I said slowly. "Is that what you mean?"

"Yeah, lingerie! I forgot the word. There were ladies in, like, old-fashioned clothes painting the walls inside, so all the mannequins were in the middle of the room."

I ruffled his dark hair, relieved that Maverick wouldn't have to explain anything more than sexy nighties. My oldest brother had been a single dad since Carter was two months old, when his girlfriend took off for greener pastures, and he'd been on plenty of dates over the years—I would know, since I usually pulled babysitting duty—but not once had he brought a woman home to meet Carter.

For all my nephew knew, those lacy nightgowns he saw next door were a woman's normal pajamas. I was content to leave it at that.

Though I hoped I'd be there to bear witness to my brother's explanations.

After he finished the granola bar, Carter pulled out his homework and we settled into our usual routine of alternately solving math problems, quizzing spelling words, and cracking jokes. I didn't mind running the store alone when my part-time employee, Rafael, wasn't working, but I loved the two afternoons each week when Carter was there with me. He spent the other two with our middle brother, Mark, who owned a bath and body product shop across town. Maverick got out of work early on Fridays to pick him up from school so they could have an afternoon together.

Once homework was complete, we were free to focus on the fun stuff—which, fortunately, was how my nephew viewed tidying up racks of comic books, organizing action figures and vinyl collectibles, and choosing which magnets and keychains would get the place of honor on the countertop display.

That day's winners were a series of geese in superhero costumes, along with some of Carter's favorite Nintendo characters. We were arranging them when Mav arrived to pick Carter up after work, still dressed in a charcoal suit and burgundy dress shirt. His eyebrows were raised in disbelief.

"Why is your car halfway down the block, man?"

I growled in annoyance. "Because someone's been parking in my spot. Every day now, for weeks, no matter what time I show up to open the store."

"But...that's your spot. You've parked there for as long as you've owned this place," Maverick sputtered.

Carter paused in shoving his homework haphazardly back into his bag to say, "Uncle Milo's name isn't on it."

"Yes, thank you for that wisdom, my son," Maverick replied solemnly. "Maybe you should leave a note on the car."

"This isn't middle school. No offense, Carter."

"None taken," my nephew said brightly.

Maverick looked almost more put out about the parking situation than I was—and I was seriously annoyed. Everyone knew that was my spot, from other shop owners to residents who'd never set foot in the shop. I'd almost managed to beat the little red SUV to it a few days ago, but it pulled in ten seconds ahead of me and I had to watch the parking spot thief in action.

I hadn't, however, caught sight of the driver, since I was busy tracking down an open spot thirty yards away. By the time I got to Dueling Dragons, there was no one in sight.

"When the hell is the place next door opening anyway? It's been weeks, hasn't it?" Maverick asked.

"No idea."

"It's a naked lady store!"

I rolled my eyes as Carter's exclamation drowned out my response. "It sounds like it's a lingerie shop. I haven't met the owner yet, but I bet that's who's parking in my spot."

"If it's one of the ladies I saw painting in there today, the owner is pretty. There were two of them, both pretty. Maybe you guys should go introduce yourselves," Carter suggested. "Are you sure you don't want to leave a note on the car? You could put your phone number on it."

Maverick and I exchanged a look over my nephew's head. Carter was anything but subtle when it came to trying to set either of us up at every opportunity. While my big brother had somehow managed to avoid falling into any of the traps his son laid, I'd gotten stuck having dinner with the kid's math teacher.

She was lovely, but not exactly a comic book fan. There hadn't been a second date.

"Buddy," Maverick began.

Carter cut him off, saying, "I know, I know. Uncle Milo met the love of his life at Comic Con and we need to give him time to get over her before he tries again."

My jaw dropped at his matter-of-fact recounting of my love life. "I beg your pardon?"

The words were quiet, but both my brother and my nephew froze, staring at one another with wide eyes in an attempt to

convey some unspoken sentiment that I could read all too clearly.

"Jesus, Mav," I muttered. "First, she was not the love of my life. We met *one time.* I don't even know her last name. Second, seriously? I confide in you and you reveal all my secrets to the ten-year-old?"

"It just slipped out, man, I'm sorry. You were sulking for an entire week," Maverick replied.

His voice was soft, like he could cushion the blow, but I shook my head as each word plunged into my body like a blade.

"Right. No, it's fine. Milo Davies shoots and misses. That's big news around here—oh wait, nope, it's just more of the same old story."

"Don't be like that, man."

"Doesn't matter. See you Wednesday, Carter," I said, laying a hand on the top of his head. "I have a shipment coming in tomorrow. You can help me put out some new stock."

Carter stared up at me, his gray eyes troubled. "Sorry, Uncle Milo."

"It's fine, buddy. Go on, have a good night, you two."

"I'm sorry, Milo," Maverick echoed.

He wasn't just apologizing for blabbing about the pathetic state of my love life to his kid. Maverick knew all too well what it was like to think you found something special and have it disappear from your life without a backward glance. I nodded, holding his gaze until he saw that I'd forgiven him.

It wasn't his fault I'd let a good thing walk away so easily.

With a lift of his hand, Maverick led Carter out of the store and I was alone once again, staring down at the daisy resting on top of my book.

Maybe it was time to move on.

T HE LITTLE RED SUV was in my parking spot when I got to work the next morning, its bumper sporting some stickers that unfortunately indicated I might actually like its owner—one read *Talk Nerdy to Me,* another was a watercolor Triforce symbol from *The Legend of Zelda.* Interestingly, the last sticker was for a local martial arts studio.

Still, annoyance thrummed through my veins as I parked even further from the store than the day before.

By the time I got inside, breathless from the muttered expletives I'd cast upon the parking spot thief, I was met with even more frustration when I found the alarm on the back door screaming at me. It was a miracle no one nearby had reported the blaring sound, but the doors were still locked and nothing appeared to have been tampered with, so I reset the device, updated the code, and set a reminder on my phone to be sure the alarm was engaged every evening when I left.

Maybe daydreaming about seeing Eden again had me so distracted that I forgot to set it the night before.

I spent half the day sorting through boxes of new comics in the limited space I had behind the counter, silently cursing whoever had moved into the bigger space next door, cat pee or not. Hell, with those extra rooms at the back, I could have had an event room *and* a room for out of print or vintage comics.

I could have done any number of things with that extra square footage, but I'd missed out. Small, intimate parties were more fun anyway, weren't they?

The bell over the door jingled and I straightened from a crouch to see a pretty blonde in high-waisted jeans and a red plaid cropped shirt enter the store, rubbing her upper arms against the chill of the January air outside. I froze, thinking about Carter's comment—*two ladies in old-fashioned clothes.* I hadn't been sure what he meant, but now that she stood before me, I was suddenly certain she was one of the women Carter saw painting next door.

Fuck. It was a painful reminder of how Eden had stood before me in a petticoat and that bustier. The memory squeezed around my heart like a vise.

"Hi there," I called, offering a smile as her dark eyes landed on me. "Let me know if I can help you find anything."

"Thanks," she replied. Her voice was bright and bubbly as she moved toward a display of vinyl collectible figures.

I debated whether it was rude to return to unpacking boxes with a customer in the store. Even after four years of owning Dueling Dragons, there were times I felt like I was brand new to customer service. When the woman disappeared from view,

I decided I'd stay standing and enter the inventory I'd already unpacked into my spreadsheet.

A few minutes later, she wandered to the counter with a vinyl collectible of Aang from Avatar: The Last Airbender in hand.

"Just this?" I asked as I scanned the barcode.

"Yeah, my godson's birthday is coming up. You have some great stuff. I'm sorry to say this is the first time I've been here." She paused, bright red lips parting when they landed on my name tag. A strange look crossed her face before she added, "Milo, is it?"

I smiled briefly and turned the card reader toward her for a signature. "Yep, that's me."

"Hey, do you know if there are any comic conventions nearby? My godson is getting really into cosplay lately, I wondered if there was anywhere I could take him."

"You just missed the one in the city last month, but there are quite a few within a couple hours of Spruce Hill." I handed her a business card. "If you check the website, there's a link to events around the area."

Her smile was blinding. "Fabulous. Thank you, Milo. It was very nice meeting you."

Before I could ask her name or verify whether she was the owner of the shop going in next door, she had flounced out the door, her blonde curls bouncing in her wake.

"What just happened?" I asked the empty store as I stared after her.

I replayed the entire interaction in my head, though she'd barely spent five minutes in the store, then shook my head and forced myself to get back to work.

Maybe mysteries were just the new fact of life around here.

Chapter Four

EDEN

Things moved quickly after Rob worked his magic on the corner of the floor. I knew whatever he'd done involved replacing the subfloor and a chunk of carpet, but it looked good as new, cost me nothing thanks to my cousin's insistence that it was a gift, and the wretched odor was officially gone.

Since Addie had declared herself my assistant, she helped out with almost every aspect of getting the store ready to open. On the Tuesday before our grand opening weekend, she strolled in with an Avatar: The Last Airbender figure in hand and an unconvincingly innocent smile on her face.

"What? What is that look?" I demanded.

"Nothing, just stopped next door to get a gift for Anna's son, Dylan. Have you been over there yet?"

"No," I said absently, adjusting the position of one of the mannequins in the front window.

Addie propped a hand on her hip when I glanced up at her. "You're coming with me to Dylan's party, aren't you? You should go over and get him a gift, support local businesses. Besides, you really ought to introduce yourself to the other shop owners on the block."

Since that was already on my to-do list, I held up my hands in surrender. "Yes, ma'am. I'll do it tomorrow. I want all of this ready to roll before we take down the paper for Friday."

"Of course," Addie murmured.

Something in her tone struck me as odd, but she turned her focus to helping me with the display and the thought went straight out of my head. In the end, though, the window displays looked absolutely immaculate. We'd decided to play up the Garden of Eden theme, draping garlands of ivy and flowers around mannequins dressed in some of my favorite items in coordinating colors—a mint nightgown with floral lace straps and a slit up to the hip, an emerald negligée set with pink rosettes across the bust and a matching robe, and a sheer black bodysuit with gold sequined snakes creeping up the ribs.

And in the center, a corset of apple-red satin with matching panties, both covered in creeping silver vines.

I just hoped my shoppers would love the items as much as I did.

By the next morning, my suspicions returned in full force when Addie called to remind me *again* about Dylan's gift. My cousin was up to something, I just had no idea what.

"I heard you the first time, Adelaide."

I had my phone trapped between my cheek and shoulder as I started attempt number three at gift-wrapping the largest box I had on hand. The last thing we needed was for me to embarrass myself in front of a customer as I struggled with a tape dispenser or the baby blue satin ribbon that matched the store logo perfectly.

"I just don't want you to forget. Dylan is a sweet kid and he *really* wants that graphic novel. It was the only one on the shelf yesterday. I'm kicking myself for not buying it."

"I told you I'd go over as soon as I finish this. Remind me again why I didn't go with those cute gift bags instead? No matter how pretty it is, this ribbon is a giant pain in my ass, Addie."

My darling cousin laughed at my pain. "I have to go, Eden, I've got a client coming. The ribbons are a nice personal touch. Any slouch can throw something in a gift bag. Text me later. I need to know if you can get that book or if I have to go search for it in the city. I want to focus on the grand opening this weekend!"

"Yeah, okay," I muttered. "Go on. I'll get the book, then I'll come back and master these stupid ribbons if it's the last thing I do. If you don't hear from me, assume this handy little ribbon dispenser strangled me."

"Ciao, babe!"

Addie ended the call before I could voice a goodbye, so I tossed the phone aside and finished tying an ugly, uneven bow. I let out a growl at the sight of it and shoved the empty box across the counter before grabbing my purse.

"Bossy, bossy, bossy," I grumbled, still uncertain why Addie couldn't have popped back over to the shop next door yesterday afternoon, when she suddenly decided her godson needed that book. I barely even knew the kid, but Addie insisted that I attend the party in a few weeks as her plus-one so she wouldn't be bored out of her mind.

Given how much help she'd been in setting up Garden of Delights, I caved. I could sacrifice a few minutes to buy a book.

I let myself out the back door, following the sidewalk around the corner of the building. Since the front door was now covered with the same blank newsprint paper adorning the windows, it was the easiest way in and out of the shop.

Friday couldn't come soon enough. I was looking forward to finally seeing the sun shining in the front of the building. Dreary gray was just not uplifting, no matter how many ugly purple bows you stuck on it.

The bitter cold of winter was depressing enough—some sunlight would work wonders.

As I rounded the corner onto Main Street, I caught sight of a piece of paper stuck underneath the windshield wiper of my car.

"Shit," I whispered, hoping it wasn't a parking ticket or a note that someone had hit the vehicle. Surely I would've heard a fender bender from inside the shop? I rushed over and pulled the paper loose, then wished I'd ignored it.

It was a Bible tract about the nature of sin.

I glanced wildly around the street, expecting to see someone staring, someone judging, but the pedestrians nearby all seemed cheerful and focused on either their destinations or their phone screens as they moved down the sidewalks. There was no sign of anyone out of place, not like the woman I'd seen from inside the sandwich shop the other day.

Not a long denim skirt to be seen, only the normal array of jeans and puffy winter jackets.

Crumpling the piece of paper in my hand, I tossed it into one of the cute barrel-shaped trash cans the town lined the street with and forced myself to ignore the pit in my stomach.

The store next to mine was called Dueling Dragons. It looked like a combination of comic books and gaming, and I had yet to venture inside. Really, if I was honest with myself, the comic thing reminded me of my idiocy in sneaking out of Milo's hotel room without leaving a note.

Since I was still berating myself for that decision, I didn't exactly need to pile on more reminders.

Window paint depicting various superheroes covered the front door and I wandered in just in time to hear a kid say, "I told you, you should put your name on the parking spot."

"It's *mine*. Everyone knows I've parked there since I opened the store. I shouldn't have to put my name on it."

"Do you want me to key the car?" the kid asked, sounding hopeful.

"Jesus, Carter, no. Don't do that. Ever, okay?"

I took a few steps deeper into the store to see the kid sitting on the counter, his Converse-clad feet swinging back and forth. Dark hair tumbled over his forehead and his mouth dropped open when he caught sight of me.

"It's one of the ladies from the naked shop!" he exclaimed.

Naked shop?

From behind him, the man I'd heard speaking rose slowly from a crouch that had hidden him from view, and all the breath left my lungs.

It was *him*. Milo. Comic Con Milo. Red-bearded Viking Milo. Sweet, attentive, funny Milo.

"Eden?" he said softly.

"I...um. Hi, Milo." Stupidly, I gave a little wave as heat flooded my cheeks.

"You guys know each other?"

We both tore our gazes away from each other to look at the kid on the counter. Milo, thank the powers of the universe, saved me from trying to answer that.

"Yeah, Carter, we do. Look, in the storage closet, there's a copy of *Absolute Batman* in one of the boxes at the back. Think you could go find it for me?"

"Sure thing, Uncle Milo," the boy said as he hopped down and rounded the counter, disappearing into a hallway at the back of the store.

I continued to stare at Milo, standing before me in a Superman t-shirt that clung to the strong shoulders I had kissed and clutched and remembered until the image was seared into my brain. His cheeks had gone as red as I was sure mine must've been, though the color was only just visible over his auburn beard.

When I finally convinced myself to break the awkward silence, it wasn't to apologize for leaving or ask how he'd been or beg for a repeat of that night at the hotel. It wasn't even to voice the stupid question of *what are you doing here in Spruce Hill* that ricocheted through my head.

What came out of my mouth was, "Parking trouble?"

His lips twitched and those eyes, just as soft and inviting as they had been at the bar that night, twinkled at me. "Let me guess. You drive a red SUV?"

"Yes," I whispered.

To my surprise, given the irritation evident in the parking conversation I'd interrupted, Milo threw back his head and laughed. The sound curled around me, coaxing more memories to the forefront of my mind.

"Of course it would be you," he said, shaking his head as he leaned his hands against the counter. "What are you doing here?"

"I'm opening a store," I replied. "Though it's not a naked shop, strictly speaking. Lingerie, actually. Kind of the opposite of naked."

Oh, god. The grin that lit his face made me want to climb across the counter and kiss him. Instead, I stood there like an idiot, frozen in place, waiting. Waiting for him to get angry, waiting for him to yell or throw out cutting comments about how I'd snuck out of his bed like a coward.

Milo did neither, just walked slowly around the counter and came toward me at that same careful pace, like he thought I might spook.

"You live in Spruce Hill?" he asked softly.

I shook my head to clear the cobwebs and saw his face fall, but it brightened when I said, "Yes, I do now. I grew up near Binghamton, but my cousins live here. We're close, so I moved to town about six months ago from Rochester."

"Cousins," he repeated, cocking his head when he paused a few feet away from where I stood. "The blonde?"

"That'd be Adelaide, yes."

"She came in yesterday. I thought it was weird, the way she reacted when she saw my name tag."

My brows shot downward as I realized just how my cousin had played me. Even in my suspicion, I'd never expected *this* to be her endgame.

"That conniving little sneak," I whispered. "She told me I had to come get some graphic novel for her godson's party—a party I had no intention of attending before yesterday, since I barely know the kid. She set me up."

Milo's teeth flashed when he smiled. "Remind me to thank her. I can't believe you've been next door this whole time. And that *you're* the parking spot thief."

"I'm just glad the kid didn't key my car."

"That's my nephew, Carter. He talks a villainous game, but he's a good kid. I don't think you were in any real danger."

"Milo, I—"

My apology cut off abruptly when someone entered the store behind me, exclaiming, "Shit, man, you're parked half a mile away! Oh, sorry, I didn't know anyone else was here."

Milo's eyes narrowed and I turned to see an absurdly handsome man with long black curls pulled into a ponytail. He was bearded, as tall as Milo, and had a killer smile. That distracted me for a solid three seconds before I realized he had the same gray eyes as Milo and his nephew.

"Hi, I'm Milo's brother, Maverick," the man said, stretching a hand toward me.

"Eden," I replied as I shook it.

Maverick looked over my shoulder at his brother. "Eden," he echoed.

"Yes, this is Eden. You can drop her hand now, Mav."

I glanced toward Milo, surprised by the low growl in his voice as he said it. He wasn't looking at me, though—the brothers had locked eyes and some kind of silent communication was passing between their steely depths. Since my relationship with my brother was anything but typical, I wondered if this was a learned behavior or something innate.

"Dad! You're early!"

The nephew, Carter, came sprinting out from behind the counter. Now that I'd met his father, the resemblance was clear. It was harder to compare the two adults because of the difference Milo's auburn hair made, but needless to say, they were clearly an attractive family.

Carter paused before passing me, straightened his shoulders, and stuck out a hand. "I'm Carter."

As I had with his father, I clasped his hand. "Hi Carter, I'm Eden."

"That's a pretty name. How do you know Uncle Milo?"

"Oh, um..."

Maverick only cocked his head like he was fascinated to hear my answer, but Milo cut in, "We met at an event."

"Oh?" his brother murmured. "Comic Con, maybe?"

Another growl from Milo's throat thrummed over my skin, followed swiftly by a hot, uncomfortable flush of embarrassment.

The brother knew. They'd talked about me.

It was no different from me telling Addie, but sudden panic clawed at my throat at the realization that someone other than my cousin knew I'd spent the night with this man, knew that I'd propositioned a stranger at a hotel bar and had run away the next morning without even getting his last name.

A stranger who owned the shop next door to mine, who lived in the same town, who I'd probably be seeing nearly daily for the foreseeable future.

It was more than I could handle just then, the rush of shame I thought I'd long since moved past. Oily and familiar, it crept up my throat until it threatened to choke me.

"I have to go," I said abruptly.

Every social nicety flew out of my head as I spun on my heel and hightailed it out the door, brushing past Maverick while Milo called my name. I lifted a hand in farewell, called out a quick apology, and fled.

Again.

Chapter Five

MILO

"**D**ammit, Mav," I ground out.

The only thing saving my brother from my elbow in his gut was the stricken look on his face. And maybe his son, who was staring with wide eyes at us both.

"Did I say something wrong?" Carter asked.

"No, buddy, it was me." Maverick grimaced. "I'm sorry, Milo. I didn't think."

Even if it was on the tip of my tongue to snap at him, this wasn't his fault. The shock of seeing her again, my utter delight that she wasn't a figment of my imagination, and my crushing disappointment at her departure blended into nausea roiling in my gut. I was worried about what this might mean for me and Eden. For the second time, she ran away, and this time I couldn't really blame her.

But I saw the way her eyes, that beautiful amalgam of gold and brown, went molten at the growl of frustration I couldn't quite hold back. The way her lips parted and her cheeks flushed, just as they had when we were in bed together.

Right before her horrified expression turned to stone and she bolted.

"I'll take care of it," I said quietly.

Maverick shoved a hand through his hair. "Maybe I can smooth things over."

"I said I'll take care of it and I will."

Something in my tone must have gotten through my brother's thick skull, because he and Carter just studied me in silence for another minute. I couldn't take my eyes off the shop door, staring out toward the busy street like Eden might reappear at any second.

"It's okay," I said, managing a smile for Carter's sake. "She wasn't expecting to see me and I think she was a little overwhelmed."

"Right. Buddy, grab your backpack. Milo, if you need anything," Maverick murmured, "I'm here. I swear I'll make it up to you. And her."

I managed a nod, ruffled Carter's hair when he passed, and waited until they were gone before moving toward the door. The sidewalk was empty when I stepped outside, and the red SUV I now knew belonged to Eden was gone from the prized parking spot on the street out front. I turned to look at Eden's shop, but behind the papered windows and door, I could tell the lights were off inside.

What were the chances? How impossibly unlikely was it that we would become neighbors when I'd been so sure I would never see her again?

I thought back to how I'd been drawn to her across the hotel ballroom, how she'd sought my company at the bar, how gutted I felt at finding she'd disappeared after an unforgettable night together.

Then I thought about the look on her face when she first saw me behind the counter today, her eyes shimmering brighter than ever thanks to the green blouse she wore, the unmistakable flare of hope within them as her surprise melted away.

I recognized it because the same parade of emotions had marched through my chest.

Something else followed, though. I saw it as I came toward her, an uncertainty that was nothing like those hints of vulnerability at the bar that night. She looked like she expected me to rip into her, like she was bracing for it. Who had made her expect anger instead of forgiveness?

I didn't like that, not one bit.

When I smiled and moved closer, though, she'd softened, loosened up, looked more like the woman I'd had in my hotel bed for far too short a time. Maverick and his impeccably bad timing had interrupted whatever she was trying to say.

God, I hoped it was something like, "Milo, I want to see you again," or, "Milo, leaving without getting your number was the stupidest thing I've ever done."

The threat that it might have been more along the lines of, "Milo, what happened was a mistake and we should never speak of it again," almost knocked me on my ass.

Sighing, I went back into Dueling Dragons to start closing for the night. I needed a plan, preferably one that would lead to spending more time with Eden. I wouldn't invite my brother into my plotting, but Eden's cousin...that might be an avenue worth exploring. The woman was bright enough to put two and two together when she came into the shop and invested enough to send Eden to my door.

Adelaide could be just what I needed to ensure I got a chance to have a real conversation with Eden—preferably *before* she ground my heart into dust by admitting our night together didn't mean as much to her as it had to me.

"**P**SST! CAN I TALK to you?" I whisper-yelled the words from my back door as Adelaide rounded the building, headed toward the door to Eden's shop.

Her immediate smile was radiant. "Of course."

I peeked around the heavy steel door to make sure Eden wasn't watching, then gestured for Adelaide to precede me into the dim hallway at the back of Dueling Dragons. There wasn't much of a resemblance between the cousins, though they were each gorgeous in a very different way and both of them dressed like pin-up girls from the 1950s. Adelaide was tall and slender in contrast to Eden's dramatic curves, but she had that same regal assurance about her.

Somehow, I couldn't imagine this woman looking alone in a crowd the way Eden had.

"Sorry, watch your step," I muttered as we moved around the piles of boxes that lined the hall.

"You need a bigger space," she replied, then her head snapped up. "Oh, shit. You were one of the other interested parties, weren't you? The landlord said he had a couple applications from other people and needed a decision quickly."

I sighed. "Is there any chance of you not mentioning that to Eden?"

Adelaide wrinkled her nose at me. "I'd like to say yes, but she's a super sleuth and we don't keep secrets from each other. I won't go blabbing to her, that's all I can promise. If—no, *when*—she figures it out herself, I'll have to confirm."

That shouldn't have made me even more desperate to get to know Eden, but it did. I wanted to see her mind at work, get to know her true self as well as I'd gotten to know her body in our hours together.

I needed to know if I had a chance at that.

"You're really into her," she mused, her gaze searching my expression. It was clear she was adept at uncovering secrets herself.

"I am, yes."

"She regretted it," Adelaide said.

The words plunged into my gut so forcefully, I almost doubled over. Her shoulders jerked and she held up her hands as she frantically shook her head.

"No, no. Jesus, sorry. She regretted leaving like that, I mean. Regretted not getting your number or saying good-bye."

The pain receded fast enough to give me whiplash. "She did?"

"I don't like talking behind her back," Adelaide said gently, "but you certainly made an impression. Getting the shop ready to open has distracted her from dwelling on it quite as constantly, but...yeah. She's not a one-night stand type of gal. To be honest, I was shocked as shit when she told me about it. I think she just freaked out that morning and convinced herself that leaving was the right thing for both of you."

"It wasn't," I said firmly.

"I'm glad you think that, because she's been beating herself up over it for weeks now."

"I think she was embarrassed yesterday when she was here, and she ran off before I could smooth things over. I need to talk to her. Alone. Do you think you can help make that happen?"

Adelaide smiled slowly, looking for all the world like her dearest wish had just come true. "Oh, yes. What time are you done with work tonight?"

Chapter Six

EDEN

"**A**DDIE, YOU'VE BEEN WEIRD all freaking day. What is going on?" I demanded, adjusting the angle of a framed watercolor painting until it finally hung straight.

It was my favorite of the half dozen now decorating the walls. This one echoed the shop colors of lavender and baby blue, depicting sensual curves that mimicked the shape of a woman's hips. The rest were similar, all in varying shades of blue and purple, but this particular image spoke to me—subtly sensual, just the barest hint of passion hidden within those serene colors.

It was now in a place of honor behind the checkout counter.

"Nothing is going on," my cousin called, dancing around with a satin bustier clutched to her chest. "I'm just excited for your opening!"

"You're a liar, that's what you are," I grumbled, but I was excited, too.

With the artwork up, the meeting rooms furnished, and the shop's signage finally unveiled out front, we were ready for action. I'd managed to avoid talking to my cousin about my trip to Dueling Dragons the day before, and she had stayed miraculously silent about her godson's gift.

Miraculous? Or suspicious?

"Adelaide," I drawled, "we really should talk about how you played me yesterday."

Addie hung the bustier back on the rack and blinked wide, innocent eyes in my direction. "Eden, I haven't the slightest clue what you're talking about. Besides, I'm famished and I have a client at six, so I have to run! I'll see you bright and early tomorrow, darling!"

My mouth dropped open as she twirled her way toward the front door, then snapped shut when she held the door open for Milo before locking it with her key and dancing down the sidewalk.

Even surrounded by lacy underwear, he looked completely at ease, smiling at me as he approached the counter. He was wearing what I'd started to think of as his uniform, jeans and a graphic tee depicting a superhero logo, though this time it was underneath a brown canvas jacket with cozy sherpa trim at the collar. In the late afternoon sunlight coming through my now-uncovered front windows, his auburn hair blazed copper, the ends of it curling just below his ears.

For the second time in as many days, I stood frozen in place, trapped by my own insecurities.

Milo didn't seem to mind, though, as he strolled toward me. "Eden," he murmured.

"Milo."

"I believe I have something of yours," he said, reaching into his pocket.

When he pulled out the hair clip I'd been wearing the day we met, my breath stalled in my chest. I stayed perfectly still as he reached out and carefully clasped the flower into my hair, but the smile that crinkled the corners of his eyes sent the air whooshing back out of my lungs.

"I was saving it as a souvenir, but with you right next door, I think seeing you in person is an even better reminder."

His voice was a low rumble that made my insides quiver. I tried not to remember the way it raised goosebumps on my skin when he'd used it to coax and praise and urge me on in my exploration of his body.

"But if you keep looking at me like that, I'm going to forget that I came over here to ask you to have dinner with me this evening."

My head jerked in surprise. "Dinner?"

"Yes, the evening meal. Surely you've heard of it?"

"Very funny. You want to have dinner with me?"

Milo moved closer, his eyes focused on my face until he paused with only a few inches between us, then his gaze swept down to my wide-legged overalls and cropped black t-shirt. I bit my lip until he reached out and gently released it with his thumb before dropping his hand.

"I want that and more, Eden, but what about you? Was it just one night for you?"

I sucked in a breath. "No. I didn't—I'm sorry I ran out on you."

"What do you want, Eden?" he asked, no longer touching me but still holding me in thrall with that impossibly sexy voice.

Of everything that happened between us, it was the memory of his voice that crept up on me unexpectedly as the days passed. He had been sweet, generous, impressively talented, and utterly devoted to pleasing me—but that low, deep timbre of his haunted my dreams, the way my name rumbled from his chest and whispered past his lips.

"Dinner," I squeaked, then kicked myself for being a ninny.

Milo's lips tipped up at the corners, barely visible through his beard, and he murmured, "That's a start. Do what you need to do, lock up, and I'll bring you back to your car later."

Much to my extremely strict parents' dismay, I was not built for following orders. When they were issued by Milo's low baritone, however, I couldn't resist.

Everything was ready for the grand opening tomorrow morning, so I just checked the back door, grabbed my coat and purse from the little room we'd turned into the employee lounge, and met Milo back in the shop.

However at ease the man looked amidst lace and satin and the occasional marabou feather trim, I felt anything but. My pulse worked double-time as I approached his spot in the center aisle. I wondered which of the store's offerings he might like best and what his reaction would be to seeing me wearing them.

When I came to a halt, he reached out and stroked his knuckles down the side of my throat.

"Relax," he whispered. "I know you don't know me very well yet, Eden, but we'll remedy that over dinner, okay?"

With a breathless laugh, I nodded. "Okay. I'm sorry I made things awkward."

"Things are awkward because I know what you taste like, but I don't know your favorite food," Milo teased, but the words were gentle. "We'll get past that, and then it will be smooth sailing while we see where this goes. Sound good?"

"Yes. Good. Just, um, if you could not mention tasting me while we're having dinner, I might be able to act like a regular human being."

That grin. It got me every time. I remembered how soft the beard surrounding it was, thanks to some hipster beard oil he'd joked about, one that smelled faintly of pine.

"I'll behave like a perfect gentleman, Eden. Tonight is just dinner and getting to know each other. You have my word."

I was still mere seconds away from hyperventilation, but I nodded. This was Milo—sweet, generous, kind Milo. He didn't hate me for leaving him alone in that hotel room, wasn't holding a grudge because I'd made a split-second decision that hurt us both. In fact, he seemed nothing but pleased to have found me again.

I took the hand he held out to me and led him out the front door, locking it behind us. The brisk January air did very little to soothe me, but when we passed my car, Milo squeezed my hand and chuckled.

"You know, even when I was annoyed at losing my parking spot, I was afraid I might actually like the owner of that car based on the bumper stickers alone. I didn't peg you as a Zelda fan."

Lifting my chin, I said, "Don't tell me you're one of those gamer dudes who looks down on girls that can kick their asses at video games."

"Oh ho," he protested, "I certainly am not. In fact, I welcome video game ass-kicking. Why don't we pick up dinner, head back to my house to eat, and you can kick my ass at your choice of games while we get to know each other better?"

Normally, I'd assume a first date at a guy's place was just a ploy to get into my pants, but Milo had already done that—at my very explicit request—so I said, "Okay, but don't say I didn't warn you."

"Consider me warned," he replied solemnly, but he winked. "What would you like for dinner?"

Part of scrimping and saving to open the shop meant I didn't get takeout very often unless I was with Addie, who refused to ever let me pay. "I've been wanting to try that new Thai place on the next block. Do you like Thai?"

"Thai Me Down?"

I choked on my laughter. No matter how many times I drove by the sign, it always made me giggle. "Yes."

"The first non-sexual thing for you to learn about me, Eden, is that I like food. Full stop. Specifically, however, I do love Thai food, so that's settled. I've only ordered from their food truck, but everything I've tried has been delicious."

We continued up the street, holding hands in a way that normally would make me feel awkward but for some reason comforted me instead. When Milo stopped so I could peruse the menu taped up in the restaurant's front window, I slanted a glance in his direction.

"What?" he asked, cocking his head at me.

"Nothing. Thai food is definitely not the first non-sexual thing I've learned about you, that's all."

This time, the grin crept across his face slowly, giving me a chance to savor the entire process. We were close enough for me to catch a whiff of pine, close enough that I could have lifted up on my toes to kiss him. Though his gaze dropped to my mouth, he gave a tiny shake of his head, like he was reminding himself that he'd promised to be a gentleman tonight.

"There's plenty more to learn, Eden, for both of us. Let's order so we can get started."

Chapter Seven

MILO

E DEN WAS QUIET DURING the short drive to my house, but she seemed to have moved past the nervousness from when I first invited her to dinner. Whether the smell of our takeout or the promise of video games had soothed her, I wasn't sure, but I was willing to roll with it either way.

"This is where you live?" she asked, peering through the twilight toward the little ranch I'd bought several years back.

"It's not much to look at, but it gets the job done."

"Not much to look at? It's adorable. And...landscaped."

She sounded so shocked that I laughed, then tipped my head in an attempt to view the house objectively. It was small and squat, with white siding and red brick accents. The yard was tiny, so it was easy to keep up with mowing in the summer, and the interior hadn't needed a single renovation when I bought it, which was the major selling point.

But along the front of the house was a small, mulched garden bed lined with various shrubs and ornamental trees.

"The landscaping is only because my mom is so into gardening, she insisted on planting all of that stuff for me. Which basically meant she went to the nursery, came home with a trunk full of bushes, and told me where to dig and haul things to."

"Your family is local, then?"

There was something in the way she said it—not wistful, exactly, but pensive. It made my heart clench in my chest, wondering what her family was like.

"Yeah, they're all still in Spruce Hill. Mom and Dad live at the other end of town. Maverick and Carter are about two miles from here, and our middle brother, Mark, lives a few blocks away with his wife, Libby. Mark has a store in town where he sells body products."

"Maverick and Carter," she repeated. "Just the two of them?"

"Carter's mom left when he was just a baby. Mark and I helped out a lot back then, but my mom took care of him during the day until he started school. Maverick works in business banking, something unspeakably boring like that. Our mom still handles any activities Mav can't make it to, but Carter likes to hang at the stores with us, so we alternate days watching him after school."

"I'm glad you have a close family like that."

Sincerity was written on every inch of her beautiful face, but so was something else. Longing, maybe? I wanted to ask questions, but I was afraid I'd scare her off.

"Ready to go inside and eat? I'm starved."

Eden nodded, but she fell silent, staring at the house. I turned off the engine and shifted my body toward her, wondering if her nerves had returned. It was a long moment before she met my gaze.

"Eden," I said softly. "It's just dinner. And video games, and I think I have some ice cream in the freezer if you want dessert. Just because we…"

"Had a wild night of incredible sex?" she suggested.

I laughed even as the reminder sent heat rushing through me. "Yes, that. Just because we had lots of incredible sex doesn't mean you're under any obligation to repeat the experience. Not now, not ever. That night was just that—the choices we made for one night."

Eden's brows lifted and she asked, "Are you concerned I'm feeling pressured to sleep with you again?"

"I…I mean, yes, I was getting a little concerned about that, but now I'm sensing I read the situation completely wrong."

The bags of takeout were on her lap, but she reached out a hand to brush her fingertips lightly over my beard, a whisper of a touch that barely reached my skin but one I felt everywhere else in my body all at once. I managed to stay still until her thumb touched my lips, then I breathed her name against it.

"I like you, Milo. If I seem nervous, it's because I'm afraid I screwed things up for us by putting the horse before the cart, or however that saying goes," she admitted.

"Not possible," I replied, still speaking around her thumb and not minding it one bit, since that meant she was still cupping my face in her ridiculously soft hand. "You didn't screw anything up. There were two of us there that night, and there are two of us here now. Together."

"Together." The whispered word sounded weighty coming from her lips.

Before her hand dropped away from my face, her fingers curved, combing gently through my beard. I remembered her doing it several times that night—and I remembered liking it just as much then as now. A low hum of contentment purred in her throat as I tilted my head to nuzzle her palm.

"Okay, then. Let's eat," Eden said.

"Stay there. I'll come around for the food."

As I opened the door and took the bags from her lap, I saw the uncertainty had fled, leaving in its place a spunky, grinning woman with a mischievous twinkle in her eye. It was sexy as hell and I had to remind myself of all the things I'd said to her—gentlemanly behavior, just dinner, getting to know each other.

Okay. I could do this.

I let her into the house, not realizing she'd stopped in the doorway until I reached the countertop dividing the big open space into living room and kitchen. When I turned to look at her, she stood stock still, staring down at my slender black cat, who gazed up at Eden in return.

"You have a cat."

"I do. Shit, you're not allergic, are you? I didn't think," I said, moving toward the two of them.

"No, I'm not. But...you have a cat."

"Yes," I said, drawing out the word in my confusion. "That's Jiji."

Eden's gaze shot to my face. "Not my favorite Studio Ghibli movie, but it's up there."

The fact that she recognized it made something in my chest shift and settle. My last girlfriend, if you could call her that when we'd only gone out a few times at Maverick's insistence, had been of the belief that cartoons were for children.

"What's your favorite?"

"Howl. I'm a sucker for a man in a poofy shirt."

"Duly noted. I try to save mine for special occasions, but maybe you'll get lucky. I could be persuaded to pull it out of storage."

Eden smirked in my direction. "You really are a nerd."

"Takes one to know one," I teased. "You *were* at Comic Con, after all."

"True, and I enjoyed it, once I figured out what the hell was happening. I accidentally booked a room at the wrong hotel. I had a meeting with a supplier the next morning in the city."

"Is that why you left?" I asked softly, hoping she wouldn't think it was an accusation.

Eden nodded, glancing back toward Jiji just as the cat completed his inspection of my guest and sauntered toward her. Without hesitating, Eden dropped to her knees on the ugly brown carpet and held out her hand for the cat to sniff.

"He's a little particular, so don't be offended if he…"

My warning trailed off as my finicky cat started rubbing his face against Eden's fingers like he'd found a long lost friend. As she scratched his cheeks, he edged closer until he was almost on her lap. Even from a few feet away, I could hear Jiji purring, but Eden's responding coos flooded my veins with warmth.

Nothing could convince me this woman was a perfect fit more than that.

Then Jiji rolled onto his back, inviting Eden to rub his belly, and before I could issue a warning, the cat latched onto her wrist with his teeth and all four limbs.

"Oh, you are ferocious," Eden whispered. "What a fierce kitty you are. Fierce *and* pretty, you sweet baby."

Jiji licked the base of Eden's palm, then bolted across the room to eviscerate the bottom post of his climbing tree.

As I offered a hand to pull Eden to her feet, I said, "That settles it. You passed the ultimate test."

She beamed up at me. "Excellent news."

I unpacked the bags of food, offered Eden her choice of beverages from the fridge, and popped the tops of two cherry colas as we settled at the breakfast bar to eat. Eden dug into her pad thai, so I gave her a few minutes before I launched into conversation.

"You got my family overview in the car. What about you, is yours still in Binghamton?"

Eden slapped a hand over her mouth as she sputtered around a mouthful of noodles. "Wow, okay, starting right in. Um. I think so, yeah."

My body stilled at the implication that she didn't know. "Oh."

"We're not in contact. My brother called once, a few years ago, but it didn't go well. I haven't heard from any of them since."

"I'm sorry," I said quietly.

"Don't be." She shrugged and twirled her fork in the noodles. "Addie and Rob are my family, and their parents. They've more than made up for any shortcomings of my own."

My heart ached at the prospect of Eden being cut off from the kind of love and support I received from my family, but her grip on the fork had tightened and her frame had gone tense.

Time to change the subject.

"Right. Okay. Martial arts?" I asked.

"Yup. I do Brazilian Jiu-Jitsu."

I let out a low whistle. "How long have you been doing that?"

"I started a couple weeks after I got here, so not quite six months. Right before we left the city, I let Addie talk me into hosting a girls' weekend in Rochester. It was basically a big sleepover at our tiny apartment, but one of her friends got mugged before she came home. She was fine and the police recovered her purse, but it freaked us all out."

"Oh, shit."

"Yeah," she said, making a face. "I know Spruce Hill's not a big city, but bad things happen everywhere. I decided I should know how to defend myself."

"So you're a badass and could kick my ass." I grinned at the thought.

"I could," she agreed solemnly, "but I probably won't. At least not if you keep feeding me."

"I'll try to stay on your good side. Since I'm happy to feed you to maintain my spot in your good graces, favorite food?"

"Well, this is ranking pretty high right now. I'm also a sucker for nachos. You?"

"Perfect, next time we'll get nachos, because I love Mexican food. There's a great little place over in Oakville. You moved here six months ago? Where did you live before?"

"Adelaide and I went to college together in Rochester and ended up staying there after we graduated, though she always wanted to move home. When her friend Monique opened the crisis center here, she recruited Addie to come work with her and I decided to come along, too, since I was having a hard time finding a good retail space in the city."

"Are you guys still roommates?"

"No," she said, grinning. "Addie is living above her parents' garage at the moment, and I love her, but we definitely each need our own space. I got an apartment off Canal Street. It's not great, but it'll do for now. I didn't want to blow my savings on rent when I need to put that money into the store."

"So how did you get into the lingerie business?" I asked, tilting my head at her.

"Lingerie business?" she repeated, laughing. "Jumping from family to favorite food to my career. I'm going to get whiplash."

I shrugged. "I want to know about everything that makes you who you are."

"Okay, then. It's not just about selling sexy underwear. It's about empowerment, making sure people can feel beautiful no matter what their size or shape. The lingerie is the face of it, but we'll be offering more than that. Addie runs support groups for survivors of sexual assault. Monique offers sexual education classes and, ah, other things."

"Other things?" I asked, wondering why her cheeks grew pink when she said it.

"Parties."

I stared at her, turning that over in my head. "Parties. Like, birthday parties?"

"Sex toy parties," Eden mumbled. She stabbed her fork into her noodles, avoiding my gaze. "They're pretty popular, and I'll get a cut of the sales."

"Oh, I see," I breathed.

Her blush deepened, streaking scarlet along her cheekbones, and dozens of enchanting images filled my head—as if all those sweet, lacy nightgowns in the shop hadn't been fodder enough for my imagination.

"Right." I cleared my throat and repeated, "Right. Cool."

Eden finally looked at me again, hazel eyes bright against her red cheeks, then she burst out laughing at whatever she saw on my face.

I tried to remember if I'd heard her laugh at all that night at the hotel. She had giggled, yes, when I stroked my hands up her sides and discovered how ticklish she was there, but nothing like this sweet explosion of sound from those pretty red lips.

I was mesmerized.

Eventually, the laughter died away. Eden shook her head and lifted her can of cola in my direction, her expression turning serious. I braced.

"You wanted to move into that space?" she asked softly. "How long have you had the store?"

"I opened about eight years ago now. And don't feel bad about the space. I waited too long. You got there first, fair and square. Besides, I needed the push to expand my website offerings, get some new ads up. I got space on some digital billboards throughout the state, which seems to be driving a fair amount of traffic to the site."

She smiled and said, "That's great, Milo."

"It all worked out in the end." I gave a quiet laugh. "Is that the news you were celebrating that night at the hotel?"

Eden blanched. "Shit. Yes."

"Good. I'm glad I got to be part of that celebration, Eden. You're doing something incredible with that storefront. That's more important. Though I am curious…how exactly did you get the cat pee out of the rug?"

"Oh, man," she groaned, nudging her shoulder against mine. "Addie's brother, Rob, replaced a chunk of the subfloor and found a scrap of the same carpeting to fit in there. Before that, I spent a lot of time on my knees."

"That's what she said?" I ventured.

She burst out laughing again, adding another checkmark to my Perfect Fit list, and we finished our dinner.

Maybe that night at the hotel counted as our actual first date, but this one felt like it—the most perfect first date I could have imagined.

Chapter Eight

EDEN

MILO MIGHT NOT HAVE fit anyone else's definition of a perfect gentleman based on some of the jokes he cracked throughout the evening—or the simmering heat in his eyes when I knew he was recalling our night together—but it had been a long time since I enjoyed myself quite that much. He showed no signs of being a sore loser, even when I whooped him at two different combat games, though he managed to beat me in a couple rounds of each.

"You're good," he said, tossing his controller onto the coffee table. "I'm ready to admit defeat."

I tucked my feet under me, turning toward him on the overstuffed couch. "I graciously accept your surrender."

"Well then, you won. What do you want for your reward?"

"I get a reward?"

Milo grinned at me as he ran one of his big hands along Jiji's sleek back where the cat lay sleeping on the cushion between us. "Of course. You earned it."

What I needed was to get home so I could attempt to get a good night's sleep before opening day tomorrow, but I didn't want the evening to end. Especially when Milo was smiling so temptingly, petting his adorable cat and gazing over at me with that soft light in his gray eyes.

I decided a few more minutes wouldn't hurt.

"A kiss," I blurted.

Milo's eyes darkened. "A kiss?"

"Yes. One goodnight kiss, then I really do need to get going."

"One kiss," he mused, rising to his feet as Jiji gave a feline glare and bolted from the room.

He held out a hand and tugged me up from the couch, his grip gentle but firm. I collided with his body, every nerve ending inside me lighting up like a Christmas tree. There was still a hint of a smile playing across his lips as one of his hands slid to the small of my back and the other sank into my hair, threading through the thick locks until his fingers curved at the back of my neck.

"Paradise," he whispered.

I blinked up at him, too distracted by the feel of him against my front to process what he meant. "What?"

His head dipped until his lips were a hairsbreadth from mine, so close that I felt him speaking against my skin. "When you told me your name at the bar that night, that's what I thought. It fits you perfectly."

"Oh."

I breathed the word just as his mouth settled on mine. For the first few seconds, he didn't take advantage of the fact that my lips were already parted, kissing me lightly instead, almost playfully. As soon as my hands went up over his shoulders, linking at the back of his neck, he dove in, deepening the kiss, reacquainting us.

God, this man was good with his mouth.

One kiss from Milo was worth a dozen kisses—or more—from anyone else I'd ever been with.

Fortunately, I went into this knowing just how good and applauded myself for my clever choice of reward.

By the time he ended it with a teasing nip of my lower lip that sent electricity zinging through my veins, I was ready to abandon all hope of a restful night and beg him to take me to bed. His lips curved up as he drew back, like he knew exactly what I was thinking, and he dropped a chaste kiss to the tip of my nose.

"You have a big day tomorrow," he said gently. "Let's get you home."

I groaned in protest but Milo only laughed, keeping hold of my hand as he pulled my reluctant body toward the door. When we got there, I slipped my shoes back on, still pouting. Milo lowered his head until his breath tickled my ear.

"I guess that answers my question about whether you're still interested," he whispered.

"I didn't realize there was any doubt," I admitted. "I had to restrain myself from leaping over the counter and tearing your clothes off that day I walked into your store."

"That definitely would have saved me from worrying that you regretted our night together."

My head shot up. "You were worried about that?"

"Yes. I guess I should have kissed you as soon as you were back within reach. It would've cleared things up quicker."

"Yeah, you should've," I mused. "But since your nephew was there, I guess it would have been extra inappropriate to go at it right off the bat."

His low laughter raised goosebumps along my skin. "Unfortunate, really."

"You're telling me."

"God, you're cute. Are you sure you didn't mean to claim *two* kisses as your reward?"

"I did mean that, actually. Yes. Please."

Milo's hands gripped my hips, pulling me flush against him, and he kissed me again. This one was hotter, harder, a little more desperate than the last. My body caught fire, burning right along with him. When it ended, I chased his mouth, rising on my toes to follow him as he pulled away.

"Now I know how you taste *and* your favorite food," Milo murmured. "I'd say we're making good progress."

I leaned back to look him in the eye and burst out laughing.

T HAT NIGHT WAS NOT restful.

Instead, I tossed and turned, alternately wishing I could forget Milo's existence and regretting that he wasn't there to calm me down—or exhaust me—so I could finally get some sleep.

I was up with the sun, freshly showered and staring down at three different outfits I'd laid out on the bed. One was a fitted burgundy dress that made a clear statement supporting my business model—that I embraced my size and loved my curves, which I did. The other dress was deep purple, soft and swingy with a flared skirt that would definitely be easier for moving around the shop all day. My final option was a pair of wide-legged navy sailor pants with gold buttons up the hips that I'd paired with a floral blouse sporting a big, floppy bow at the neckline.

The pants won out. They were cute and professional, and without knowing what the day might actually look like, comfort was key. We could be slammed with customers from open to close.

Or it might be a ghost town. Shit, I hoped this dream of mine wasn't a total bust.

When I got to the shop, I parked around the corner, leaving Milo's spot open for him. Maybe it was silly, but I wanted him to start his day with a smile on his face. I might not be so generous in the future when I was wearing heels or dealing with snow, but today, with the sun shining despite the chill in the air, a pair of silver flats on my feet, and plenty of time to spare, I'd do what I could.

I was in the store alone for approximately three minutes before Adelaide came in, her arms full of bakery boxes.

"What is all this?" I asked my cousin, taking a box from the stack before she could bump into a display and send them all soaring.

"Cupcakes. There's a little folding table in my trunk, I'll have to run back out to get it. I ordered these from that food truck you love. Wait until you see them."

She laid the other boxes on the counter, then threw back one lid, revealing dozens of cupcakes frosted with lavender and baby blue. There was some kind of edible glitter sprinkled on top of them, along with tiny silver candy stars. They were beautiful and smelled amazing.

"Oh, Addie," I said quietly. My breath hitched, something my cousin did not miss.

"No tears! You look fabulous. Don't start crying over cupcakes. Besides, we have an hour before opening and you are going to tell me all about your dinner with Milo while we set these out."

The mist in my eyes evaporated as I glared at her. "Right, we've got a few things to talk about concerning Milo, Adelaide Harrison."

Addie blinked her big brown eyes at me, cherry-red lips in a pretty pout, but finally muttered, "Yeah, okay. Let me grab the table and we'll talk while we unpack."

I helped her unfold the table in a corner of the store where the frosting wouldn't pose a threat to any merchandise, then narrowed my eyes until she heaved a dramatic groan.

"It all worked out, didn't it? Was last night truly horrible?"

"Last night wasn't horrible at all, but that's not the point, Adelaide. That's twice you've gone behind my back to set me up. Why not just tell me you found Milo working next door?"

"Eden," she said softly. "Would that really have been enough to get you over there?"

"Of course!" I exclaimed, then swore under my breath at her pointed look. "No. Maybe not. But I would've liked the option, Addie. Blindsiding me wasn't cool. Not the first time, and definitely not the second."

"I'm sorry. It's just...the way you talked about him after that night, Eden, it was different from anything I've ever seen. Like you've been wearing a veil for your entire life, keeping you from living full out, and then you finally threw it off. It was beautiful, girl."

I stared at her in surprise. How the hell did she see those things? My throat grew tight for a moment, until it became a real battle not to burst into tears.

"They scarred you, Eden," Addie whispered. "Your parents made you feel like you needed to fit into a tiny box, live your life a certain way, play by all their rules. Even when you fought against it, that echo was still there in your head. It kept you from being free to be who you are. And you're incredible. You deserve to show that to the world. To show it to yourself."

"Ugh, I'm definitely going to have to fix my makeup," I muttered, rolling my eyes toward the ceiling to try to stem the flow of tears.

Addie wrapped her arms around me as I breathed deep, waiting for the threat of ruined makeup to pass. Every word she said struck my heart like a gong, reverberating through my body until it reached my fingertips and toes. We might be the same age, but Addie had always been wise beyond her years.

"I didn't mean to play you, babe. You deserve great things and I thought maybe I could surprise you with one. I thought you'd want to see him again."

"That night was amazing."

A soft laugh escaped her lips. "I'll bet it was."

"I'm afraid," I whispered into her shoulder.

She pulled back, framing my face with her hands. "Afraid of what?"

"Afraid it won't be the same. Do you remember that spring break when I stayed with you guys so my parents could go to some church member's wedding in Saratoga Springs? All the kids in your neighborhood got together and we played that game of Capture the Flag. It was just different, somehow. Magical. Like we were really defending our castle, and every kid was so invested, it was like the real world melted away."

Addie grinned at the memory. "Yeah, I do."

"Or when I came out during the summer before senior year. We went to that bonfire, and some girl started singing campfire songs and suddenly we were all joining in and dancing in the moonlight?"

"I remember that, too. What's that got to do with Milo?"

I drew a shaky breath. "Those moments, they were magic. And afterward, no matter how many times we played the game again or how many bonfires we went to, it was never the same. We were never able to bring back those feelings. It was like the magic had disappeared."

"You're afraid the magic between you two will be gone," Addie said slowly.

"I—I think so, yeah. That night was incredible, Addie. Like nothing I've ever experienced. What if it just can't be recreated?"

"Eden." My cousin smushed my cheeks until my lips puckered. "Those moments were magical because we were kids. Trying to recreate a moment from childhood is very different from enjoying the first in a string of countless amazing nights with a guy you're into. You can't hide from disappointment, babe, or you'll miss out on so much good. Please, give him a chance to show you the good."

If last night had proven anything, it was that our chemistry remained just as strong as it had been that night at the hotel. Those kisses hadn't been a disappointment—no, they were just as magical as the ones I'd been reliving for weeks.

Could I do what Addie suggested? Open myself up to marring the memory of that one perfect night if things went bad?

Before I could come up with an answer, our first customers of the day entered through the front door, a tinkling bell announcing their arrival, and it was time to embrace the future.

Chapter Nine

MILO

WHEN I GOT TO work that morning and found my parking spot open, my first reaction was panic—had something happened to Eden after I saw her safely to her car the night before? Then I caught sight of her little red SUV parked around the corner and a wave of relief crashed over me, followed by something warm ballooning inside my chest.

Now that I knew she was the parking spot thief, I planned to tell her to keep parking there, but the fact that she'd made the gesture of leaving it open for me was sweet.

"She likes me," I whispered to myself, unable to hold back a grin.

Throughout the day, I saw plenty of people going in and out of Eden's shop. The thing that surprised me was the number of shoppers who then stopped into Dueling Dragons, all of them carrying lavender shopping bags from next door.

I considered visiting Eden at work, but I was hesitant to intrude on her first day of business, especially since I wasn't exactly her target market and didn't want to make any actual customers uncomfortable with my presence. My curiosity was finally satisfied when Olivia strolled through my door carrying her own glossy lavender bag in one hand and a canvas tote of artwork in the other.

"You did *not* tell me that your rockabilly goddess moved in next door, you jerk," she scolded, handing over the art. "And shit, she's even more gorgeous up close."

"Yes, she is," I muttered.

Unfortunately, that caused Olivia's gaze to snap to my face. "Oh, you've been keeping things from me, Milo. Spill the tea, bro."

"Liv, I love you, but I don't kiss and tell."

"So there was kissing," she pressed, a broad smile spreading across her face.

"I'm not talking about this," I replied, unpacking the plastic-sleeved prints from the tote bag. "I take it you did some shopping over there?"

"The place is called Garden of Delights. Of course I did some shopping. I also scored a date with the blonde. We're going out next week."

My head lifted. "Adelaide?"

"Mm-hmm. You gonna ask out your dream girl or what?"

"We had dinner last night." I sighed when her expression lit, realizing she'd never stop hounding me until I told her the rest of it.

A truncated version of the rest of it, anyway.

"And we might have had a thing at Comic Con."

Olivia mimed a swoon. "A *thing*, huh? That sounds promising."

Was it? After last night, I certainly hoped so. My fear that Eden had only been looking for a no-strings hookup dissipated under the intensity of those kisses—kisses *she* had requested, then responded to like she couldn't possibly get enough.

I recognized that need, because I felt the exact same.

"How's it going over there?" I asked, both to change the subject and because I wanted to know that Eden's first day was going well.

"Place is hopping. Lucky for me, I snagged the last celebratory cupcake. Your girl told me a bit about the other offerings she plans to have over there—brains as well as beauty."

"She has a name," I grumbled.

"Oh, yes, and what a name. *Eden,*" Olivia sang out. "Temptation personified, and she's right next door."

"You're really not helping."

Olivia just grinned at me. "Well, her store closes at six tonight, just in case you wanted to pop over and say hello. Oh, and I'm working on getting another fantasy role-playing game up and running. Are we good for alternate Tuesdays from my other game nights?"

"Yeah, definitely. Just let me know when you're ready to start."

With a jaunty wave, Olivia took off, swinging her lavender bag. Technically, she rented the space to run her game nights, but we'd worked it out in trade for a higher percentage of her art sales in the shop. Most of her players purchased stuff from the store when they wanted new dice, books, or miniatures, so it worked out to be a beneficial exchange all around.

Fortunately, the foot traffic to Eden's shop proved to be beneficial, too, even though I wouldn't have foreseen so much overlap in our target customers. Still, I had a fairly steady stream of shoppers for a Friday afternoon. My business card stash dwindled while my sales climbed.

I took my time closing up at five, trying to delay until closer to six so I could poke my head in to see Eden without it being too hideously awkward. After placing Olivia's new art around the store, I locked up and headed over to Garden of Delights, trying very hard to act like walking into a lingerie shop was an everyday occurrence.

"Milo, you're just in time!"

My head jerked at hearing my name, but it was Adelaide who'd called out. Eden stood behind the counter, shaking her head at her cousin even as she smiled at me.

"Ignore her. Contrary to Addie's plans, I have not actually incorporated 'closing time dance party' into the daily schedule."

I grinned, moving toward her like a magnet. "I mean, it's not a terrible idea."

"Only because you haven't seen me dance," Eden mumbled.

Adelaide was twirling around the shop, singing along with the Sir Mix-a-Lot song blasting over the store's speakers. I choked back a laugh when I recognized it and Eden rolled her eyes toward the ceiling.

"Don't encourage her. We've been fighting over the music all day. My choice was jazz, which fits the atmosphere we're going for here. Addie prefers songs featuring explicit descriptions of women's bodies."

"This sounds like the kind of disagreement I should stay out of," I mused, leaning a hip against the counter. "Hi."

Eden's expression softened. "Hi."

"How was your first day? Looked like you got a lot of people in here."

"We did, yeah. It was good. Really good. I'm sure a lot of people just wanted to see what kind of monster would put a lingerie shop in the middle of Spruce Hill, but we did pretty well," she said. "A bunch of Addie's friends came by. They said they were going to talk us up to everyone who would listen, so hopefully business will be steady."

"You should come out with us, Milo," Addie called across the store from where she was repositioning a mannequin, though she swung her hips toward it as she danced. "We're going for celebratory drinks at The Mermaid!"

"Oh, I wouldn't want to intrude," I started, but Eden grabbed my hand.

"Please, for the love of all that is holy, don't leave me alone with her for another minute. It has been a very, very long day. I need you there."

It was a simple statement, but it sent a burst of pleasure through me. I curled my fingers around hers and nodded. "In that case, the first round's on me."

"Rock on!" Addie shouted.

For a second, Eden just smiled up at me, a soft expression that made me want to kiss her—but I wasn't sure where she stood on PDA, so I didn't want to start something in front of her cousin.

"You're a lifesaver," she whispered, squeezing my hand.

"You did buy the last round," I replied, my voice low. "It's my turn."

Just as I'd hoped, the reminder caused Eden's hazel eyes to heat. Her cheeks grew pink as she leaned toward me across the counter. The neckline of her top came all the way up so her collarbone was covered with a floppy bow, but the silky fabric brushed over my arm when she got close.

Eden bit her lip for a second, then whispered, "I had a really good time last night."

"Me too," I whispered back. "And thank you for the parking spot, but I want you to take it from here out."

She drew back. "Why? You said you've parked there since you opened your store. It's yours."

"Well, you see, there's this gorgeous woman who I really like. Sometimes she wears these sexy shoes with heels, or sweet little dresses, and it might make me a chauvinist pig, but I like the idea of her not having to walk so far to get to her shop when my work uniform is jeans, sneakers, and a graphic tee."

"How gallant," she murmured.

I lifted our joined hands and rubbed my beard over the back of her knuckles, grinning when she shivered at the sensation. "If you hate gallantry, we'll come to some other arrangement, but I mean it. I like knowing you're parking there."

Eden's lips parted to respond, but her cousin abruptly turned off the sound system and we both jerked in surprise at the sudden silence.

"Let's blow this popsicle stand, lovebirds. Time to celebrate!"

Though Eden rolled her eyes, she reluctantly pulled her hand from mine. "I'll go get my purse. Adelaide, I'm trusting you not to give Milo the third degree," she warned.

"Who, me?"

Her cousin assumed a look of pure innocence, which earned an exaggerated sigh from Eden before she headed into the back. Adelaide practically skipped to my side to whisper-scream, "I still cannot believe you work next door! This is the greatest thing that's ever happened to me."

"To you?"

"To me by proxy. Seeing Eden happy. This is the best possible scenario, even better than I could have dreamt up myself." Her radiant smile evaporated and her brows drew together in a threatening scowl. "Make her happy or I'll cut you."

Startled by the sudden change in tone from bubbly to ominous, I blinked at her as Eden emerged from the back of the store, but while Eden glared suspiciously at her cousin, I gave Adelaide a tiny salute to indicate my agreement.

I had no intention of throwing away a second chance.

Chapter Ten

EDEN

M Y COUSIN WOULD BE lucky to survive the weekend. Low-key drinks with Addie and Milo turned into an ambush when we walked in to find half a dozen of Adelaide's buddies sitting around the bar at the back of the restaurant. The only one of the group who I'd previously met was Addie's friend, Monique. I stiffened as soon as I spotted them all.

Milo's hand settled on my lower back just before he murmured in my ear, "It's okay. I'll shield you if you need it. I know most of them from school, but if you want to escape after one drink, say the word and I'll whisk you away."

Since Addie couldn't see the daggers I was shooting from my eyes as she skipped toward the bar, I grumbled my acquiescence under my breath and let Milo propel me forward.

The rest of them introduced themselves, greeted Milo with hand clasps or hugs, and then every one of them eyed the two of us curiously.

Just what I needed. More scrutiny.

The bartender was a young guy named Lucas, probably only in his mid-twenties, but he, too, knew Milo. "Hey, man! I'm joining Liv's new game on Tuesday. I haven't played Dungeons & Dragons since I was a kid, but Liv is…"

"Tenacious?" Milo suggested.

"I was going to say persuasive, but yeah."

The two of them shared a grin as we ordered our round of drinks—fortunately just for the three of us rather than the whole group, or I would've ripped into my cousin for costing Milo a small fortune. I decided on the evening's special, a bourbon-based cocktail, and Milo smirked in my direction.

"You're a bourbon girl, huh? Not champagne, to celebrate?"

I shrugged. "I don't drink very often, but I know what I like. The champagne that night was more symbol than preference."

"Good to know," he mused.

Though Addie proposed a toast to the shop's success, which resulted in the entire restaurant erupting in cheers, her friends diverted her attention enough that Milo and I were left mostly to our own devices.

He reached over, his fingers gently tugging the bow at my neck. "I like this."

"You do?"

"Mmm."

The low sound was somewhere between a murmur and a growl. Those gray eyes darkened when goosebumps rose along my bare arms and a shiver danced up my spine.

"You look like a gift, just waiting to be unwrapped."

I sucked in a breath as that fantasy spun before me. Milo let go of the fabric, but he trailed one fingertip along my throat as his hand moved away. Focused as I was on his expression, a mixture of heat and longing, I didn't realize Addie was calling my name until Milo tipped his head in her direction.

"What?" I asked, swiveling on my stool.

Addie was smiling at me, but it wasn't the triumphant smirk I expected. It was soft, pleased. Loving. All my remaining irritation fled under the warmth of that smile.

"Sorry about the crowd, babe. I just told them we were coming out and they wanted to celebrate your success today. You did great. I'm so proud of you."

"Be proud of us," I replied. "You've done more than your share of the heavy lifting. I couldn't have managed this without you."

"Nonsense. Take note, Milo. Eden Rosalie Campbell has a will of solid steel. Whatever she sets her mind to, it doesn't matter how long it'll take to make it happen—if she wants it, she will get it."

Milo grinned at me and said, "I'd noticed that, actually."

Addie burst out laughing while I shot him a glare, but I couldn't hold onto it long. Aside from Addie, Rob, and Monique, I hadn't built a whole lot of community in Spruce

Hill while I worked toward my goal, but here I was, sur-rounded by people ready to cheer me on.

Including Milo.

With him at my back, I let Addie and her friends draw us into their conversations. As I relaxed into this whole being part of a group thing, I felt Milo shift, turning on his stool with one knee on either side of my hips. I moved without thinking, settling myself there between his legs, reveling in the heat of his chest against my back and the weight of his hand when it squeezed my waist.

"I'll walk you out when you're ready," he murmured into my ear, just as my sleepless night and chaotic first day caught up with me.

I stifled a yawn. "I think I'm ready now."

Addie had a sixth sense for anything that involved getting me alone with this man, so she smiled brightly and said, "I'll catch a ride with Monique. Have a good night, you two!"

Though I rolled my eyes, the chorus of farewells and wishes for continued success on opening weekend distracted me from my cousin's meddling. Milo's hand closed around mine as we left the restaurant, walking into a startling burst of chilly air. I recoiled slightly, bumping into Milo's firm chest.

"If I had a jacket, I'd offer it to you," he said.

"I guess I should still be bringing one to work. It's been so nice out during the day this week, I thought maybe we were in for an early spring. I can't wait for warmer weather."

He wrapped his arm around me, tucking my body into his side as we hurried toward his car. God, he was warm, even in a t-shirt and jeans. I tripped over my own feet just as we reached the car, saved from falling only by Milo's quick reflexes.

"Easy there. Are you okay to drive? I can take you home."

I wrinkled my nose. "That's probably a good idea. You'd think a single drink wouldn't be a problem, but I have zero tolerance for alcohol. Addie had offered Monique as our driver and said she'd bring me to work in the morning if I needed it."

Milo's expression shifted as he led me toward his car instead. Once my door was shut, he jogged around to the driver's side, settling into his seat before he spoke. "Eden, that night..."

Before he could even finish the sentence, I started shaking my head. "No. Nope. If you'll recall, I didn't even finish that glass of champagne. I'm not drunk now, Milo, I would just rather be safe than sorry when it comes to operating heavy machinery."

"Okay," he soothed. "Just making sure."

"Do you regret hooking up with me?" I blurted out, then wondered if I might be drunker than I'd thought, since my verbal filter had apparently abandoned me.

"Do I regret—fuck no."

The words carried enough force to reassure me, though he looked a little hurt that I'd even asked the question. I wasn't sure what exactly my face was doing, but as his eyes searched mine, whatever he saw there caused his expression to grow soft.

"Eden, that night was amazing and my only regret was not waking up with you so we could exchange information before you left. But for what it's worth, this—hanging out, talking, letting you kick my ass at video games—this is amazing, too."

My eyes narrowed. "What do you mean, *letting* me?"

"By giving you the opportunity to use your vastly superior but slightly concerning button-mashing skills."

"Mm-hmm." I glared for another second, then reached out to stroke his beard, silky soft under my fingertips—but still rough enough to leave pink marks on my skin, as I recalled all too clearly. "You're lucky I like you."

"Was that so hard to admit?" he whispered, covering my hand with his own and nuzzling his cheek into my palm.

"Yes," I whispered back.

His eyes looked black in the dark interior of the car, but I saw them sweeping across my features. After a long moment, he nodded, kissed my palm, and released my hand.

"We'll work on that. Can you direct me to your place, or should I put your address in my phone?"

"I can direct you," I replied, but his words were still bouncing around inside my brain.

We'll work on that.

Like it was a given he would be by my side to do just that. Like he didn't mind my idiosyncrasies, like this was the start of something real and true. Like somehow, together, we could make our way forward.

It sounded like a promise, like a lover's vow, and damn, I liked that.

I IGNORED EVERY ONE of my cousin's curious looks the next morning when she picked me up, but I knew I wasn't fooling either of us.

"I'm sorry again about the crowd," she said, "but I'm glad Milo was able to make it."

"You're just glad he's a gentleman and offered to drive me home."

Her immediate grin was confirmation enough. "I don't believe in questioning serendipity, and you shouldn't, either."

Though I rolled my eyes, she had a point. After the best night of my life, I'd let my upbringing cast its ugly shadows over what happened between me and Milo, let that imagined shame frighten me away from a night of sheer joy.

Never again.

That's what I'd started telling myself even before I left home at eighteen. Never again would I let someone else's beliefs destroy my happiness.

It hadn't been easy, shedding that skin, melting into a messy pile of goo inside a chrysalis as I fought my way into independence so I could emerge as something new, something stronger. Addie had been at my side through all of it—the therapy sessions, the late night crying jags, the tentative emergence of a bolder Eden who moved through the world with confidence and poise. An Eden who embraced her sexuality, who wore what she wanted, who didn't have to hide herself away from constant criticism for fear of being locked in her room as punishment for her imagined misdeeds.

The fact that I'd let that new me slip away in a moment of panic at the hotel room still grated on me, but now I had the chance to fix things. I had the chance to seize hold of what I'd found with Milo, even if I had almost thrown it away because of everything my parents had embedded deep into my psyche before I knew any better.

I drew a deep breath, washing every trace of them from my mind, and smiled at my cousin. "You're right. I'm certainly not complaining."

That smile lingered until we pulled up around the corner from Garden of Delights where I'd parked the day before, and I noticed my car looked weird.

"What the hell?" Addie muttered angrily, throwing the gear shift into park and jumping out of the driver's seat to stalk toward my SUV.

"Son of a motherless goat," I whispered as I hurried over to inspect the car.

Every single tire was completely flat. Aside from the flappy, deflated rubber, the rest of it looked unharmed, but even if I'd wanted to change a tire in my work clothes, I only had one spare.

Maybe fate wasn't actually on my side after all.

Chapter Eleven

Milo

T HE NIGHT BEFORE, I drove Eden to her apartment at the far end of town, walked her to her door, spent a heavenly few minutes kissing her, and barely—just barely—managed to bid her goodnight before things got too heated. With hazy eyes, she murmured the words back to me and I had to fight the urge to tug her back into my arms.

This was a marathon, not a sprint.

It was slightly more difficult to keep myself distracted on Saturday, since that was the day Rafael worked the store alone unless we had a special event on the calendar, and Dueling Dragons was closed on Sundays. At home with Jiji, I was all too free to let thoughts of Eden occupy my mind.

Thoughts, fantasies...and memories.

Sunlight glinting auburn in Eden's hair. The curve of her thigh peeking from beneath those petticoats. Her black satin corset falling to the floor. The sweetness of her mouth, the sounds tumbling from her lips.

I killed a few hours doing laundry, cleaning up the house, and cuddling with Jiji, all while trying to keep myself from texting Eden. As though he could hear my agitation, Maverick invited me and Mark over for a Davies game night at his place, and I immediately accepted.

Of course, Mark's wife, Libby, had a standing invitation to these game nights, but she usually took the opportunity to enjoy the peace and quiet at home instead. She'd attended often enough over the years to hold her own, even if she wasn't quite as good at video games as Eden.

I couldn't wait to introduce the two of them. My sister-in-law was an amazing person and I had a feeling she would hit it off with Eden right away.

Unfortunately, Mark waited too long to confess his undying love to Libby in their youth—she and their other best friend, Henry, started dating in high school and got married in college. Somehow, they all managed to stay friends despite my brother's heartbreak.

When Henry and Libby realized they weren't right for each other after only a year of marriage, they got divorced. Mark eventually gathered the courage to speak up about his feelings, but it took almost a decade before he overcame the fear of messing things up further.

Miraculously, their friendship survived that hurdle, too. It was like our own Spruce Hill soap opera.

If Maverick's experience had taught me to be careful about not giving my heart to the wrong person, Mark's taught me that when it was right, it was right, and hesitation might mean losing everything.

Carter threw open the door when I showed up, his eyes alight. "Uncle Milo! I was just telling Uncle Mark about your girlfriend."

"Of course you were," I grumbled, tousling his hair.

"How did I get so far out of the gossip loop that this is the first I'm hearing about a girlfriend?" Mark demanded as I threw myself down on the other end of the couch.

"First and foremost, she's not actually my girlfriend." *Not yet, anyway.*

"Dad said she's the one from Comic Con," Carter cut in, dark brows scrunched together. "I thought she was the love of your life."

Maverick showed up with three beer bottles and a can of Sprite, shaking his head. "I don't think those were my exact words, buddy, and I learned my lesson. I'll be keeping my big mouth shut about Milo's love life from here on out."

"Wow," Mark breathed. His gaze darted between us as he absorbed the information. "I missed more than a little gossip, I think."

I rolled my eyes and grabbed a game controller from the coffee table. "When it's official, I'll let you know."

"She owns a lingerie shop," Carter whispered to Mark.

"Lingerie, huh? Do you even know what that means?"

Carter's expression was perfectly serious. "Nightgowns and stuff for ladies, I think."

"Does she do gift wrapping?" Mark asked. "Maybe I should stop in. Libby's birthday is coming up."

"Seems like a better gift for *your* birthday," Maverick muttered.

Carter blinked at him. "Why?"

"I think we should stop talking about lingerie. And Eden. And my love life," I suggested, though I should've let Maverick sweat longer under his son's guileless gaze.

The three of them fell silent while Carter loaded up the game, then he gave me a quick side-eye and said, "She's really, really pretty."

My brothers burst out laughing.

"I'm going to have to crush you for that," I said to Carter, keeping my eyes on the television screen.

The game proved to be a distraction for about half an hour before we took a break to eat some pizza, then Mark tipped his head at me between bites.

"How serious is it?" he asked softly.

Though our middle brother looked like a surfer with his tanned skin, sunkissed blonde hair, and the laid back charm to match, he'd always been astute, able to read people at a glance. Whatever he saw in my face must have been enough to answer the question, because his lips curved upward.

"Excellent. I look forward to meeting her."

I sighed, but part of me looked forward to that, too. If my gut feeling was correct, that our connection went beyond one hookup and a couple sorta-dates, I wanted her to get to know my family. We were tight, like Eden was with her cousins, even though she'd made it clear she wasn't close to her family beyond that.

My brothers might love any excuse to rag on me, but they did occasionally know when to let a subject drop. Since they didn't bring her up again, I decided it was my lucky night.

Sunday morning, I hit the grocery store in town, did some meal prep for the week, and lounged around until I couldn't stand it anymore. Eden had given me her phone number during dinner at my house, but I didn't want to interrupt her at work. Besides, I knew she had shorter hours on Sundays and would be closing up at three, so I forced myself to be patient.

I had just stretched out on the couch when Jiji hopped up and settled himself on the center of my chest. Stroking a hand over his sleek black fur, I stared up at the ceiling, completely ignoring the mindless television show playing across the living room.

At five after three, my phone buzzed, startling us both. Jiji's claws tensed into my skin, but I managed not to dislodge him as I wrestled my phone from my pocket and read the text from Eden.

What are the chances you're free tonight?

I blew out a breath, grinning stupidly at the screen. *Extremely high. Jiji misses you, he wants me to make dinner for us. What do you think?*

I think that sounds amazing, though I didn't mean to invite myself over.

Don't worry, I was going to text the invitation once I was sure you were done at work. Five o'clock good for you?

She didn't respond immediately, so I closed my eyes and imagined her in one of those sweet outfits of hers, locking up the store and walking to her car. My mind rotated through a few clothing options, from the swingy retro dresses to the prim and professional look she'd sported on Friday, then my phone vibrated again.

Absolutely. See you then.

DINNER PREPARATION WAS WELL underway when my doorbell rang. Jiji sat perched on the back of the couch, grooming himself like he wasn't as excited about Eden's arrival as I was.

At least, that was my interpretation of his twitching ears and big yellow eyes.

I swung open the door to find Eden wearing black leggings and a bright turquoise shirt that fell off one shoulder, revealing the wide strap of a black bra or tank top underneath. She looked like she'd stepped out of an eighties-themed exercise class, minus the legwarmers, and *damn* if this look didn't do it for me just like everything else I'd seen her wearing.

"Hey," I said, my voice coming out lower than usual.

Eden's eyes warmed. "Hi."

"Come on in. Jiji's been waiting for you."

I tried—I swear to God, I tried—to keep my gaze from dropping to her ass, but when she bent down to nuzzle Jiji, I lost the fight. It hadn't even been forty-eight hours since the last time I saw her and I felt like I was starved for her.

"Dinner smells wonderful," she said as she straightened.

Though my gaze shot to her face, I knew she'd caught me. Her lips tipped upward, she crossed her arms over her chest, and those twinkling eyes narrowed. I fought the urge to cover the distance between us and kiss that adorable smirk off her face.

"See something you like, Milo?"

"Fuck yes," I muttered.

A startled laugh burst from her lips, then it was Eden closing the distance, rising up on her toes as her arms tangled around my shoulders. My hands went to her waist, slipping under the fabric of her shirt so I could brush my fingertips over bare skin.

"Then what are you waiting for?" she whispered against my lips.

I couldn't manage more than a growl before I captured her sweet, laughing mouth. It took less than a heartbeat for her to melt into me, each soft curve of her body molding against my frame. When I stroked my tongue into her mouth, she purred deep in her throat, and I let one hand slide down to cup the perfect ass she'd caught me admiring.

A persistent beep from the oven timer cut through the bliss of having her in my arms, and we drew reluctantly apart. Eden's cheeks were pink, her eyes a dark, hazy gold. I couldn't resist another quick touch of our lips before taking her hand and leading her into the kitchen.

"What are we having?" she asked as she climbed onto a stool at the breakfast bar.

"Herb-crusted chicken and rice pilaf, with fresh buttermilk biscuits and corn. I hope you're hungry, because I'm not used to cooking for two people and I might have overestimated a bit."

She laughed. "I'm starving, so extra sounds great."

It felt good, having her here with me as I moved throughout the kitchen. I enjoyed cooking because I enjoyed eating, but it wasn't often that I had company to appreciate the fruits of my efforts. As I was flipping the chicken breasts, Eden's voice broke through the quiet.

"I hate cooking."

I reset the timer, then cocked my head at her. The pink in her cheeks had turned to a deep crimson, like she was embarrassed by her admission. After tossing the oven mitt onto the counter, I came over to where she was sitting and cupped my hand around the back of her neck, leaning close to her ear.

"Then it's a good thing I like doing it."

Eden laughed and relaxed under my palm. "I guess it is, yes."

"What was that look on your face?" I asked gently. "Did you think I'd be upset that you hate cooking?"

For a second, she bit her lip, then her gaze lifted to mine, shining with that vulnerability I'd only caught glimpses of before. I stroked the side of her throat with my thumb until she nodded.

"Why? Because it's a traditionally female job or something?"

A tiny shrug was her only response, so I leaned in close until our foreheads were touching and her eyes locked on my face.

"I know we don't know each other that well yet, but let me assure you I give zero shits about gender roles or societal expectations. I know how to cook not only because my mom refused to raise helpless man-babies, but because I enjoy it. I'm more than happy to feed you, okay?"

"Okay," she whispered.

"Anything else you hate doing?"

Her lips quirked. "I don't ever make my bed."

"A rebel," I mused, kissing the tip of her nose. "You should know I find rebels very fucking sexy."

When bright laughter finally burst from her lips, I vowed to spend as much time as she'd let me making her laugh, whether that turned out to be days or weeks or the rest of my life. I managed not to voice that thought and scare the hell out of her, though.

"How was your first official weekend?"

Her nose wrinkled and her eyes dimmed slightly. "Fine, but my tires were all flat when Addie drove me in yesterday."

"What?" I blinked at her. "All of them?"

"Yup. They weren't slashed, just deflated, like someone let the air out."

"Why would anyone do that? Especially while it was parked on the street and anyone could have seen," I muttered, shaking my head.

She offered a tiny grin. "You think Carter has an alibi?"

"I think Carter would go to war against anyone who tried to mess with you," I replied. "Were you able to get them fixed?"

"Yeah, a mechanic from that Saucy Wrench place came by to replace them. Apparently my old ones were verging on bald anyway, so I guess whoever it was did me a favor, because now I have four brand new tires to get me through any lingering snow we might get."

I frowned. "Did you file a police report?"

"They stopped over and took a statement, but it was probably just kids messing around. Though they did say if I'd been parked in your spot, some of the cameras on Main Street might have caught it."

"Then park there," I said firmly. "Please. All the more reason for you to take that spot. I don't want anyone messing with your car, Eden. Or you."

She narrowed her eyes at me, but finally heaved a sigh and replied, "Okay, fine."

I stroked her cheek, reveling in the softness of her skin and the way her lips parted at my touch. If I didn't focus on dinner, we'd end up doing something other than eating together, and she'd said she was starving.

Time to change directions again.

"So, Garden of Delights—which is a killer name, by the way—is closed on Mondays?" I asked, hoping to sound casual.

"Yes, and I'm not sure it's as cool as Dueling Dragons, but thanks. With a name like Eden, I figured I might as well play it up."

So far, she'd spoken very little of her parents and only mentioned her brother once. I didn't want to dig too deep, not when things were still light and easy between us, but I hoped she might throw me a few crumbs.

"I mean this in the nicest way possible, but it sounds like a hippie name," I ventured.

She scoffed. "My parents are far from hippies. They're extremely religious. Like, a woman's place is in the home, wearing long skirts and having lots of babies and being sub-servient to her husband."

"Hence the assumption I'd want a woman to cook and clean for me," I said softly. When she nodded, I grimaced. "Shit, I'm sorry. That had to be tough."

"We don't have much of a relationship. It's fine. I had Addie's parents growing up, and they always treated me like I was one of their own."

Running a hand over my beard, I said, "I guess your par-ents aren't terribly supportive of you owning a business then, huh?"

"Being thirty-two and unmarried? Not supportive. Going to college instead of finding a godly man to guide me with a firm hand? Not supportive. Owning a store that sells sinful, immodest lingerie? Unforgivable. Needless to say, I haven't told them and have no intention of doing so."

"Eden," I murmured, rubbing my thumb over the soft skin under her ear. "You're an incredible human being and that store is already a smashing success. Your parents are the idiots missing out on all that is you."

She sucked in a breath and dropped her forehead so it hit my shoulder. Though she didn't speak, her shoulders shuddered under my other hand. It was a long moment before she lifted her head again and met my eyes.

"I don't want to give them another minute of this time with you," she said firmly.

"Then we'll stop talking about them."

Her resulting smile was a bit tentative, but that didn't make it any less beautiful—or any less tempting. I gave in and kissed her, slow and soft and sweet, until I knew she was as tempted as I was to forget all about her parents, about dinner, about everything outside of the two of us.

When I lifted my head, I bit back a triumphant grin at her dazed expression, brushed my thumb over the flush in her cheek, and set about serving up our dinner.

This is a marathon, I reminded myself.

Then again, I'd never been a very good runner. Maybe a few little sprints were a fine addition to my slow but steady jog toward the future. I had long legs—I could even manage a few hurdles in my way.

Most likely, I'd have to let Eden decide our pace as we journeyed onward, and if the look in her eyes was anything to go by, she had some very definite ideas about that.

Chapter Twelve

EDEN

MILO WAS A PHENOMENAL cook. I ate two servings of rice pilaf and made him give me the recipe, but it was dessert that tipped me over the edge.

The man had made us chocolate chip cookies. From scratch.

We brought the container of cookies over to the couch, agreed on a superhero movie we'd both already seen, and somehow ended up overstuffed and stretched out along the length of the sofa. Milo's head was on the armrest, mine on his chest, with my body tucked between him and the back cushions.

Sometime before the hero triumphed in his final battle against the villain, I fell asleep. The sun was shining when I reluctantly peeled my eyes open, only to see that Milo had extricated himself from under me and was in the midst of tucking a blanket around my shoulders.

"Hey," he said softly. "I was going to leave you a note. I need to go over and open the shop, but you're welcome to stay here as long as you want. You looked so sweet, I didn't want to wake you."

I rubbed my eyes, then realized he was wearing glasses with thick black frames. "Oh my god. I didn't think you could get any hotter, now this?"

Milo laughed. "I didn't put my contacts in yet. Shockingly, I might have overslept a bit, thanks to an excellent couch companion. You're an expert snuggler, you know."

"Hmm. I should go." I burrowed under the blanket while my brain slowly fired up, not quite getting the memo that my body should be moving off the couch instead of sinking into it.

"Seriously, stay as long as you like. There's coffee, cookies. Cereal, uh, maybe some Pop Tarts."

"Coffee?" The endearment warmed me even more than the blanket, but coffee was my morning lifeblood.

Milo's beard twitched as he grinned. "Yes, coffee. C'mon, I've got enough time to have a cup with you before I go."

My clothes were rumpled and my hair almost certainly a disaster, but his gaze was warm as it traveled over me, top to toe. With his hand wrapped around mine, he led me toward the kitchen, laughing softly when I slumped onto a stool.

"Not a morning person, huh?"

"I'm a morning person when I wake up at home in my bed with my programmable coffee pot ready to roll," I corrected. "I can't even remember the last time I fell asleep during a movie, nevermind on a couch. How are you so spry this morning?"

"Mostly because I had a beautiful woman draped over me all night, but the fact that I've been up long enough to shower and drink my first cup of coffee helps."

"Am I going to make you late?"

Milo poured me a mug of coffee, slid a sugar bowl and two different creamer options toward me, and grinned. "If you did, it'd still be worth it, but no. I've got another fifteen minutes before we hit critical mass."

We sat there together, sipping coffee and eating cookies, settling into the kind of easy conversation that I'd come to associate with Milo. In fact, everything felt easier when I was around him, more natural, like I'd spent my life in the wrong climate and finally found the environment where I could thrive.

It was unsettling, even if it was also a relief.

By the time Milo needed to leave for work, my muddied thoughts had cleared enough to drive home and figure out what exactly I was going to do with my day off. At the door of my car, Milo kissed me, light and sweet.

"Carter comes to the store after school on Mondays, but I'm alone until then. If you're around the shop, I mean, and want to visit."

"I just might take you up on that. Thank you again for dinner. And breakfast."

"It was my pleasure, Eden," he murmured.

With that, Milo grinned, planted one last swift kiss on my lips, and stepped back so I could get behind the wheel. I gave a stupid little wave before backing out of his driveway, then it hit me that we'd spent another night together.

Asleep. On his freaking couch.

MILO'S PARKING SPOT WAS open when I pulled up in front of the stores, so I decided I'd take him up on the obvious offer, especially to protect my four new tires. I couldn't quite see into Dueling Dragons from there, but I was more nervous about walking in to visit Milo that afternoon than I had been about approaching him at the bar during Comic Con.

It was silly and ridiculous and I couldn't stop replaying the scene from that morning, waking up to Milo gazing down at me.

Here I'd been worried about it being impossible to recreate the magic between us, and he just kept gifting me with more magical moments.

So instead of going next door like a grownup, I puttered around Garden of Delights, restocking the racks that had been depleted over the weekend, cleaning smudges from the mirrors in the two dressing rooms, updating spreadsheets, and doodling window display ideas for the future.

Finally, when I had nothing left to do, I locked up and made the short trek to Milo's store.

His face lit when I walked in, though he teased, "I was afraid maybe you weren't going to show up."

"Am I that transparent?" I asked.

I didn't have it in me to tease back, but Milo must have sensed that, because his expression turned serious. Leaving his seat behind the counter, he came around to take both my hands in his.

"I'm sorry, Eden. I didn't mean anything by it."

"Does it bother you that I'm not the same woman who propositioned you in that bar?"

Milo's head jerked back in surprise, but he didn't release my hands. "What are you talking about?"

"I just...I was bold that night. Decisive. That's not who I am."

"Eden," he admonished gently, "that's exactly who you are. You struck out on your own, opened a kickass store, made plans that will help people live their lives to the fullest. If that's not bold and decisive, I don't know what is."

I blinked at him. "I never thought of it that way."

"It's so innate, so integral to who you *are*, I'm not surprised you didn't see it. Not only are you the exact same woman who walked up to me in the bar, every moment I spend with you shows me more and more of what's beneath the surface. And I like what I'm finding, Eden. A whole hell of a lot."

"Oh," I replied, catching my lip in my teeth.

"Oh," Milo repeated with a grin. "I don't know if you've caught on, but that was my first surprise hookup too. I guess it's not really a one-night stand if we're dating now."

"Are we dating?"

His grin widened. "I mean, we've had dinner twice, went out for drinks once, you slept over at my house last night, and my cat is obsessed with you."

A giggle bubbled up in my throat and escaped before I could lock it down. "Right. Dating, then. I guess if we hadn't been dating, those cookies would have forced the issue."

Milo burst out laughing just as his nephew tore open the door and careened to a stop beside us. The kid grinned up at me as he shoved a pile of mail into Milo's chest. Though Milo let go of my hands to grab the stack of envelopes and catalogs, he slipped one arm around my waist.

"Hi," Carter said. "Are you Uncle Milo's girlfriend now?"

Even though we'd just cleared up the dating issue, I hesitated long enough for Milo to answer for us both.

"Yup. Got homework to do?"

Carter ignored the question to ask me, "Are you gonna hang out with us for a bit?"

"Am I going to distract you from your homework?" I countered.

"Nah, I did some of it on the bus already. I only have a page of math problems left to do. I heard you beat Uncle Milo at Mortal Kombat. Even Dad can't beat him most of the time."

I allowed myself a moment to feel smug, then nodded. "Sure, I'll hang out for a while, if it's okay with your uncle."

Milo grinned, squeezed my hip, and murmured, "Absolutely. Come on, as the guest of honor, you get the un-wobbly stool."

Once we were all situated behind the counter, Milo started sorting through the mail. This row of storefronts shared a big, rusty mailbox outside of Dueling Dragons' front door, and Carter explained that it was his job to bring it in on the days he came after school. After Milo sorted it, Carter would deliver it to the shop on the other side, which did custom framing for photos and artwork.

"If you're closed on Mondays, what should I do with your mail?" Carter asked, frowning. "Maybe you should come over to visit us so you can pick it up."

The kid's gray eyes were wide and innocent, rimmed with thick black lashes. I wondered if he was playing me, but he looked hopeful rather than devious.

Just when I opened my mouth to agree, Milo muttered, "What the hell?"

I turned to see what he was looking at. Two piles of mail were stacked on the counter, one for Milo and one for the framing place, with just a local coupon circular beside them for me. In Milo's hand, though, was a crumpled white envelope addressed to "Peddler of Evil."

"Oh, shit," I whispered, then my gaze shot to Carter. "I mean, shoot."

"You can swear in front of me, it's okay."

"I think that's one for my pile," I joked weakly.

Milo frowned at the envelope, then at me. "What? Why would you think that?"

"The phrasing. That's the kind of stuff my parents and the people from their church used to say. Milo, it's no big deal. I knew the shop might draw some negative attention, especially in a small town."

"Your shop has been open for three days, Eden. Getting hate mail three days in seems like a big deal to me. Look, I'm going to open it," he said quietly.

I sighed. "Be my guest."

Part of me wanted to see what was inside, but the other part wanted to throw it straight into the trash. Just because I knew people might hate what I was doing didn't make it easier to realize it was going to hit home so quickly.

The envelope contained a preachy orange flier calling for repentance, offering redemption in the eyes of God for turning away from Satan. There was no identifying information on it, though, not even the name of a church or organization. That struck me as odd, having seen my share of that kind of thing before. Usually they hoped to gain congregants seeking a second chance.

In fact, now that I thought about it, that little tract left on my windshield hadn't had the name of a church on it, either.

Milo crumpled it into a ball and threw it in the garbage can under the counter. His lips were tight, hands clenched into fists even after the flier was out of sight.

"I'm sorry," I said quietly.

Both of them swiveled to look at me in surprise.

"What are you sorry for?" Milo asked.

Carter set his small hand on my arm and said, "Haters gonna hate. You just gotta shrug it off and keep your head up."

For a second, I just stared at the boy, my lips parted in shock. He held onto his solemn expression for a long moment, then he finally cracked a tiny grin and Milo slung one arm around each of our necks.

"Thank you, oh wise one," he intoned, "but more importantly, who do you guys think would win in a battle between Superman and One-Punch Man?"

I couldn't help it—I started laughing, turning my face into Milo's shoulder. With the two of them telling jokes and chatting about all things superhero, I forgot all about the hate mail and let myself simply enjoy the afternoon.

Chapter Thirteen

MILO

THE WEIRD PAMPHLET HAD me tweaked, but Eden's nonchalant response to it freaked me out even worse. I didn't like thinking that this gorgeous, successful woman had dealt with enough hate in her life to make her barely bat an eye at the hellfire and brimstone bullshit in that envelope.

Carter's energetic presence acted as a buffer for the afternoon, forcing me to not make a big deal out of the incident. At one point, when Eden left to use the bathroom at the back of the store, I told Carter that if he saw anything like that envelope again, he was commissioned to make sure it got to me instead of Eden.

"Like a secret mission?" he asked, eyes bright.

I nodded solemnly. "Top secret. Vital importance."

"You got it, Uncle Milo," he whispered.

Maybe it was uncool to involve the kid in my newfound quest to keep Eden from experiencing that pain again, but my nephew seemed proud of his new job as my lieutenant.

When Maverick showed up to get Carter after work, he issued a quiet, sincere apology to Eden for upsetting her at their last meeting. Carter and I pretended to be busy sorting his homework folder, but we were both shamelessly eavesdropping.

"It's fine, Maverick. Really. It was a shock to see Milo again and there was a lot going on in my head," she murmured.

My brother looked like he wanted to say more, but he caught my eye over Eden's shoulder and smiled at her instead—not his usual flirtatious charm, but an expression filled with warmth, one that conveyed his happiness for us both in finding each other again.

"Dad, did you know Eden beat Uncle Milo at Mortal Kombat? You haven't beaten him since that time last summer when he was recovering from the flu!"

Maverick's brows dropped ominously low at that. "She did, huh?"

When a giggle burst from Eden's lips, my heart lifted. I slid my arm around her waist and nodded at my brother. "She absolutely did. Best button-mashing I've seen in decades."

"Stop insulting my technique," she grumbled.

"I'm sorry, Eden, but I have to see my brother being humbled up close and in person. You should come with Milo to our next game night. As long as you don't mind a little friendly competition."

"Friendly, my ass," I said against her ear.

Eden looked uncertain about the invitation for a split second, then her eyes lifted to mine and a radiant smile spread across her face. Those smiles were like a drug, each one making me want more.

"That sounds like fun. I'm in."

"We'll get Libby to join us. Maybe she'll be a civilizing force on Mark and Mav," I said, grinning back at her.

"Yes! Then we can play tournament style!" Carter cried.

He threw his backpack over his shoulder, gave me a fist bump, and then offered the same to Eden. When she bumped his fist with hers, my chest threatened to burst wide open.

Maverick lifted his hand in farewell, winking at us both, and ushered Carter out of the store. Though music played from a speaker in the back corner, the sudden quiet had Eden fidgeting as she joined me behind the counter again.

"I should probably go, too," she said softly.

Instead of responding, I lifted her hand and set it on my chest. She slipped it upward, over my shoulder, until her palm cupped the back of my neck. It was only another second before she stepped closer, fitting the front of her body against mine.

"But maybe I have time for a kiss goodbye," she whispered. "If you don't mind, I mean."

"Not at all," I whispered back, and I set about prolonging that goodbye for almost half an hour.

Garden of Delights had an interesting impact on my business that week in the form of another huge influx of customers toting lavender bags. No one expressly stated that Eden had sent them, but most of them ended up making a purchase. Several inquired about upcoming event nights, half of Olivia's newest prints were sold, and three people placed special orders for products I didn't have in stock.

None of them felt like pity-shoppers.

I was contemplating the phenomenon when Olivia showed up Friday evening with a new batch of artwork—with Adelaide in tow.

"Can't stay and chat, we have a reservation," Liv called as she passed me the bag of prints. "But in case this uptick in sales continues, here's a new batch for you."

Adelaide grinned at me. "Who knew there'd be such a crossover between nerds and naughty underwear?"

Olivia leaned in close to Adelaide's ear and whispered, "I did."

I laughed and waved them off for their date night, then hurriedly closed the store so I could pop over to see Eden before she locked the doors. Maverick had managed to coordinate another game night for Sunday evening at his place, but I hadn't gotten a whole lot of private time with Eden during the week. I wanted to make sure she was really okay with being surrounded by the vast majority of my family all at once.

Two women were leaving Eden's store as I arrived, so I held the door for them and then met Eden's smirk from across the shop. She tossed her hair over her shoulder, which gave me a chance to admire those long, dark locks against the pale blue fabric covering her upper half above the counter.

"What's that look for?" I demanded.

"Just thinking that chivalry is definitely *not* dead."

I headed straight for her, ignoring the racks of satin and lace on either side of me as the rest of her dress came into view. It was a different style than I'd seen on her, but no less mouthwatering. The wide neckline exposed just a hint of the tattoo on her collarbone, and I admired the way it clung to the curve of her hips before kicking out in a little ruffle at her knees.

"I'm thinking some very unchivalrous thoughts right now," I growled.

Her lips, glossy pink and utterly kissable, curved upward. "Oh? So I shouldn't wear something like this to game night?"

After ascertaining that we were alone in the store—I probably wouldn't have noticed a brass band in the corner after I caught sight of her—I circled the counter until her hands landed at my waist, then I bent my head and brushed a kiss to her tattoo.

"You could, but I'd definitely embarrass myself in front of my brothers. Carter would get a pretty graphic anatomy lesson and I might end up dragging you into the coat closet to make out instead of playing video games with my family."

"Not much room in a coat closet," Eden mused, but she shivered under my lips.

"We could always skip game night and have dinner at my place again."

"No can do, cowboy. I promised your nephew I'd show him a master in action. But if you want to cook for me again, I wouldn't turn down an invitation for next week."

Oh, I could work with that.

"Count on it, then. You, me, no interruptions. Maybe we'll both stay awake this time."

"If I recall correctly," she teased as she twirled away from me and started her closing routine, "you have a number of tricks up your sleeve that would *definitely* keep me awake."

"Christ," I muttered, closing my eyes as blood rushed immediately away from my head.

Eden's laughter was light and carefree in a way that more than made up for my inconvenient reaction to those mental images. My eyes were still closed when I felt her dress brush my arm, so I reached out and snagged her around the waist.

"Temptation personified," I muttered. "That's what Olivia called you."

Her lips lifted at the corners. "Did she? The one who's out with Addie tonight?"

"Yeah. She had a table of artwork at Comic Con and caught me staring at you across the room that day. She referred to you as my rockabilly goddess. As soon as you walked up to me at the bar, I thought it fit you perfectly. And you're definitely a walking temptation."

"No one's ever called me a goddess before."

I rubbed my thumbs against her sides. "Do you mind it?"

"I don't think so," she replied, a pink tinge creeping along her cheeks. "Not from you, at least. Addie might have a fit if Olivia keeps calling me that, though."

"Now that Addie is in the picture, I doubt Olivia would be caught dead calling anyone else a term of endearment. She's loyal as hell, even if she is a pain in my ass."

"Then they're a match made in heaven, because Addie's a pain in mine," Eden said with a laugh.

I grinned and, before I could think better of it, asked, "Your parents let you spend time with your cousins even though Addie is gay?"

"She's bi, but believe me, we went to great lengths to keep them from ever finding that out. Aunt Jocelyn is my mom's sister. They grew up Lutheran or something, very low-key. My mom didn't start her descent into the hellfire and damnation side of religion until she met my dad, and Jocelyn never gave up hope that she'd be able to pull her back from it."

"But that didn't happen, I take it?"

Eden sighed. "No. And once I left home, my mom cut all contact with Jocelyn. She blamed her for leading me astray. Aunt Jocelyn would have tried to shield me from that, but we were in the house while they were on the phone and my mom's screaming was so loud, we could all hear it."

"Shit. I'm sorry."

"Me too. When I was a kid, I didn't question how they convinced my parents to let me visit so often, but as I got older, I realized they created this perfect display that they put on for Mom and Dad. All of them, including Addie and Rob, would pretend we were attending church twice a week while I was with them. Everybody dressed a particular way when I was dropped off or picked up. Jocelyn was determined not to give them any reason to keep me away."

"And your parents bought it?" I asked.

"Yes. Maybe? Sometimes I think they just pretended to accept it all at face value because it got me out of their hair," she replied, shrugging.

"Baby," I whispered.

"Nope. No. We're not going there, Milo. It's over, I never hear from them. It doesn't matter anymore. And you're only allowed to call me baby when you're being sweet, not when you're pitying the sad little girl I once was."

"I'm always sweet, am I not?"

She smirked, then it blossomed into another beautiful smile. "We'll see how sweet you are when I'm kicking your ass in front of your family on Sunday."

Chapter Fourteen

EDEN

PICKING OUT CLOTHES WAS not usually a hardship for me. I dressed for style or for comfort, but almost everything I owned fell into both categories. Except, maybe, for a couple pairs of shoes I reserved for occasions when I wanted to look hot but knew I wouldn't be on my feet very long.

Dressing for an evening with Milo's family had me stumped.

He insisted it was low-key, just a relaxing night with his brothers, his nephew, and his sister-in-law. We'd be eating pizza, playing video games, and lounging around Maverick's living room. All I'd managed to do so far was pull on a pair of charcoal gray leggings.

I was still staring blindly into my closet when my doorbell rang.

"Shit, shit, double shit!" I yelped, grabbing a tunic-length green sweater and yanking it over my head as I ran toward the door. "I'm coming!"

When I threw open the door, Milo's gaze roamed over my features, immediately spotting the panic that threatened to choke me. Instead of waiting for me to throw on my coat and join him on the porch, he gently nudged me back into the apartment with one hand on my belly.

"I couldn't decide what to wear," I whispered.

"Eden," he murmured, stroking his fingers along my jaw. "Take a breath."

Caught in the soft look in his eyes, I drew oxygen into my lungs and exhaled on a sigh.

"You look perfect, but this is just us hanging with my brothers. Carter will probably have pizza sauce all over his shirt by the time we finish eating. Maverick will most likely be in sweatpants because he spends his weekdays in suits and ties. You have nothing to worry about. There's no one to impress, okay?"

That edge of panic receded a bit, more due to his touch than the reassurance itself. I closed my eyes and leaned into his hand, sighing softly when his thumb swept across my cheek.

"Right. Okay. I just need my coat."

"Hey," Milo whispered as he tipped my chin up. "I know what will help you relax."

There was no need to ask what he meant, because he showed me, dropping his head to capture my mouth in an achingly sweet kiss. I was realizing that very few things couldn't be helped by one of Milo's kisses. It ended too soon, but I let out a slow breath when he drew away.

"You're a magician," I told him.

He grinned. "Go on, get your coat. Mark and Libby are picking up the pizzas."

On the ride to Maverick's house, I twisted my fingers together to keep from tapping them against my legs, but after parking the car in his brother's driveway, Milo lifted my hands to his lips and kissed each one in turn.

"They're going to love you. Especially if you ruin my record of destroying them all during the tournament. No pressure, though."

I laughed and the knot of tension eased another notch. "Right."

"Did you hear from Addie about the big date last Friday?"

"Only that it was fantastic. I guess they really hit it off. Addie can be a handful, but she has the biggest heart of anyone I know. I want her to be happy."

Milo smiled over at me. "Olivia is always digging for details about you, but she tends to be suspiciously close-lipped about her own love life. Even so, she texted me yesterday with nothing but heart-eyes. I hoped that meant it went well."

Carter greeted us before we got two steps into the front hall. "Uncle Milo! Eden! Come in, come in."

"Sorry guys, he's hyped up on sugar. Made the rookie mistake of stopping for candy while we were out shopping earlier,"

Maverick said as he clasped Milo's shoulder. He then leaned down to kiss my cheek and muttered, "Rookie mistake."

Oh, god. They were a cheek-kissing family. Okay. I could do this.

I managed to smile, but Milo caught my elbow and widened his eyes at me until I huffed a laugh, then we followed Carter and Maverick into the living room. He held me back just enough that his brother was out of earshot.

"If you don't want him touching you, just tell me. I'll let him know," he murmured in my ear.

I shook my head. "It's fine. Just surprised me."

"I'll warn you right now, Libby is a hugger. It's rubbed off on Mark over the years, but no one's going to force physical contact on you, Eden."

"Milo, it's fine. Really. Addie is as touchy-feely as they come, but Rob is pretty reserved and my brother...well, we never hugged, so I wasn't expecting it. I promise you that I'll let you know if I'm uncomfortable, okay?"

He studied my face, then nodded. "Can I just mention how gorgeous you look in this sweater? Your eyes look extra bright tonight."

I gave him a warning look as we reached the overstuffed couch, but as soon as we were seated, Carter took over the conversation, telling us about the neighbor's new foster puppy and his quest to convince Maverick that they needed a dog. He was still talking when I heard the front door open and close.

"Do you like dogs, Aunt Eden?" he asked, then his face went slack. "I mean, Eden."

The newcomers had reached the living room just in time to hear it and I felt the weight of everyone's gaze on my face. I had no intention of embarrassing the kid, and some hidden part of me was touched to be called aunt. It was one more tiny symbol of inclusion, of welcome, tattooing itself on my heart.

I leaned toward Carter and said in a stage whisper, "Don't tell Jiji, but I'm usually more of a dog person."

Milo squeezed my knee as everyone laughed. Mark and Libby moved further into the room and we stood to greet them. I almost snorted when I saw that Mark was very blonde. The three of them somehow shared those gray eyes, each as handsome as the last, but all with such different hair colors.

"Eden, this is my other brother, Mark, and his significantly better half, Libby," Milo said.

Despite his earlier warning about hugs, both of them only shook my hand. Libby was the most stunningly beautiful woman I'd ever seen, with smooth brown skin and gorgeous black curls, but it was her smile that went the distance toward soothing my nerves at meeting Milo's family.

"It's so good to finally meet you, Eden," she said warmly. "I can't wait to come check out your store, I've heard it's fabulous. I'm planning to stop in on my next day off."

"Libby is a doctor. She runs the clinic in town," Mark told me.

"And you have your own store, right?"

He smiled broadly. "Davies Soap Emporium, yeah. Maybe we can do a collaboration sometime. It'd be cutting it pretty close for this Valentine's Day, but I bet we could create some kickass gift offerings for future holidays."

Milo grumbled under his breath, "Comics would be hotter."

The rest of that knot in my chest released when the brothers started roughhousing and Libby moved closer to my side, rolling her eyes at the tangle of limbs before turning to wink at me.

"Welcome to the chaos."

The Davies crew took their game nights seriously—we decimated the pizzas Mark and Libby had brought, then got straight to the video game tournament. Even the ribbing between brothers had a gentle edge to it, an undercurrent of a love so strong, it nearly bowled me over.

And somehow, they kept me from feeling like an outsider, gently pulling me into their teasing. Addie and her friends had always welcomed me into their group, but this felt different.

Like I was actually a part of it all, rather than being included by default. Like I was valued for who I was, rather than who my cousins happened to know.

I won enough rounds in fighting games to secure the praise of the family, then joined forces with Libby to insist on a different game. We switched over to MarioKart and an unspoken alliance grew between me, Libby, and Carter. Between the three of us, we kept the Davies brothers from winning a single race.

"I think it's time to declare a new family champion," Mark said finally, lifting a beer to toast my success. "To Eden."

"To Eden!"

Amidst the chorus of cheers, I stood from the couch, dipped a little curtsy, and dropped back down next to Milo. He tickled my side, but his expression was soft as he tugged me closer to him on the cushion.

"You're a total badass, Eden Campbell."

Though I wasn't sure I believed him—about being a badass *or* about being bold and decisive—I decided to embrace it. I might not see it yet, but if other people did, who was I to argue?

Besides, I'd spent my life feeling like an outsider, never quite fitting in even with my closest friends, who happened to be my cousins. Here among Milo and his family, I felt like I was part of something bigger than myself.

Only time would tell if that feeling would last.

Chapter Fifteen

MILO

IT WAS ON THE tip of my tongue to ask her to spend the night with me, but Eden started yawning before we even left Maverick's house. I swallowed my disappointment and tried to remind myself we had plenty of time, even if every cell in my body longed to have her in my arms again.

As soon as we were buckled into my car, though, she glanced over at me from beneath those long lashes, her fingers tangled on her lap again.

"I threw a change of clothes into my bag," she said quickly.

Slowly, my lips curved in the darkness. "Does that mean you're sleeping over?"

"It means if you invite me to stay over, I'm prepared to say yes."

"Okay, then. Eden, would you like to spend the night with me?" I asked, reaching over to cup her cheek.

The breath she drew was ragged enough for me to hear it, then she nodded against my palm. I could only just see her features in the lights from the dashboard, but I felt her cheek lift with a smile.

"Yes, I would."

"Excellent," I breathed, grinning at her. "Jiji will be very happy."

Eden laughed. "Well, anything for Jiji. As long as it doesn't include sleeping on the couch again."

I fought back the giddy wave of excitement that taking Eden home with me inspired. Last time, we'd only slept—and I'd be fine with a repeat, if that was all she wanted this time. Cuddling up in bed together and whispering in the darkness sounded like a perfect end to the evening.

But if she wanted more...my hands tightened on the steering wheel and my body tightened in anticipation.

When we pulled into my driveway, Eden grabbed her bag from the floorboards while I jogged over to open her door. Mark did stuff like that for Libby all the time, and even when she rolled her eyes over it, she still gave him the same pleased little smile that lit Eden's expression as she stepped out.

Jiji ignored my presence, weaving between Eden's feet the second we crossed the threshold.

"Ungrateful beast," I muttered.

Eden laughed, bending down to scratch the cat's cheeks and giving me a perfect view of her ass. Presented with such bounty, I couldn't stop myself from appreciating it, though I did manage to keep my hands to myself.

Barely.

As she stood back up, Eden gave me a look like she knew what I'd been thinking. Instead of being offended, though, she moved closer and hooked her thumbs in my belt loops. I circled her waist with my arms, not pulling her in but following her lead.

Once we were pressed together, she propped her chin on my chest so she was gazing up at me.

"I want you," she whispered.

"Thank fuck." Relief nearly buckled my knees.

"You have an actual bedroom, right? Not just a couch?" One dark brow arched upward even as her lips twitched.

I dropped my head to nip the edge of her jaw. "I do. Would you like to see it?"

"As long as Jiji doesn't mind being locked out temporarily, yes."

Before releasing her, I kissed her smiling lips, slow and deep. She opened immediately, pressing herself closer, her hands shifting so her fingers could twist in the sides of my t-shirt. When I finally lifted my head away, I remembered what I'd been meaning to tell her.

"We can sleep in tomorrow. Rafael, my part-timer, wanted a few extra hours a week, so he's going to open the store on Mondays."

Her expression, already soft and a little dazed, melted into a smile. "That is fantastic news."

"And I programmed my coffee pot."

"Even better," she muttered, then tried to tug me back down for another kiss.

I shook my head, untangled her hands from my shirt, and pulled her toward the bedroom, saying, "If I keep kissing you out there, I'll end up tearing off your clothes and Jiji might destroy them out of spite."

"Can't upset the kitty, can we?" Eden laughed as she skipped along behind me.

When we hit the bedroom, I spun and caught her in my arms. Her laughter faded into a low purr as I trailed my lips down the side of her neck and back up again.

"We should talk first," I murmured into her ear.

"About what?"

At her breathless question, I grinned against her skin. "About what you liked or didn't like at the hotel. We didn't know each other then, so I was going on instinct."

"Milo, let me assure you, your instincts are outstanding."

"Yeah?"

"God, yes."

I skated my hands up to her waist, taking the hem of her sweater with them. Eden raised her arms and I pulled it over her head, then tossed it onto the dresser beside us. That night at the hotel, as extraordinary as it had been, hadn't involved a whole lot of conversation. It was one thing to read her cues and adjust as needed; making sure she got exactly what she wanted was another.

"I took charge," I said, running my gaze over her bare skin and following the path with my fingertips. "You're okay with that?"

"Yes," she breathed as she shivered under my touch.

"Anything you didn't absolutely love from that night?"

Her head fell back as I ghosted my thumbs across the black satin of her bra. "No, I loved all of it."

"Anything you wish I'd done but didn't?"

"Milo, for Christ's sake, please can we stop talking and go back to kissing?"

I laughed and released her just long enough to pull off my t-shirt. Eden's lips parted, the tip of her pink tongue sneaking out to wet them before she reached out to run her palms over my chest.

"Beautiful," she whispered.

"I want you bare and spread out on my bed," I replied, my voice low.

Eden shivered, her lashes sweeping down for a second. After a half step backward, she reached behind her, unhooked her bra, and let it tumble from her shoulders. I fought the urge to cup her full breasts in my hands, toy with those plump nipples as they tightened under my eyes, instead of waiting as she shimmied out of her leggings and a pair of lacy black panties.

"Fucking hell," I whispered.

She tossed me a grin. "I do own a store full of sexy underwear."

"Starting to see the benefits of that," I replied, taking a step closer to her as she backed away toward the bed.

Though I'd become well-acquainted with her body at the hotel, it wasn't the same as seeing it in my bedroom, draped across my sheets. With her dark hair fanned out over my pillows, I felt a surge of satisfaction, followed by a rush of possessiveness that threw me, because I'd never felt that way over a partner.

Eden's expression shifted from shy to sultry when she caught sight of my face. I moved slowly to the foot of the bed, studying every inch of her. In the light of my bedside lamp, her skin glowed almost golden, though a rosy flush stained her cheeks and chest.

"Paradise," I murmured. "Spread your legs for me."

Biting her lip, she did, and I swallowed a groan. Those dark curls, the wet heat I knew I'd find there, the way she responded to each quiet command—fuck, she was perfect. As I stroked my gaze over her body, her fingers clutched at the navy comforter beneath her.

"I want to taste you."

Gasping out a laugh, she replied, "Be my guest."

I grinned and planted one knee on the mattress, sliding my palms from her ankles to her knees, opening them wider.

Though her skin was wonderfully sensitive, she wasn't ticklish anywhere but her ribs. Even when I trailed my fingertips up the insides of her thighs, she only sighed with pleasure.

When I dropped my head and ran my tongue over her, she shifted restlessly and a quiet moan escaped her lips. I repeated the caress, determined to have her writhing and desperate before sending her over the brink.

"Milo," she whimpered as I slid a finger inside. "Please."

"No need to beg, doll. I'll give you everything you need." I swirled my tongue over her clit and added another finger, curling them in the way I knew would force her closer to the edge.

Fuck, I could listen to her all night long. Every helpless noise she made only inspired me to prolong this moment forever.

But I also couldn't wait to be inside her again, so I sealed my lips around her clit and fluttered my tongue over it. Her hips bucked, then her thighs quivered on either side of me, a sure sign she was getting close. I rotated my wrist, sucked hard, and drank in her cry of release as her back arched off the bed.

"That's it. Fucking beautiful," I growled against her trembling flesh, remembering how she'd responded to little comments like that the last time. A quiet purr of pleasure from her served as confirmation.

God, I'd missed this.

I kissed each hip bone as I crawled up her body, nuzzled the soft roundness of her belly, and drew each dusky nipple into my mouth until they were peaked and glistening. The sounds she made were like a symphony, soft gasps and little whimpers and low, sexy moans.

"Gorgeous, you know that?" I whispered against her throat as I slid my fingers back between her legs. "The only thing sexier than seeing you laid out like this is the look in your eyes when I sink into you."

She groaned, the sound vibrating against my lips, and said, "Then maybe you should do that. Right now. Please."

I lifted up and kissed her until her legs wrapped around my hips, the fabric of my jeans barely muting the heat of her as it pressed against me.

"I think that can be arranged."

Chapter Sixteen

Eden

WHILE HE LEFT THE bed to pull off his jeans and boxers, I realized I was wrong to think we couldn't recreate magical moments.

That was definitely *not* a problem with Milo.

The magic was inside him, I decided. As I watched the auburn hair on his chest and between his legs shimmer like flames in the lamplight, though, I conceded that maybe it was outside of him, as well. Between the sensation of his beard against my inner thighs, his talented tongue, and those questing fingers, he spun every moment between us into a dream.

I rolled onto my side when he approached the bed, staring down at me like the triumphant Viking I had called him. His expression was intense, his gray eyes like storm clouds as emotion rolled through them.

My entire body thrummed with need in response to that look.

"Milo," I said hoarsely, holding out my hand to him. "Please."

"Sweet Eden," he murmured as he climbed into bed beside me and hooked my leg over his hip. "Do you trust me?"

I blinked at him. "Yes. Of course."

He dipped his head and kissed me while he slid his hand along the back of my thigh, over my ass, then back down. I wiggled against him, pressing myself into the rough hair of his thigh until he pulled away to laugh.

"So impatient. Roll onto your belly."

Without a word, I obeyed, though I wondered what it was about his commands that made them so hot, what exactly made me want to follow his directions when I'd spent my life defying orders from everyone else. Maybe it was that he was so sweet and solicitous outside the bedroom, radiating those *good guy* vibes that drew me to him in the first place.

The shift from that into this, slightly dominating and extraordinarily sexy, made me tingle in anticipation.

When he coasted one palm along my spine, running from the back of my neck to the top of my ass, I realized another part of it was probably that he had proven himself time and again during our night together. Every suggestion, every command, had resulted in pleasure unlike anything I'd experienced.

"This ass," he growled, squeezing gently. "Do you have any idea what it does to me?"

Peeking over my shoulder, I batted my lashes at him. "No?"

"Every time you bend down to pet Jiji, I can't take my eyes off you. It makes me want to do dirty, dirty things, and I think you enjoy teasing me with it, don't you?"

I wiggled again when he started trailing his fingertips from one cheek to the other. He laughed against the back of my shoulder, then grabbed my hip and rolled me onto my back.

"Later, I'll take you from behind. I'm not missing the chance to watch you this first time. I've been dreaming about that look on your face again ever since Comic Con, right when I'm buried to the hilt."

"I guess that'll be okay," I said as he reached toward the nightstand to grab a condom from the drawer, but my breath hitched with anticipation.

He grinned. "Oh, it'll be better than okay. I seem to remember you quite enjoyed both positions last time."

Since it was one hundred percent true, I didn't argue, just watched as he tore open the package and rolled the condom on. He kissed me, plucking at one nipple with his fingers as he settled between my thighs. I reached for him, tangling my fingers in the hair curling at his nape, and wrapped my legs around his waist.

Before he pressed forward into me, he paused, lifting his head so he could watch my eyelids flutter to half-mast under the teasing of his fingers. Then his hips drove forward, his gaze burning into me when he plunged so deep pleasure radiated through my entire body, but I threw my head back at the perfect fullness of it and lost sight of him.

"That's it. So good, Eden," he murmured, and when he started moving, I had to agree. "Like fucking paradise every time I get inside you."

Each thrust sent tingles skittering along my skin, especially when he hitched one of my knees higher up his side. The new angle tore a groan from my throat and I dropped my fingers to his strong shoulders, tightening my grip until I was sure my nails must be marking his skin. He didn't seem to mind, though, growling against my jaw as he increased his pace.

"Milo," I gasped.

"Right here, beautiful."

He lifted up slightly on his knees and braced one arm next to my head. A strangled sound caught in my throat when he reached between us, stroking lightly, playfully, despite the deep, powerful thrusts. His fingertip circled, a barely-there touch that shouldn't have been enough, but the contrast had my muscles quivering as the tension ratcheted higher.

Just before I could demand he stop playing around and get down to business, the most intense orgasm of my life shuddered over me. I sobbed out his name as the waves rolled through my body, seeming endless, overwhelming, overpowering.

"That's it, let go," he whispered, then he moved his hand away and drove faster, harder, riding the final waves with me until his head arched back with his own release.

Each breath came so rapidly, I was almost hyperventilating, but Milo drew me back down, gliding gently in and out until we recovered. My body felt like it was drifting through space, anchored only by the spots where he was pressed against me.

"Eden," he murmured. "You okay?"

"Okay? I think you've ruined me. That...that wasn't sex."

"What was it?" he asked, finally stopping that slow glide to settle his hips flush against mine.

I stared up at him. Tremors still buzzed through me, but I finally managed to say, "Metamorphosis."

Milo dropped his forehead to my collarbone, nuzzling his beard against the sensitive skin there. He was silent for so long that I thought the conversation was over. My eyelids drifted shut, my pulse finally slowed, and I felt like my body had melted into the bed beneath me.

"Sweet Eden," he whispered. "Do you have any idea how fucking grateful I am that you walked back into my life?"

I threaded my fingers through his hair, overwhelmed by the rush of emotion in my chest. It was another moment before I could respond.

"Yes, because I feel the same."

T HE MAGIC DIDN'T FADE.

It wasn't like fumbling to recreate a memory—no, it was like worldbuilding, expanding our experiences until the result was all-encompassing. Milo was both anchor and rocketship, keeping me safely grounded while letting me soar.

At some point, I fell asleep tangled up in him, but he must have slipped out of bed to let Jiji in and turn off the lights, because I woke up with the cat curled into the small of my back. My head was tucked into Milo's neck, the soft pine scent of his beard wafting over me with every breath. I stayed awake only long enough to think that he was right about this being paradise, then dozed off again.

The next time I woke up, Milo's thigh was wedged between my legs. Without intending to, I rocked sleepily against it. His heavy lids lifted in the dark, his hand found my breast, and the next round began.

Throughout the night, the cycle repeated a few times, dreamlike in its perfection, each interlude more magical than the last.

A plaintive meow from outside the bedroom door filtered through my hazy thoughts as I blinked the world into focus. I was on my side with Milo's warmth curved along my back and his arm draped over my middle.

Every muscle in my body was deliciously sore.

The meow came again and I tried to ease myself out from under Milo's arm, which tightened around me. A low, sleepy rumble accompanied the soft abrasion of his beard against my neck.

"Where are you going?"

"Your cat is yelling for breakfast."

Milo's lips feathered over my shoulder. "I'll feed him. I want you here, all soft and sleepy and warm, when I get back."

"If you insist," I mumbled, but my exhausted muscles were glad for the reprieve.

Though I lost his heat at my back, he tucked the blanket around me as he slipped out of bed. I cracked an eyelid to watch him pull on a pair of black sweatpants.

"You should go shirtless more often," I called out before he rounded the bed.

When he grinned, I opened both eyes to soak in the glory of it. He strolled back toward me, dropped a kiss to my lips, and went to take care of Jiji.

I breathed deep, drawing the scent of him into my lungs, then snuggled into the cocoon of blankets and closed my eyes again.

Magic, or paradise? Maybe this feeling was simply...both.

Chapter Seventeen

MILO

THE NIGHT I MET Eden had been the best night of my life—until having her spread across my own bed, tucked safely in my arms, knowing she wasn't going to disappear again.

That definitely topped it.

Last night was different from the first, but in all the best ways. This time, I knew more about who she was, and we were both clearly more comfortable with one another. That threw our already off the charts chemistry into the stratosphere. I'd never experienced anything like it, physically or emotionally.

Her trust was an aphrodisiac of the highest order.

We hadn't slept much at Comic Con, either, which meant I didn't learn until now that Eden was as much a cuddler as I was. I loved that about her, loved the way she tucked herself against me, even in sleep. It felt like another layer of intimacy, a closeness that ran deeper than just the outrageously good sex.

But fuck, that part was otherworldly, as well.

I lost myself in thoughts of all the things I loved about Eden while Jiji continued to scold me until I'd smushed up his morning can of food on a plate. I refilled his water bowl, checked that the coffee pot was brewing, then hightailed it back to the bedroom.

Eden was exactly where I'd left her, but when I slipped under the covers, she rolled toward me. In the morning light, her hair gleamed as it had at Comic Con, a full palette of red and gold highlights against its usual darkness. I tucked a lock of it behind her ear.

"Good morning," she said softly, a smile playing across her lips.

"Good morning. Did you sleep well?"

The smile widened. "During the parts where I actually slept, yes. Very well, actually. Must have been all that exercise. Or this mattress, which is really awesome, by the way."

"You're welcome to sleep over anytime," I told her as I wrapped my arms around her body and tugged her so she was curled into my chest.

"I think I'd like that," she murmured.

"Good. Standing invitation to enjoy my awesome mattress." I hadn't been inside her apartment yet, but since I had Jiji to consider, sleepovers were less complicated if Eden was willing to stay at my place.

Her nose brushed slowly back and forth along my sternum. "I don't know if my body can handle marathon sex every night, though."

"I'm sure we could scale things back, especially if you're spending the night regularly. The weeks since finding you again have been like prolonged foreplay."

"You're quite good at foreplay," she muttered.

I laughed, stroking my hands up and down the silky skin of her back, and she nestled closer. "No pressure, Eden, but I'm more than happy to have you here whenever you're willing, whether it involves sex, cuddling, or just sleeping. Though preferably not on the couch."

"Now that I've experienced this bed, there's no way we're sleeping on the couch again."

When she tilted her head to smile up at me, I tangled my fingers in her hair and kissed her. Sleepy, soft, and pliant, she purred against my lips, and I decided I could quite happily live out the rest of my days in bed with her.

Unfortunately, we each owned a business and that made it impossible to stay in bed full time, but Eden was definitely on board with sleeping over as often as possible in the days that followed. I had to stay late for Olivia's game night on Tuesday and Eden had Addie's first support group on Thursday, but we managed to steal moments to ourselves even on the days she didn't spend the night—coordinating lunch or dinner breaks, the occasional makeout session in a storage closet.

I was falling. Fast.

After a week and a half of this careful dance, Eden and I were driving to work together, joking around about the sex toy party her cousin's friend was hosting at Garden of Delights that weekend.

"Are you going to buy anything?" I asked, glancing over to catch the flush in her cheeks.

"Is there something you'd like?"

Christ. Talk about a loaded question. I shifted in the driver's seat, thinking I should have waited to start this conversation in a place where I could haul Eden onto my lap. She might be bold and decisive, but she was also an expert tease.

Two could play that game, if I'd been free to use my hands and mouth to coax it out of her.

"Anything you want to try out, I'm more than happy to oblige," I told her.

"Anything at all?"

Fuck. This conversation was making it very difficult not to pull over and drag her into the back seat. "Eden, I promise you that I can work with whatever you choose."

As we turned onto Main Street, I saw a wicked smile curve Eden's lips, but it faded as we caught sight of road closure signs and orange traffic cones. There were at least a dozen uniformed bodies milling about, more cops than Spruce Hill's small police department even employed.

Not a good sign.

"What the hell?" Eden muttered.

I put down my window as one of the officers I recognized walked over. "Rose, what's going on?"

Detective Rose Hanson had known me since I was in diapers, and she'd never let me forget it—even though she was only three years older than me. She was in Mark's grade in school, had dated Maverick briefly before he went off to college, and was one of the smartest people I'd ever met. When the Spruce Hill Police Department finally grew enough to support a detective position, she was the first to get promoted.

"Morning, Milo. This must be the infamous Eden?"

Eden gave a tentative smile and said, "That's me."

"I'm Detective Hanson. Why don't you park over here so we can talk?" Rose said, gesturing toward a space near the barricades. "This concerns both of you, so it's good that you're here."

My blood pressure skyrocketed, wondering what the hell had happened. It must be something to do with the stores, but I didn't see or smell smoke, and if there was a break-in, why would they block off the entire street?

Eden scrambled out of the car as soon as I parked, then gripped my hand so tight I almost flinched. I tucked her against my side as Rose approached us, her expression solemn.

"We were about to call both of you, so this was good timing," she began. "About an hour ago, we got an anonymous tip about a bomb threat. As you might know, we don't have those resources within the department, so we had to call in the county sheriff for assistance. There was a backpack leaning against your building. We shut down the perimeter, but we had to wait for their bomb squad to show up before we could take a look."

"A *bomb* threat?" Eden whispered.

Rose glanced at her and her expression softened. "Chances are it's nothing. Happened a couple times over at the high school in recent years, but every instance turned out to be unsubstantiated. Usually someone who didn't finish a project on time or forgot to study for a test called in the fake threat."

Though Eden looked shell-shocked, my mind went straight to that letter she'd received. *Peddler of Evil.* Spruce Hill might be a small town, but most people here were pretty progressive, aside from some of the older generation. I tried to imagine ninety-year-old Mrs. Horowitz from down the street calling in a bomb threat, but there was a likelier explanation.

"There was a letter in the mailbox a couple weeks ago," I said quietly, "and before you tell me I'm an idiot, I realize now that I'm an idiot, because we threw it out. It had a weird, preachy flier inside about hell and repentance."

"Who was it addressed to? Did it have a stamp, or was it just shoved in there?"

Eden answered, "It was for me, but it was addressed to 'Peddler of Evil.' I don't remember it having a stamp though, do you?"

I shook my head. "No. I didn't think of that at the time, but I'm pretty sure it was just the street address on there."

"Unfortunately, not much we can do without seeing it, but I'd like you both to make an official statement so it's on record.

If this little stunt is related, I want to be sure we have a full account of what's gone on. Rumor had it there was a third bid for the empty storefront. You know who it was, Milo?"

"No," I said slowly, "but Jim can tell you if he's coming to open the framing shop."

"I'll ask him. Hang tight, you two."

Eden and I both nodded as a young officer who looked vaguely familiar jogged up to the three of us.

"Coast is clear. Backpack contained a modified clock radio. No explosive devices found," he said, then directed a smile in Eden's direction. "Officer Huxley Ford, ma'am."

It was a testament to how shaken up she was that she didn't even attempt to smile back. Eden was friendly in a sincere, thoughtful kind of way that drew people to her—I imagined her success as a business owner owed quite a bit to that trait. Customer service was second nature for her. The tight nod she managed to give Officer Ford spoke volumes.

"Can we go inside?" she asked.

The young officer shook his head and said, "I'm afraid not, at least not yet. If you have your keys, the bomb squad wants to sweep all of the stores on this block. The owner of the place on the other side of you is on vacation, Milo, but the landlord is coming to open the door."

Eden stayed huddled against my chest as we passed the policeman keys to both stores. I shook hands with Rose after she promised to let me know when we could go inside and guided Eden back to the warmth of the car. Once we were enclosed in silence, I hooked my hand around the back of her neck and clasped her against me over the center console, wrapping my other arm around her.

"You doing okay?" I murmured into her hair.

Her shoulders lifted and fell, but she said nothing, another uncharacteristic reaction that concerned me even more than a fake bomb threat.

"Eden, baby, it'll be fine. They'll get everything cleared away and we'll be all set to open. In fact, we'll probably both end up with a rush of customers because this town thrives on gossip."

"Yeah," she replied quietly. "Probably."

"Eden, look at me."

It wasn't sharp or forceful, but that low tone of voice I used in the bedroom had an immediate effect. She straightened and met my eyes, her own swirling with uncertainty.

"Everything is going to be okay. Do you trust me?"

She nodded right away and relief swept through me. Though I didn't like the note of defeat in her agreement, I had no idea how to reassure her. Hopefully, she'd see firsthand that this wouldn't negatively impact her bottom line, and then she'd be back to her usual self again.

"My beautiful Eden," I whispered.

I felt the shiver that ran along her spine, trembling under my palm. God, she enjoyed praise as much as I enjoyed giving it. Like she was made for me.

"Everything is going to be fine. I promise you that."

Whatever it took, I would not let her down.

Chapter Eighteen

EDEN

B Y THE TIME THE bomb squad finished up and all the barriers were moved off the street, it was only an hour past my normal opening time. I could tell Milo didn't want to leave me in the store alone, but I forced myself to shoo him off to Dueling Dragons so I could rush through my morning routine.

He was right—from the minute I opened the door, I had a stream of customers that didn't dwindle until late afternoon. I barely grabbed a moment to scarf down a snack around lunchtime and deflected as many questions as I possibly could.

Addie wasn't scheduled to work that day, but she showed up anyway and made a beeline toward me.

"What the hell happened?" she whispered.

I glanced toward the customer perusing a rack of filmy silk nightgowns before muttering, "Nothing. Someone faked a bomb threat. Just a stupid prank."

"I know about the bomb threat," she replied tartly. "But what's this about a threatening letter?"

"Who told you about that?" I asked, frowning.

"I have my sources, but *you* should have told me, Eden Rosalie Campbell. So I repeat, what the hell?"

"Addie, it was nothing. Remember the crap my parents used to hand out at Halloween? Those pamphlets about hell and damnation?"

Addie flinched. "Christ. Yes, I remember. That's what was inside?"

"Not the same exact thing, but similar enough."

"You think they sent it?" Her blonde brows drew together. "I thought they didn't know about the store."

"They don't," I replied. "At least, as far as I know—I don't even think they know where I'm living, nevermind about the store. I doubt an anonymous pamphlet would be the extent of their reaction if they found out, but from what I recall, all the shit they passed out had the name of the church on it. This had nothing."

I'd known Addie my entire life, so I knew the expression creeping across her face never boded well for anyone. It was equal parts devious and determined.

"Adelaide, don't do anything stupid," I warned.

"What makes you think I would do something stupid?"

I huffed out a laugh. "Thirty-two years of experience, for a start."

"I'm sure as shit not going to let them find out where you are or what you're doing, Eden," my cousin said softly. "I don't want them within a hundred-mile radius of you. All I'm going to do is find out where they are and what they've been up to. And Isaiah."

"How are you planning to do that?" My brother, Isaiah, had been just as embroiled in the church as my parents, the last I knew.

"I have my ways. You're not the only super sleuth in the family, but it's nothing for you to worry about. Besides, you're probably right, just a stupid prank."

Addie beamed at me as I cashed out the customer, who gave no sign of having overheard our conversation, then apologized when she told me she had to get back to her other job.

With a jaunty wave, she called out, "Looking forward to the party on Saturday!"

Once I was alone in the store again, I let out a long sigh and forced my attention to my to-do list for Monique's event. Addie and I were responsible for snacks, so I'd need to get my contributions sorted during my break on Saturday afternoon. I tidied up the store, replenished a rack of the emerald green nighties from the front window which had become one of my bestsellers, and set up a rack of party exclusives in the back room so it was ready to go for the weekend.

I had picked out an array of purple options to match the Pleasure Players logo, including a pale lavender teddy, a deep eggplant corset set, and a lilac ruffled cami with matching boyshorts—which I'd already snagged for myself for a special occasion.

Milo, unsurprisingly, managed to take my mind off of hate mail *and* bomb threats that night. He cooked another stellar meal, took advantage of my wandering attention to beat me in a dirt bike racing game, then practically carried my exhausted self to bed.

When I told him about Addie's plan to check up on my family, he nodded calmly and said, "I was thinking about doing the same thing. It'll probably be easier for her, though."

"I feel like I should have kept tabs on them myself," I admitted.

He shook his head before I even finished talking. "Let someone else carry this weight for now. You don't need any more stress on these lovely shoulders."

"How did you get so amazing?"

He laughed. "I'm not. I just happened to find a woman who brings out the best in me."

"Milo," I muttered, propping myself up on my elbow to glare down at him.

"Eden."

"You need to know something about me."

His lips curved. "I know a great many things about you already, but go on, enlighten me."

"I'm not good at flowery," I admitted quietly. "Compliments and...lovey-dovey stuff. Not good at giving it and not really good at receiving it. I don't want you to think that means I don't feel the same. It's just hard for me to express it like that."

"Eden, beautiful, I already figured that out on my own," he replied, a sweet smile curving beneath his beard as he stroked his fingertips over my cheek.

"Oh."

He rolled us so he was looking down at me, gray eyes soft as summer rain. Beneath that gaze, I felt like I was blooming, blossoming into some new version of myself.

It was extraordinary.

"I don't ever want to make you uncomfortable, so if my flowery words do that, I'll try to scale it back. But I know who you are, Eden, and I don't need the words back. You have the most expressive eyes and face of anyone I've ever known. Believe me, those give me all the reassurance I need."

I blinked up at him, processing that. Milo's gaze swept over my face, then he dropped his head and kissed me.

Maybe I wasn't so bad at flowery after all.

S ATURDAY FOUND ME IN a tizzy of preparations for Monique's toy party. Addie had dragged me to one years ago, long before I moved to Spruce Hill, but I'd been there strictly for moral support and hadn't purchased anything. At that point, I was working my ass off to save up for the day when I could finally open my own store. I couldn't afford to drop necessary funds on vibrators or flavored lube.

Rent here was cheaper than in the city, and the store was doing better than expected, so I had a little bit of money set aside for things like this. Monique was the sales rep, but I was ostensibly hosting the event. That meant I'd get some hostess bonuses based on the party's sales, along with some serious discounts.

Which led me to speculate about what Milo might enjoy using with me.

Business picked up again in the last hour before closing, distracting me from my thoughts, then Addie showed up with the snack trays I'd ordered earlier in the day and a rolling cooler of beverages. It took us three trips just to haul it all inside.

"Just how many people are we expecting?"

Addie shrugged. "Better to have extra leftovers than run out in the middle of a party, right?"

Though she hadn't mentioned my parents again, I knew better than to think that meant she'd abandoned her plans. Even if she'd rarely spent any time around them, she knew enough about my childhood to despise them on principle.

"Is Olivia coming?" I asked.

A pretty pink blush accented my cousin's cheeks as she locked the front door and flipped the sign to announce the store was closed. When she finally met my eyes, hers were sparkling.

"Yep."

"So things are going well?"

"Yep."

I narrowed my eyes at her. "One word answers, really?"

"I don't want to jinx it," she whispered, dragging me into the back room to start laying out our spread of snacks and desserts. "I really, really like her."

"Addie, that's great. I'm happy for you. She and Milo are tight, from the sounds of it. Maybe when you're ready, we can all have dinner or something."

She flashed a blindingly bright smile. "I'd love that."

A knock sounded at the back door, sending my cousin hurrying to let Monique in with her suitcases of goodies. We chatted while she set up a separate table for her stuff, giggling like middle schoolers as Addie and I flipped through one of her catalogs, then I finally mustered the courage to admit something I hadn't said out loud before.

"I think I have a praise kink."

Monique smiled at me and said, "Nothing wrong with that, girl."

"I'm not even remotely surprised by it, either," Addie added gently.

"You're not? What does that mean?"

"Babe, did your parents ever approve of a single thing you did? Validate your strengths, tell you that you were doing a good job?"

I frowned at her. "No."

"Milo is into you in a way that extends well beyond a hookup, Eden. He values you—your heart and soul as much as your body, if not more. It makes perfect sense to me that him offering up a verbal confirmation of just how much he appreciates you would be insanely sexy."

Monique nodded along with every word. "Absolutely. And if you light up when he offers praise, he'll see that and make sure he keeps giving that to you. Do you feel like he's noticed?"

"Yes," I said slowly. "Even before we started really dating. I think he understood it before I did."

"I liked him for you before, babe, but I like him even better now," Addie said, grinning at me. Then she bounced her eyebrows. "And I think you should pick out a little something tonight to show him your appreciation. Something extra special."

I blew out a long breath and nodded. "I think you're absolutely right. Let's do this."

We joined Monique at the table to arrange party favors like flavored condoms, penis-shaped candles, and travel-sized bottles of Bombastic Lube.

I flinched when I read the label, and Addie wrapped her arm around my shoulders.

"It's okay, babe," she murmured. "We can swap those for something else if you want, right, Monique?"

"Absolutely. I should've thought of that, Eden, I'm so sorry."

Steeling my spine, I shook my head and pasted on a smile. "No, it's fine. These are adorable and I think people will love them. Besides, it's not every day that name will be so on point, you know?"

Addie snorted and though Monique looked skeptical for a few beats while we all stared at each other, we ended up bursting into peals of laughter that washed away some of the bomb threat trauma.

The party ended up with a group of seven guests, plus me, Addie, and Monique. A few of them were women I'd met that night at The Mermaid, a few were unfamiliar, but everyone was chatty and enthusiastic enough to make it feel like a circle of friends before the night was over.

Nothing said bonding moment like comparing dildo models, from colorful silicone tentacles to a plaid behemoth called The Big McIntire, and debating the advantages of vibration versus suction.

Catching Addie and Olivia making eyes at each other throughout the night was a special treat, and the snack trays were almost completely depleted by the time we wrapped up. During a quiet moment as we filled out order forms, the woman next to me leaned over just as I set my pen down.

"Thank you for setting this up," she said quietly.

I smiled at her and dropped my eyes to the sticky name tag on her shirt. "Thanks for coming, Simone."

"You know," she mused, "I'm a photographer. I mostly do weddings, family photo shoots, that kind of thing, but I've been thinking about venturing outside of my comfort zone and offering sessions for boudoir photos."

"Oh?" My eyes shot wide as I imagined gifting Milo with a sexy photo of myself wearing some of my favorites from the shop.

Her lips quirked. "Yeah. You've done an amazing job with this place. Maybe we could come up with some kind of collaboration for your customers, like they buy one of those hot as fuck numbers out front and then we do a photo shoot of them wearing it."

"Holy shit," I breathed. "That's an amazing idea."

The woman on the other side of Simone leaned forward and raised her hand. "I volunteer as tribute."

That got the attention of the rest of the circle, which meant Simone and I ended up with an entire lineup of interested women who had killer suggestions for how to promote these photo sessions.

Even though Addie and Aunt Jocelyn had done their best to give me the education and support my parents denied me, being so enthusiastically included by this new community who celebrated my passions instead of smothering them was like taking flight for the first time—terrifying and thrilling, poignant and astounding. My heart soared, even if I still couldn't shake the fear of an eventual crash landing.

It felt like the dawn of a new era. I hadn't smiled so much in years.

I wasn't sure how to handle going from zero friends to a room full of them, but if I'd learned anything from my relationship with Milo, it was that opening myself up to new experiences could lead to beautiful things.

And I did, in fact, pick out a few extra special items to surprise him with.

Chapter Nineteen

MILO

KEEPING MYSELF BUSY WHILE Eden was shut away in a room full of sex toys proved nearly impossible. Every time I got a handle on my imagination, a new fantasy would pop up and I'd have to distract myself all over again.

Jiji watched with casual disdain as I cleaned the entire house, washed and dried my bedding, and baked a batch of Eden's favorite cookies.

"You like her just as much as I do," I muttered at the cat, then shook my head. "No, probably not quite as much, but whatever."

Eden would be coming over after the party and her store was closed the next day—she'd decided to take off Sundays as well as Mondays, now that she had a clearer view of her customers' shopping habits. Since that would give us a day off together, I was in full support of that prospect.

I paced the living room like I was waiting for my prom date to show before finally collapsing onto the couch.

Just before eleven, her car pulled into my driveway and I jumped to my feet, displacing an aggravated Jiji so I could throw open the front door. Eden grinned at me, lugging a backpack so she could stay until Monday. She was wearing a polka-dot dress that flared out from her hips and swished around her thighs.

"Hey, you."

"Hey," I replied, as enchanted by the cheeky look on her face as by the thought of bunching that skirt up around her waist and bending her over the couch. "Did you have fun?"

"I did, in fact. Unfortunately, the surprises I got for us have to be shipped and won't be here for a week or so."

"Surprises? What kind of surprises?"

She rose up on tiptoe to kiss me before passing through the doorway. "The kind of surprises that you'll learn about when the package arrives."

"I have to wait a whole week? Not even a hint?" I asked, closing the door and taking the bag from her shoulder so I could tug her against me.

"Not. Even. A. Hint." She punctuated each word with a kiss. "But I promise you'll like all of my choices. Will that satisfy you?"

I brushed my cheek along her throat until she shivered at the sensation. "Not even close, but I'll let you make it up to me."

"Oh? And how will I do that?"

With one hand at her waist and the other inching up under the full skirt of her dress, I leaned in and whispered in her ear, "Maybe I'll tease you the way you're teasing me, spend all night edging you until you beg me to let you come, and then fuck you until you come so many times, you're begging for mercy."

"I think I could get on board with that," she replied with a grin, tangling her fingers in my hair. "By the way, what are your thoughts on boudoir photos?"

I blinked at her, images of Eden modeling every sexy item in her shop playing rapidfire through my mind. "Favorable. Very favorable."

"Good. One of the guests at the party, Simone, is a photographer who's looking to branch out a bit. She suggested we could work together on creating some photo packages—clients could come to the shop to pick out some items, maybe at a discount, then do a photo shoot with Simone and I'd get a cut of each session."

"That's an amazing idea," I said, realizing just how many connections Eden had made in the short time since her store opened.

"Anyone who wants to will get an extra discount if they let us use the photos for advertising or display in the store. Simone said it's easy to frame shots so their faces aren't visible and the models aren't identifiable."

"And are you going to do a test run for her?"

Her grin was as wicked as it was promising. "You bet your ass I am."

I ran my lips along her jaw and murmured, "Excellent. I can't wait to see how they turn out. In fact, I'd very much like to see photos of you in nothing but a pair of sexy little panties and a Wonder Woman comic book."

"What an intriguing idea," she replied, tipping her head as I moved to her neck. "You know, I've been thinking…"

My body went tight at her tone even before her hands moved to the zipper of my jeans. "Oh? Thinking about what?"

"About how much I enjoy all the things you've done to me, and about certain things I haven't done to you."

"I'm listening."

A groan tore from my chest when she dropped to her knees in front of me, smirking up at me and looking no less like a goddess for kneeling before me.

"And I wanted to show my appreciation, you know?"

I threaded my fingers through her hair, sifting it back away from her beautiful face. "I'm not going to stop you, if that's what you're worried about."

"Good."

She flashed a grin and dragged the zipper down, and the only speech my brain could handle after that was a steady flow of praise and encouragement that had her humming happily around my cock until I was finally able to haul her into the bedroom and show my own appreciation.

W ITH ALL OF SUNDAY and half of Monday to laze around together, I had plenty of opportunities to try to convince Eden to spill her secrets, but she held firmly onto her plan to surprise me with her purchases. I tried to wager a hint as reward if I could beat her in a round of Super Smash Bros, but she annihilated me. I offered a daily cookie delivery; she shot me down.

In the end, I accepted my fate and looked forward to learning just what she'd chosen.

The only update we received about the investigation into the bomb threat was that the third party interested in Eden's location was an older couple from the next town over who ran a Lutheran summer camp in Oakville and wanted to open a Christian gift shop in Spruce Hill. Hanson had found no connection between them and Eden's parents or their church, and the couple had a solid alibi for the days around the bomb threat, when they were spending the weekend at a meditation retreat in Lake Chautauqua, so it felt like a dead end.

I hadn't found a moment to have a private word with Adelaide about Eden's parents, either, so it was time to get creative.

Olivia showed up at the store just before closing time on Tuesday to do some game prep, and I pounced.

"Has Addie mentioned anything about her reconnaissance mission on Eden's parents?" I asked as soon as she set her bag down on the folding table we popped up for her game nights.

"Hello to you, too," she muttered. "No, and before you ask, I'm not pumping my girlfriend for information for you, either."

"Girlfriend." I grinned at Liv, who'd been single almost as long as I had.

She rolled her eyes at me, but she couldn't hold back a smile. "Yeah, look at us, dating the hottest cousins in town."

"Pleased for you, Liv."

"Back at you. Hey, Eden wouldn't happen to be into table-top RPGs, would she?"

I almost laughed at the thought of Eden joining a role-playing game. "Why?"

"My new campaign starts next week and Addie said she'd like to try it out. Most of my other players have some experience, so it might be nice for her to have another newbie around."

"I'll ask, but I'm not sure that's her style of nerdiness. She might be interested in hanging out during the game, since I'll be here."

Olivia laughed. "I'd call the two of you sickeningly cute, but I have a feeling Addie and I aren't much better."

"Hey, you were there on Saturday." I tapped my fingers against the table.

"Don't even try it, Milo. I'm sworn to secrecy. But from what I remember, you're going to have a real good time when those orders come in," she teased, her tone a little too gleeful for my liking.

The first of Olivia's players arrived, so I opened the door for them and then retreated to the stockroom to update inventory while the group got down to business.

I'd gone weeks from my first taste of Eden until seeing her again, then even longer before I finally had her in my bed—I could handle waiting a few days to find out what she had in store for me, for us.

Knowing Eden, it would be paradise for us both.

Chapter Twenty

EDEN

"**P**LEASE, PLEASE, PLEASE!"

I glared at Adelaide, who was draped dramatically over the checkout counter. "Is there any way to undo three decades of caving to your whining?"

"Sadly, no," she replied. "Aside from doing what I ask."

"I have no desire to play Dungeons & Dragons, Addie. I'm not into role-playing, end of story."

"Ever? Not even with Milo?"

The singsong words inspired a number of dirty thoughts, but I held strong. If I couldn't manage to offer Milo pretty words when he was being ultrasweet, there was no way I could play a character in front of strangers.

"Not like that. Look, if it won't be too awkward, I'll come next week and hang out with Milo during the game, but I'm not going to join it, Addie. That's my final offer."

"I'll take it." She bounced upright and beamed at me. "Though you really do need a life outside of the store and banging Milo's brains out."

I pinched the bridge of my nose and muttered, "Adelaide."

"Well, it's true. I've always had to drag you out of the house, but now that Liv and I are a thing, I feel like I'm falling down on the job."

"Or," I said gently, "I'm really, really happy with my life the way it currently is, and Milo respects that I don't enjoy going out the way you do, Addie. That's not a dig at your lifestyle, either. I don't like bars and clubs or hanging out with strangers. You know that's never been my scene. I'm happy you're happy, truly I am. But I'm happy, too."

Addie's smile practically burned my retinas, and I had about two seconds to brace before she threw her arms around me. My parents had avoided public displays of affection like the plague; the fact that I tolerated them at all was owed solely to Addie and her family. I wrapped her up in a hug until the bell over the door chimed.

"Sorry, should I come back?" Milo called. We had a lunch date scheduled, so he came in bearing brown paper bags of takeout.

"No!" Addie leapt away, squeezed my hands one last time, and grabbed her purse off the counter. "I'm just heading out. Toodles!"

I rolled my eyes as we watched her saunter out of the store, but then Milo set the bags on the counter and slid one hand around the small of my back to pull me toward him.

"Good afternoon," he murmured. "Everything okay with you two?"

"I just agreed to hang out during the game on Tuesday. She's been begging me all day to join in, but after her reaction just now, I'm guessing I've been played. Again."

He raised a brow. "So all she really wanted was you to be there during the game?"

"Seems that way. She's convinced I'm a hermit and it's her job to lure me out of my cave."

"There's a lot to be said for chilling in a cave, as long as the cave is my bed."

I laughed, but he was absolutely right. "I guess if I have you to keep me company, it won't be too awkward. Are they going to do voices and stuff?"

"Some of them might. Liv only tends to do them here or there for side characters, but I don't know all of her new players except Addie and Lucas, the bartender from The Mermaid."

I nodded, biting my lip until Milo gently freed it with his thumb.

"We'll have fun, and if you don't, I'll take you home. But we can always slip away to a dark corner of the store and make out," he offered, smiling down at me.

"Now, that idea has some merit."

Milo laughed as he kissed me, the taste of mirth on his tongue turning to fizzing champagne bubbles in my brain. It always surprised me how firm his body was under my hands compared to the softness of his mouth, moving so tenderly, so masterfully. He made each kiss feel like something more, something deeper.

Those kisses made me feel like I'd transformed into someone new. The word *metamorphosis* echoed through my head.

When he eased back, he brushed his nose along mine. "Hungry?"

"Famished," I replied.

Milo gave me a pointed look and muttered, "Insatiable," but there was a clear glint of amusement in his eyes.

"Well, *that* hunger will have to wait until later. For right now, I need actual food."

We settled behind the counter with falafel wraps and pita chips, drinking the cherry cola Milo remembered was my favorite, and once I was relaxed and feeling good, he dropped the bomb.

"My parents asked if we'd come for dinner sometime in the next couple weeks."

My entire body froze. This was not something I had done before—mostly because I'd had very few long-term relationships, though also because my last one was with someone whose parents lived in California. What if they hated me? What if they felt I wasn't good enough for their son? A trickle of panic crept up my spine even as I tried to remind myself that my own parents' opinions about me were not universal.

"Eden, breathe," Milo murmured.

I sucked in a huge breath, then nearly choked on the pita chip I'd been chewing when he tipped the world on its axis. As I coughed until my eyes watered, Milo rubbed his hand between my shoulder blades, staring at me with a mixture of horror and concern.

"Really, it's okay. I'll tell them we need more time. I didn't think it would be a big deal, since you already met the rest of the family."

"No!" I yelped, my voice hoarse from choking. "No, you can't postpone. They'll be insulted. They'll think I'm rude for putting them off. They'll—"

"Eden," Milo interrupted, using that low tone that cut straight through my freakout. "Take a breath, one that hopefully won't require the Heimlich, okay?"

I grabbed my soda, sucked down a sip to soothe my throat, then tried to draw in enough oxygen to clear my head. Milo still had one hand on my back, moving in soft circles, and the other was on my knee, his thumb brushing slowly back and forth.

"Sorry," I whispered.

"Nothing to be sorry for. I didn't mean to spring anything on you. I promise you, though, they won't think anything bad about you even if we need to push it off, okay? My brothers and Libby have already vouched for how awesome you are. Mom and Dad won't mind waiting."

I rotated in my chair so I could drop my forehead against his shoulder, but Milo only laughed softly into my hair as his arms came around me. After I pulled myself together, he tipped my chin up with one finger and placed a chaste kiss to my lips.

"You know I'm crazy about you, right?" he asked.

"I got that impression, yes."

He smiled sweetly. "Then you know you have nothing to worry about."

I tried for a scowl and grumbled, "I wasn't worried."

"No? You almost choked on pita chips because you're totally nonchalant about meeting my parents?"

"My epiglottis betrayed me."

"Eden," he said, grinning now, "you freaked out, and I appreciate that you want to make a good impression, but they're going to love you."

"Fine. Set a date. Can we just please stop talking about it now and finish our lunch?"

My disgruntled expression apparently did nothing to fend off his good mood, so Milo just captured my lips for a more thorough kiss, winked at me, and took his arms back so he could grab his food. I sighed as I reached for my own.

Opening a store, starting a relationship, finally making friends—what was one more milestone on top of it all?

Chapter Twenty-One

MILO

I FELT TERRIBLE THAT I hadn't eased Eden into the idea of meeting my parents, but I couldn't stop thinking about how adorable she was, worrying about whether they'd like her, afraid they might think she was rude. Though I had only told them a little bit about her, they'd heard much more from my brothers and my nephew.

After game night, Carter practically worshipped the ground Eden walked on, so he'd shared plenty.

But she was the first woman I *wanted* to introduce to my parents, the first woman I felt this strongly about. They'd adore her, and I wanted her to experience even a fraction of the love and support I'd grown up with.

She deserved all that and more.

While our lazy Sundays together were my favorite day of the week, Monday afternoons were a close second because Eden always stopped in to hang out with me and Carter after school. They'd trade book recommendations or draw together or play rummy, which was another one of those games where Eden remained utterly undefeated.

For the first time in my life, I was thinking about the future—building a life with someone else, marriage, maybe having kids of my own. I wondered if Eden wanted those things, but her freakout over meeting my parents had put the brakes on any discussion of that nature with her.

Hell, I'd be happy with her in my future, whatever form that took.

Maverick, on the other hand, had zero qualms about bringing it up when he came to get Carter later in the week.

"So she spends more than half her nights at your place, and all of her time off—when are you gonna ask her to move in?"

"I told you what happened when I mentioned dinner with Mom and Dad," I grumbled under my breath, wondering if there was any chance Carter wouldn't overhear this conversation.

Maverick rolled his eyes. "Milo, we both saw how she bolted when she realized I knew you two hooked up. Why were you surprised she freaked over meeting the parents? You're usually more observant than that."

I didn't like to admit Maverick was right, but I'd been wondering the same thing all afternoon. Why *was* I surprised? That boldness I so enjoyed about Eden hid a soft, vulnerable center. Sometimes, it was so well hidden that I forgot about it.

"I screwed up," I admitted, rubbing my forehead.

"You did, but fortunately, I think she'll come around. You're pulling a Mark, bro, falling hard and fast. My guess is Eden can see that, but if you think she's the one, you need to be sure she's on the same page."

I sucked in a breath and nodded. "You're right. I guess you're not as stupid as Mark says you are."

"I could take both of you at once, asshole," Maverick muttered as he slapped the back of my head, but he grinned. "Get your shit sorted, Milo. Carter's already calling her Aunt Eden."

Aunt Eden. Christ, I liked the sound of that.

After Maverick and Carter left, I pondered just how to ascertain that The One was truly The One. And, more importantly, how to know whether The One felt you were also The One for them.

Just before closing time, Eden sent a text that made me grateful it was almost the end of the day.

Package arrived. Hope you're ready for some fun tonight.

"Fuck me."

After involuntarily whispering the words, I jerked my head up to make sure no one else was in the store. Fortunately, I was very much alone.

So, SO ready, I replied, tacking on the eyes emoji.

Eden, the little tease, went radio silent after that, but she strolled in just as I flipped the off switch on the neon OPEN sign. Today's outfit consisted of a black scoop-neck tee tucked into a patterned skirt that fell between her ankles and knees. A large tote bag was thrown over one shoulder, a sure sign she was planning to spend the night.

My gaze snagged on the shoes, which were much higher heels than she normally wore for work.

"Is it my lucky day?" I asked, locking the door. "I don't think I've seen these shoes before."

"It is, and you haven't. They're not terribly comfortable, but I decided they would suit the occasion. I changed before I came over here."

Dropping my head, I kissed her hard and deep, then grabbed her hand and pulled her along behind me until we reached the back door of the shop. Eden laughed, but I forced myself to slow down so she didn't break one of her pretty ankles tripping over those sexy heels.

I barely remembered the drive home. Before I could blink, we were inside the house, plastered together against the front door. Jiji meowed loudly at such blatant disrespect, so I tore myself away to give him a quick cuddle and a fresh bowl of food.

Eden and her bag disappeared into the bedroom.

The game was on.

I followed more slowly, giving her time to prepare whatever surprises she had in store, but walking in to find her naked except for those sexy fucking heels, standing in front of the mirror over my dresser with some kind of fluffy makeup brush, sent all the blood in my head straight to my dick.

"Are we doing makeovers?" I asked, shoving my hands in my pockets so I wouldn't toss her over my shoulder and throw her on the bed then and there.

Humming quietly, she dipped the brush in a little jar and then trailed it teasingly across her nipples. Unable to look away, I pulled off my shirt before strolling closer.

"That smells like lemon bars," I mused, watching as she dusted a path from her collarbone down over her belly. "What is this?"

"Edible body powder."

"Edible, hmm?"

When she turned to me, light glinted off the iridescent trails over her torso and I licked my lips. My eyes locked on the sight of the shimmery powder dusting those dark curls between her legs as I kicked off my jeans and boxers.

"Your turn," she replied, dipping the brush again before sweeping it along the side of my throat.

Holding still while she stroked the soft bristles over my skin took gargantuan effort. Her expression was serene, like she was painting a masterpiece, as she dusted the lemon-scented powder across my shoulders, over my nipples, along my ribs, and then finally—*finally*—painted it along my painfully hard dick with long, teasing sweeps that I hoped she intended to follow with her tongue.

But not yet.

The second she set the brush down, I dropped to my knees, licking and kissing a path along every brushstroke on her body.

Her fingers tangled in my hair as I laved her skin with my tongue, reveling in the tart sweetness and the woman underneath.

I took my time, moving top to bottom, collar to navel, sucking and nipping even after the lemon powder was gone, then I eased two fingers into her.

"Fuck, beautiful, you're soaked."

Her head fell back as I curled them inside her. "Remember when I said you were an expert at foreplay? It's true."

"Foreplay is all well and good, but I need you to sit on the dresser so I can clean all this lemon stuff off your sweet pussy, Eden."

A shuddering breath slipped from her lips at the command, but she shifted until her ass was perched right at the edge of the wooden dresser. I spread her knees wide, drinking in the sight of shimmering powder and glistening arousal.

"So fucking pretty," I breathed, blowing a stream of air across her clit.

Her thighs twitched beside my head. "Milo."

"Right here." I leaned in and gave her one long lick. "I'll take care of you, don't worry."

The lemon was long gone by the time she sobbed out an orgasm that had her whole body trembling, leaving me desperate to get inside her, but when I reached for a condom, she tutted at me.

"Not yet. It's my turn. Then I'll show you what else I got. Go lie on the bed."

I grinned, always happy to oblige when that boldness surfaced, and Eden took her sweet time cleaning the body powder off of my skin.

Every inch of my skin.

By the time she finished, smirking at me from under a veil of the tousled waves that had been wrapped around my fist, I was harder than I could ever remember being, but she had more tricks up her sleeve.

"Show me." My voice was hoarse, my whole body quivering.

She grabbed the small paper bag out of her tote and dumped it onto the bed, presenting a host of options I had every intention of using on her in turn. I assessed them quickly and came to a decision.

"On your knees," I ordered. "Facing the mirror."

Licking her lips, she moved into position—a position where she couldn't see which toy I picked out. There was a suctioning rose, a small wand, one with bunny ears, and a vibrator with a moving tongue attachment.

"Oh, Eden, what fun we're going to have."

I moved behind her and slid my hands up the outside of her thighs, then over her belly until I was cupping her breasts, my chin on her shoulder to watch us in the mirror. She arched back against me, filling my hands, displaying all that beauty for us both to observe.

Then I released one breast to reach behind me, turned on the first vibrator, and set it between her legs.

One after another, I wrung at least one more orgasm from her with each toy, until I couldn't stand another minute of not being inside her. I guided her down to her hands and knees, rolled on a condom, and buried myself inside her before the last orgasm had faded.

Each ripple of her muscles threatened to demolish my self-control, but I held out as I reached for the wand again. Thrusting slowly, lazy but deep, I curled my body over hers so I could press it to her clit.

A low moan escaped her throat as her hips jerked at the contact.

"Go on," I growled in her ear. "You know what I want, Eden. Give it to me."

She sobbed my name, but her muscles clenched and quivered around me, and I knew she was close. So close. I wanted to push her over the edge one more time before giving into my own body's demands.

"Milo," she whimpered, those sexy goddamn heels pressing harder against the outside of my thighs.

"One more. You can do it."

Her back arched as she came hard one last time, pulsing so tight around me that I had to grit my teeth in order to hold out.

"That's it, just like that. My beautiful, sweet Eden."

Even if I hadn't been used to giving it, the way she responded to that gentle praise, even more than the dirty encouragement that turned her on so readily, would have kept me offering it. I felt her reaction, from the way her muscles clenched around me to the purr of pleasure that rumbled in her throat.

Tossing the toy aside, I continued gliding in and out, slow but steady, murmuring soft words in her ear and against her skin, until I finally picked up the pace. Her body continued to ripple around me as I thrust harder, faster, soaking in her whimpers and moans as she rocked her hips back to meet each one.

When I couldn't hold out any longer, I planted myself deep, came so intensely my vision blurred at the edges, and collapsed carefully over her.

Eden turned her head to smile at me and breathlessly mumbled, "I take it you liked my choices."

"Fuck, yes. When's the next party?"

Beneath me, her body shook with laughter. I reluctantly untangled our limbs, unbuckling her shoes before I shifted her up toward the pillows and pulled her into my arms.

"I could sleep for a week," she said, her words muffled against my throat.

"That sounds like a good plan, as long as it's in my bed. I'm sure the town will understand if we have to close both stores for recovery time."

Eden snuggled closer. Just when I thought she might have drifted off to sleep, she sighed, her breath tickling my skin. "Set a date with your parents for dinner, okay?"

"Baby, I told you, it's fine if we wait."

"I want to meet them," she replied.

The statement was firm, resolute, so I kissed the top of her head and said, "Okay. I'll set it up."

"But let's not pull out the body powder the night before we have dinner with them."

I laughed, my arms tightening around her. "That's probably for the best."

"Thank you," she whispered, relaxing against my side. "Thank you for being awesome."

"My sweet Eden. Whatever you need, I'll make it happen. I hope you know that by now."

As she settled into my side, her body soft and loose after our marathon evening, my mind quieted until a single thought remained.

Eden was definitely The One.

Chapter Twenty-Two

EDEN

"**Y**ou're sure it's not too soon?" Milo asked for what had to be the tenth time in the past two days.

"It's fine, Milo. I told you it was fine when you called to check. I told you it was fine when you started worrying it was too soon an hour after that. I told you it was fine this morning, and two minutes ago, and I think you know where I'm going with this."

He grinned. "I'm thinking you're gearing up to kick my ass if I don't stop asking."

"You'd be right."

Despite my annoyance, I appreciated his concern. I was the one who'd flipped my lid when he first brought it up—I couldn't blame him for being cautious now. The Davies family already had one perfect daughter-in-law and one epic failure.

Milo had as much right to be nervous about my reception as I did, no matter how many times he insisted they would love me.

We eventually moved on to eating our lunches behind the counter at Garden of Delights in comfortable silence, until Addie burst through the front door. There was an expression on her face that I couldn't quite place, but it didn't look good.

"What's wrong?" I asked, rising from my seat.

Addie made her way toward us with her hands raised like she was trying to calm me down before she'd even said a word. Milo stood, wrapping an arm around my waist, his gaze locked on my cousin.

"You know how I was checking up on your parents, to make sure they weren't secretly stalking you and interfering with your life now that you're finally free of them?"

I blinked at her in confusion. "Yes."

"I found out something and I think you might want to sit down for this, babe," she said gently.

Milo's arm tightened, then he guided me back down to my chair while Addie circled the counter. He stayed standing, his hands on my shoulders, and Addie lowered herself into his seat.

When she didn't speak right away, I snapped, "For fuck's sake, what is it?"

Addie pulled her phone from her purse, unlocked the screen, and passed it to me. The page she'd pulled up showed a picture of my parents, unsmiling as ever. I glanced at the web address and saw it was their church's page.

"I'm sorry, Eden," Addie whispered.

I scrolled down and read the announcement. My parents had sold everything they owned, donated the money to their church, and left for a missionary trip overseas. They were scheduled to be gone for five years, and the date on the announcement was almost three years ago.

Around the time Isaiah had called me. I wondered if that was why he called, but he hadn't said a word about them.

"They're gone. The house, all of it. It's gone," I said flatly.

Milo's fingers tensed on my shoulders, then he rubbed his hands up and down my arms and asked, "They left without trying to get in touch with you?"

I lifted my head just in time to catch the look Addie gave Milo. "I don't understand."

"They're selfish assholes, babe. I'm sorry," Addie said.

"No, I know that. I don't understand why you wanted me to sit down for this."

Both of them were silent, so I handed Addie's phone back to her and stood again, feeling suddenly restless.

"Thank you for telling me, but it's fine. I took everything that meant anything to me when I left home at eighteen. This is news, but it's not upsetting. They've been gone from my life a lot longer than a few years, Addie. You know that."

"There's more," Addie said quietly. She switched to a different screen and passed the phone back.

Reverend Isaiah Campbell, pictured with his wife and daughter, announced as new head of Binghamton's Church of Eternal Light.

"Wife and daughter," I read aloud, staring at the photo.

It was dated several years ago, also around the time my brother had called me to try to convince me to rejoin the church. The woman was covered neck to ankles in the kind of ugly, shapeless dress my mother favored and the dark-haired, dark-eyed little girl—my niece, apparently, looking younger than Carter in this picture—was wearing a long skirt and high-necked blouse. None of them were smiling.

Unlike the news about my parents leaving the country, this hit me like a cannonball to the chest, knocking the breath straight out of my lungs.

"That's your brother?" Milo asked, shock evident even in his soft tone.

"He got married and they didn't tell me," I said slowly, my voice coming out strangled and rasping. "And then he had a child and didn't tell me that, either. Even when he called me a few years ago, he didn't mention any of it..."

Silence stretched around me as I studied the photo, focusing mostly on the little girl. Maybe I was projecting, but I thought there was a spark of defiance in her eyes despite the expressionless façade.

After all, I'd perfected that mask of compliance myself, back when I was her age.

"Addie," I whispered.

She moved in, wrapping her arms around me even when I couldn't tear my eyes off my niece. "I know. I'm still digging. I'll find out everything I can."

Of course she understood exactly what I wanted to know—was my brother a good man? A good father? Was his daughter loved and cared for? Or was this a new generation of the same old thing?

No matter how much Addie joked about my sleuthing skills, I'd never dug into my own family—never wanted to. I slammed the door on that part of my life long ago.

And maybe I was afraid that opening it again would lead to the same heartache that a lifetime of being an utter disappointment, an outsider among those who should've loved me best, had wrought.

"I'm sorry about your parents," Milo murmured.

His comment snapped me out of my panic over history repeating itself with my niece. Finally shoving the phone onto the countertop, I lifted my gaze to the two of them. "I'm not."

"Eden," Addie said slowly. "They left the country without a word to you."

I tidied up the wrappers from my lunch and shrugged. "How would they tell me? I made sure they didn't know where I was living. They haven't tried to make contact once since I left home."

"They could have reached out to my parents," Addie replied, still frowning.

"They could have, but they didn't. Have you told your mom yet? I hope she's not too hurt by it."

"No, not yet. I'll go over there now. Eden, babe, are you sure you're okay?"

Milo set a hand to the small of my back, a silent act of support, and Addie caught his eyes, still looking confused by my lack of reaction. Between Milo's concern about family dinner and Addie acting like the world was going to fall apart because my parents had proven once again to not give a shit about me, I lost it.

"Will you both stop asking me that? I'm fine!" I snapped, jerking away from both of them. "I have work to do, if you don't mind. Milo, thank you for lunch. Addie, thanks for the update. Now please, just let me get back to work."

There was no missing the flash of hurt across Adelaide's face or the quiet shock in Milo's gray eyes, but I couldn't deal with either of those things right then. A heavy weight settled in my chest, pressing inward until I felt like I would be crushed by it.

With one last glance at Milo, Addie mumbled a farewell and left the store. Milo caught my chin in his hand and stared hard into my eyes before dropping a light kiss on my lips.

"You know where I am if you need me," he said gently, then he left, too.

Alone with my thoughts and the invisible boulder pressing the air from my lungs, I sank back down into my chair, dropped my face into my hands, and breathed deep as I tried to quell the rising wave of emotion that threatened to burst out of that heaviness in my chest.

As I blinked to clear my stinging eyes, I told myself it was only the upcoming dinner with Milo's parents, the prospect of belonging to a family like his, that made me feel like this news was anything more than confirmation of what I already knew.

I'd been on my own for a very long time. Nothing had changed.

O VER THE FEW DAYS between my outburst and the upcoming dinner at his parents' house, Milo treated me like I was made of glass. Inside the bedroom, he was as meticulously attentive as ever, but outside of it, he acted like I was one second away from losing my cool or completely falling apart.

Even if I couldn't really blame him, it was getting on my nerves.

Fortunately, dinner with his parents proved to be a distraction and a balm toward settling both of us back into our previous state.

"Eden, it is an absolute pleasure to meet you," Milo's mom said as she opened the door for us. She was tall and statuesque, with laugh lines around the same gray eyes she'd given to her sons and the warmest, sweetest smile I'd ever seen.

"Thank you, Mrs. Davies. It's great to meet you, too."

She laughed, ushering us inside. "Please, call me Terry, and this is Tucker."

While Milo's mom was blonde, Tucker's dark hair was peppered with gray, and there were hints of red in his goatee. He was as tall and handsome as all three of his sons.

"We're so glad you could make it," Tucker said, smiling broadly at us.

Given the awkward silences of the last few days, sacrificing part of our lazy Sunday had been no hardship. Still, I smiled, thanked them for having us, and made small talk like it was my job.

Which, coincidentally, it seemed to be. Milo was quieter than usual, answering whenever he was directly addressed, but apparently content not to direct the conversation.

Eventually, both of our hosts retreated to the kitchen to check on dinner, leaving me and Milo on a loveseat in the family room. I tangled my fingers in his and lifted his hand to my lips. For some reason, that simple touch seemed to soothe him. His gaze moved over my face, reading whatever was written there—hopefully the depth of my regret for shutting him out.

"I'm sorry," I whispered.

He reached up with his other hand to cup my cheek. "Me too. I've been awkward as hell and it was stupid. Your feelings, no matter what they might be, are totally valid, Eden."

"You are extraordinarily well-adjusted, did you know that?"

"I try," he replied, grinning. "I'm sorry I was tiptoeing around you this week. I thought you might need that caution while you processed, but I think I went a little overboard."

I shifted so I could drop my head against his shoulder. "I feel like an alien sometimes."

"Good thing you're dating the owner of a comic book store. Half my merch is filled with aliens." Though I laughed, he kissed my forehead and said, "Eden, you're very much human. I know how lucky I am to have come from all this—parents who love each other and never hid how much they love us, brothers who drive me crazy but always have my back, a town that's not Pleasantville but was pretty great to grow up in."

"I'm glad you had that," I said softly.

"I'm glad, too. I wish you'd had even half of it."

"My parents don't matter, I just...I want to know my niece is safe and happy."

His lips brushed lightly over my hair. "Then we'll do what we can to find those answers. I'll help in any way I can. Addie said you're a super sleuth."

I grinned. "That's true. I never had a reason to delve into my family after I left. I thought about it back when Isaiah called, I was afraid to open that door again."

"And now?"

"That little girl is reason enough to get over my fears."

"My brave Eden," he murmured.

"I don't know how I'm supposed to feel," I admitted. "I think that's what freaks me out the most. Like Addie expected me to start crying or something. I thought she was going to show me an obituary when she walked into the store."

Milo stroked his thumb over my knuckles. "There's no right or wrong here, beautiful. My mom's dad died when we were teenagers—he was an emotionally abusive narcissist and they weren't close. No one cried at the funeral, not even her. I once overheard her telling Dad that she felt sad about all the things that could have been, but not about losing the man he was."

"I think...that sounds close to what I'm feeling."

"A couple months later, when Christmas rolled around, I walked into the kitchen and found her sobbing, because every year, she held out hope that he'd get his shit together and act like a good father, a good grandfather, instead of letting everyone down again. That was when it hit her that there was no chance of that ever happening. As far as I know, those were the only tears she shed over him," he finished quietly.

I drew a breath, still leaning into him, absorbing his warmth and his strength, and whispered, "I've always been afraid that I wouldn't know how to be a good partner or a good parent, because I came from that house. Even around Addie and Rob's parents, I wondered if I could ever find that."

"And now?"

"If your mom grew up with that and became the person she is, maybe there's hope for me."

Milo drew back, smiling at me with a tenderness that beat back the weight I'd been carrying around since Addie's revelation, then slid his hand along my jaw and kissed me until everything else fell away.

Chapter Twenty-Three

MILO

EVERY TIME EDEN GAVE me a glimpse at the softness she hid inside, I fell a little more in love with her. I understood that we weren't at a place where she could handle a conversation about the future—not even about moving in together. The last thing I wanted was to prompt another panicked response from her, especially since things returned to normal after our pre-dinner chat.

My parents, unsurprisingly, adored her. I'd told them a little about her own family, mostly as a warning not to ask about them during dinner, so their usual warmhearted charm was dialed up to the max. As a result, Eden slipped straight into chatting and joking with them throughout the meal.

And that night, after we got home, every trace of the shell she'd tried to retreat behind was gone. My sweet Eden was back, both vulnerable and bold.

I wasn't sure whether she and Adelaide had smoothed things over, but Eden was still planning to come hang out during Olivia's game night at Dueling Dragons, so I figured they must have made up one way or another. Addie and Olivia were the first to show up, holding hands and sending covert-but-heated looks at one another, and Eden slipped in just before I locked the front door.

The first thing she did was curl one hand around the back of my head, fingers threading through my hair, and kiss me. The kiss was everything Eden—daring and intrepid, yet exposing the tenderness underneath.

I didn't hear the chorus of cheers until she drew back.

Eden's cheeks were pink, but she grinned up at me as Liv and Adelaide whooped and whistled behind us. My arms had shifted around her as soon as she got close enough to initiate that fiery kiss, though I'd been justifiably distract-ed. The thing she was wearing—a romper or jumpsuit, I couldn't remember if there was a difference—was simple and black, but the fabric was impossibly soft under my hands.

"Hi," Eden whispered.

I threw back my head and laughed, tugging her closer against the front of my body. "Hi. Can I just say you have a permanent invitation to greet me like that any time you wish?"

"Noted. So, nerd mentors, is there anything that needs to be done before you get started?"

Olivia and Addie were in the midst of setting up the table, but Eden and I jumped in to help bring folding chairs out from the storage closet. Eden found little ways to brush up against me, running her fingers over my arm as she passed or nudging me with the sweet curve of her hip.

As the handful of players arrived, Liv introduced everyone to Eden and Adelaide. I watched for any signs of discomfort, but Eden was her usual charming self through the short stretch of small talk before the game got started. The two of us then retreated to a corner of the store, though Eden refused my invitation to make out where no one could see us.

"Hands to yourself," she whispered, attempting to scowl through her quiet laughter. "I want to check out the store. You're usually too distracting for me to look around."

"And that's a bad thing?"

"Hmm. Well, it did prevent me from admiring this," she mused.

I grinned as she lifted a heavy pewter dragon statue from the shelf by the front window. The statues weren't a top seller, but they were eye-catching, each one holding a twenty-sided die in its claws. The one Eden picked up had mother-of-pearl scales inlaid within its wings, glittering opal eyes, and a die made of iridescent resin that sparkled like Eden's eyes.

"These are gorgeous," she said, inspecting it carefully.

"I met the creator at a Comic Con a few years back—she isn't from Spruce Hill, but she lives close enough to deliver new stock every so often."

"It weighs a ton." Eden hefted it in her palm, then set the dragon carefully back on the shelf. "What's your favorite item in the store?"

I tilted my head, considering. "That's a hard one. I like the t-shirt that says 'Bard Kitty' with the cat playing the lute, but Liv's artwork is probably my favorite. That watercolor of Carrie Fisher, in particular. I have a poster-size copy at home that I need to frame and hang up."

Eden's gaze lifted to the art, positioned throughout the store, and she said, "Maybe I can commission her to do something for my shop. There's another artist Addie introduced to me who did the stuff I have hanging up, but I could diversify."

"Milo? I hate to interrupt, but do you have a *Player's Handbook* copy that Addie could borrow? I meant to bring mine and must've left it on the table at home," Olivia called.

"Coming right up." I leaned in to nuzzle Eden's cheek, saying, "Be right back."

"No worries, I'm sure I'll find something to entertain myself," she replied, turning back to the pewter dragons.

As I headed toward the shelf of Dungeons & Dragons books, I made a mental note to see which dragon Eden liked best so I could sock it away as a gift for her birthday at the end of February. I grabbed the book for Addie, flipped to the page she needed, and delivered it to her spot at the table.

Just when I started to head back toward Eden, a flash of headlights from the street outside nearly blinded me.

Eden was perfectly illuminated where she stood by the window. She turned to look out toward the street as the car revved its engine, then it pulled forward along the curb and a deafening crash echoed through the store as something smashed the window.

With a tinkling rain of shattered glass, I watched Eden lift her arms to cover her face and everything slowed as the fall of glass glinted like snowflakes under a streetlamp. Dimly, I heard the thud of something heavy hitting the floor of the shop, a squeal of tires outside as the car raced away down the street, and someone shouting that we needed to call 911.

I bolted toward Eden, crunching the broken window pieces under my sneakers, but I froze when I reached her side. Fragments of varying sizes glimmered in her hair and over her shoulders like fairy dust. The urge to brush it off of her as quickly as possible was tempered by the realization that it might slice into her delicate skin if I wasn't careful.

"Fucking hell," I whispered as she slowly lowered her arms. "Are you hurt?"

"I don't think so," she said dazedly.

"Just hold still for a second, let me help."

Gently, cautiously, I plucked tiny shards off of her and dropped them to the floor. Her exposed collarbone and right arm were dotted with tiny nicks in the skin, slowly reddening as blood beaded from the cuts. When I moved to her hair, glittering like she was adorned with diamonds, she lifted a hand to remove a couple bigger pieces from her cleavage.

"What the hell was that?" she asked.

"Some asshole getting his rocks off on destruction? I think your hair is clear." I stepped back to look her over, searching for the telltale twinkle of more glass.

"Police are on their way," Olivia called from the table, outside the radius of broken glass. "You two okay?"

I opened my mouth to reply as Eden reached up again to check her bra, but my assurance that we were fine died on my tongue when I saw a wash of red covering Eden's left forearm. I caught her elbow in one hand to inspect it and found a two-inch slice across the back of her hand.

"Eden, baby, you said you weren't hurt."

She blinked at me. "I'm not."

"Liv, call Mark, tell him we need Libby. We can meet them at the clinic. I think she's going to need stitches."

Eden's arm jerked in my grip as she cried, "I don't want stitches!"

Olivia was already on the phone, speaking quickly, when Addie appeared at the edge of my vision. I turned and she tossed me a clean towel from the storage closet, which I wrapped carefully around Eden's hand.

"Eden, babe, you're okay," she called gently.

"I don't want stitches," Eden whispered frantically. "It doesn't even hurt."

I cupped her face in my hand, sweeping my gaze over a tiny dot of blood along her cheekbone and another closer to her jaw. "It's going to be okay, I promise. We'll let Libby figure out what you need, okay?"

Eden's eyes were wide, still dazed, and her breath came in ragged gasps. My heart clenched hard in my chest as I tucked her into my side and led her out of the sea of shattered glass. Addie and Olivia were standing with the other gamers, arms around one another, staring at us.

"Liv, can you tell the police we're headed to the clinic? Are you okay staying here until I get back?"

Olivia nodded quickly. "Of course."

I glanced around at the destruction inside—fortunately, nothing a shop vac couldn't take care of—but there in the center of the mess lay a brick with a strip of paper and length of twine wrapped around it. Addie stepped forward to tug Eden into a hug while I squatted down to look at the paper.

"What the fuck?" I muttered.

Even with the twine across it, I could read the words scrawled on it. *Let us purify ourselves from everything that contaminates body and spirit, perfecting holiness.*

I stood and looked at the group of gamers, a range of ages from late teens to early thirties, mostly dressed in nerdy shirts like my own. No one else had been close enough to end up showered in glass like Eden, but they all looked shell-shocked.

"Everyone okay?"

From the group, I received half a dozen nods, a few verbal confirmations, and a tense smile from Addie. She released Eden back into my arms.

"Nobody touch that brick," I warned, "but make sure the police see it. We'll be at the clinic, then I'll come straight back here. I'm sorry, guys."

Olivia squeezed my arm. "Go on. We'll be fine. Take care of your girl."

It was only when I pulled up outside the clinic with no recollection of the trip over that I realized maybe I shouldn't be driving, but we arrived safely and Eden was still bleeding, so that was all that mattered.

Libby appeared on the sidewalk before I even opened my door. Though my sister-in-law possessed a killer poker face, I saw the concern in her eyes as I helped Eden out of the car, especially when Libby's gaze dropped to the towel that was now stained crimson.

"Come on inside, we'll get you sorted out," she murmured, positioning herself on Eden's other side. "Mark and your dad went to get some plywood to board up the window after the police finish up."

I sucked in a breath—the window was the last thing on my mind, but a warm rush of gratitude soothed some of my panic. We got Eden into an exam room, where Libby carefully unwrapped the towel to inspect the injury while I gave Eden another once-over to check for errant pieces of glass under the brighter fluorescent lights.

"I don't want stitches," Eden whispered.

Though she hadn't shed any tears since the incident, I heard them in her voice, fracturing the words in a way that broke my heart. Libby was the expert here; I just wrapped my arms around my girlfriend so she knew I was there for her. I'd let the medical professional handle this.

"I know you don't, but the bleeding isn't slowing down," Libby said gently. "I'll give you a local anesthetic to numb the area before we do anything, okay? Milo can stay right here with you. I promise it will be over quickly."

Eden gave a quick, reluctant nod, and Libby set to work. By the time the anesthetic kicked in, though, the police had arrived at the clinic to take our statements. I was about to refuse to leave Eden's side, but my mom appeared in the doorway and gave us both a warm smile.

"Hi, honey," she murmured, moving toward us. "The police are here and need to ask you both some questions."

"Can it wait until this is done?" I asked quietly.

She winked at me and made her way to Eden's other side. "With three boys, I'm sure you can imagine how many injuries I've tended over the years. Would you let me take Milo's place here while he gives his statement? That way you can both get out of here sooner."

I thought Eden would panic, but she nodded against my shoulder, so I pressed a kiss to her temple, offered a grateful nod to both Libby and my mom, then whispered into Eden's hair, "I'll be back as soon as I can."

"Okay," she whispered back.

I gave her a gentle squeeze, then stood and left Eden in the care of my family, hoping to hell she would feel safe and loved in the arms of the other two most important women in my life.

Chapter Twenty-Four

EDEN

I'D NEVER HAD STITCHES before, but they weren't as bad as I imagined, at least not with Terry Davies distracting me with stories about the many injuries her sons had sustained over the years. My favorite was about Milo, Mark, and Mark's friend, Henry, who had gone against Libby's advice and decided to scale a barbed wire fence outside an abandoned building when they were around Carter's age.

Libby had simply followed the fenceline until she found an unlocked gate. The boys ended up covered in scratches, but had insisted they could take care of the injuries themselves.

Terry found them cutting up the maxi pads Milo discovered under the bathroom sink to use as bandages. After calling Henry's parents and hauling them all in for stitches and tetanus boosters, the mothers had parked outside a drug store and sent the three boys in to buy a replacement box of pads.

I was giggling helplessly when Milo returned to the room.

"Oh, dammit, Mom. You told her about the pads, didn't you?"

"They *are* extremely absorbent. That was good thinking on your part," I told him.

"I didn't even know what they were," he grumbled. "I couldn't understand why Mark and Henry thought it was so funny when I pulled out the box, but their fingers were bleeding too much to argue."

Libby winked at me as she finished taping a bandage over the back of my hand. "If only there were places to seek medical treatment and professionals to deal with such things."

With the gash taken care of, Libby turned her attention to dabbing antiseptic on the tiny cuts along my arm, chest, and cheek. Terry made Milo step back out of the room while the ladies helped me undress to make sure there were no other injuries that needed attention, then I was deemed well enough to give my statement to the police.

Rose Hanson, who'd spoken to us during the bomb threat, sat beside me in the clinic's empty waiting room and had me go over the sequence of events leading up to the window shattering. I didn't think I had much to contribute, since I'd barely noticed the car outside before glass rained down over me, but Detective Hanson was incredibly patient with me.

"Did you notice anything about the car—color, make or model, license plate?"

I started to shake my head, then went still. "It was a light color, but not white or silver. It looked almost like pale gold."

"Good, Eden, that's good. Could you see inside the car?" she asked.

"Not really, especially after the headlights hit me. There was a passenger, though. I mean, you probably knew that, because they were driving north and would've had to throw the brick out the passenger window, right?"

The detective smiled encouragingly. "Confirmation helps, Eden. So you saw two people in the car, a driver and a passenger?"

I nodded and said, "Yes, but I didn't get a good look at either of them. I'm sorry. I wish I could remember more. It all happened so fast. The headlights paused on me for a minute, the engine revved, then the window broke."

"The headlights paused?" she repeated.

"Yeah, I think the car stopped. It was like a spotlight on me in that corner of the store by the window."

"The note on the brick makes it clear this was planned, Eden," Hanson said gently. "Do you think you were the target?"

I froze. "The note?"

"There was a note tied to the brick with a Bible verse about purification, something about contamination of body and spirit. I'm sorry, I assumed you saw it."

For a second, I forgot that my parents were somewhere across the world and experienced a moment of absolute terror. It faded as quickly as it hit, but there were plenty of members of my parents' church who might have taken up the baton of ensuring I didn't succeed in a business venture that might contaminate them all.

Members of my *brother's* church.

He'd found my phone number all those years ago when he called me—who was to say he hadn't found out the rest in the time since?

"Yes, I'm the target. Shit, shit, shit," I wheezed.

"Easy, easy. That brick didn't go through your shop window, Eden."

"No, but it *was* the window I was standing in front of. No one else in Milo's store was even visible. The displays blocked the game table. Milo was over by them when it happened, but I was standing by the window."

"Is there a reason you think you're the target, aside from that flier?"

I bit my lip, then nodded. "I grew up in a very strict church, the kind that doesn't approve of a woman owning a business, much less one like mine."

Her expression was gentle, but her gaze was sharp. "I understand your family isn't local, is that right?"

"Yes. But it's not like they're far away. I mean, my parents are on another continent, but we just found out my brother took over their branch of the church. He's the pastor there now, in Binghamton."

"Let's not jump to conclusions, okay? Can you give me his name and the name of the church? We'll look into any possible connection and you can focus on getting some rest."

Shakily, I gave her the information and watched her scribble it on a tiny pad of paper. She stayed silent, but my brain launched into warpspeed. Milo's shop had been vandalized because of *me*. Someone else could have been hurt because of *me*.

The past I'd fought so hard to free myself from was rising up to hurt the people I loved.

Oh, god. I love him.

The realization wasn't warm or fuzzy; it was edged in sheer panic. Milo could have been hurt, killed even, if he'd still been standing at my side, whispering into my ear, when those headlights landed on me.

"Eden," Hanson said, her voice firm and authoritative. "What happened is not your fault."

I closed my eyes, nodding even though she was dead wrong. "Do you need anything else from me?"

"Not right now. I'll be in touch if anything else comes up, and here's my card. I want you to call me directly if you see or hear anything else even remotely out of the ordinary."

"Okay," I whispered, taking the card with my bandaged left hand.

Hanson stared hard at me for another minute before she rose to her feet and left the clinic. I sat in the silent waiting room, staring out the glass front doors into the night, until eventually Milo poked his head out of the exam room and saw that Hanson was gone.

"Hey, everything okay?"

I didn't look at him—I couldn't. "I'd like to go home now."

Milo sat in the chair beside me, wrapping his fingers around my uninjured hand. "Eden, hey, are you all right?"

"Please," I whispered. "Can you or your mom drop me at my apartment before you go back to the store?"

Hurt and alarm mingled in his handsome face, darkening his eyes as they scanned my features. He lifted his free hand to my cheek and swept his thumb just below the tiny cut under my eye.

"Don't shut me out, Eden. Not again. Please."

His voice sounded wrecked and I almost gave in, but this was for his own safety. Guilt and fear pulsed through my veins as I tried to summon an excuse that would inflict the least amount of pain while still keeping him protected—away from me—for the time being.

Nothing came to mind, so I said, "I just need to be in my own space for a bit."

After a long, penetrating inspection of my features, he blew out a defeated breath. "If that's what you want."

It wasn't what I wanted, not by a long shot, but when I nodded, Milo dropped his hands and stood to go speak to his mother and Libby in hushed tones that barely registered in my ears. When the three of them came back out to the waiting room, Libby flipped off the lights and locked the door behind us, then they bundled me into Terry's car.

Before closing the door, Milo crouched down and took my face in his hands. "I don't know what's going on in that beautiful head of yours, Eden, but I don't like this. I promised I'd back off when you need time to process, so that's the only reason I'm not pushing you to talk this through right now."

"It'll be okay," I whispered.

"It will," he whispered back. "Because I love you. This wasn't how I imagined saying it, but I want you to know before you leave here. I love you and we will sort all of this out."

I drew in a shuddering breath, wishing like hell I could give that back to him, but fear tightened my lungs until I couldn't speak another word.

Milo, as always, didn't need words to see what was in my heart. He searched my expression, smiled slightly, and leaned in to kiss my forehead. Though I managed not to burst out crying, I felt one tear sneak past my eyelids and roll slowly down my cheek.

"I'm here for you," Milo murmured, "and, eventually, you'll believe that. Get some sleep. You know where to find me when you're ready."

I gave a tight nod as he backed away, closed my door, and lifted his hand in silent farewell as his mother slid behind the wheel. It took every ounce of strength I possessed to keep it together until I got inside my silent apartment, where I curled up in a tight ball on the couch and let the sobs loose.

Once everything had poured out of me, I retreated to my bed, squeezed my eyes shut so tight that pinpricks of light danced behind my eyelids, and let the aching emptiness in my chest suck me down.

If my brother was behind any of this, then I was the only one who could stop it.

Chapter Twenty-Five

MILO

THIS WAS WRONG. *I* was wrong. Letting Eden walk away was the worst mistake I could have made. I knew it the minute my mom's car pulled away from the curb, but it was too late to call her back.

If only I'd been next to her when it happened, I could have shielded her, protected her.

Now I was standing in Dueling Dragons, holding plywood against the window as my dad and brother secured it to the frame. Olivia and Adelaide had swept up the glass, one of the gamers had carefully vacuumed every shelf within the danger zone, and the brick had been bagged up as evidence and taken. Only the three of us remained.

"She's going to be okay," Mark said quietly.

I wasn't surprised he'd cottoned on to my distress, but I didn't particularly want to discuss it with him right then, either, so I just muttered, "Yeah."

Dad gave me the side-eye as he drilled another screw into the wall. "Is there something going on with you two? She seemed a little out of sorts at our house the other night."

"She's...I don't know. Not used to sharing her feelings when things go bad, I think. Not used to letting somebody in when she's hurting. When everything is good, she's affectionate and forthcoming, but I'm not sure she knows how to let others support her when things are shitty."

"You managed to turn the night around on Sunday," Dad mused. "I would think you can handle that again."

"Yeah. Except I think this time there was more to it than just sorting through her own feelings. Tonight, she was in shock when it first happened, but she seemed to be coming around again after the stitches were done. Then she went to talk to Rose, and a switch flipped."

"You think Rose said something that freaked her?" Mark asked.

"Maybe. All I know is she panicked and shut me out. Maybe she blames me for getting her hurt?"

"Not a chance," my father said with a snort.

Mark studied me for a second, then said, "You should go to her when we're done here. Clear things up instead of making assumptions."

"How can I do that when I promised I'd back off if she needed space? I don't know how to do what she asked while still trying to break through those walls."

Both of them went quiet. There was no easy answer, but that didn't mean I wasn't hoping one of them would suggest some magic fix. I leaned my forehead against the plywood, still trying to forget the sight of Eden's arm covered in blood.

"She's it for me."

The words tumbled from my lips and the silence between us grew heavy. Mark had almost lost any chance with the love of his life when he didn't speak up, and even if things had worked out in the end, we all knew he regretted losing those years with Libby as more than just a friend.

Out of respect for Maverick, we didn't talk much about what my mom called the Davies Devotion. We'd grown up hearing their love story over and over, like a family legend in the making—Dad had known from the first time he saw Mom that she was the one. As clear as an arrow through the heart, a neon sign declaring that true love not only existed but had been found.

It had been the same for Mark, and now it was the same for me.

"Then you'll do whatever you need to do to work through this, son," Dad said softly.

"We're here for you, man. Whatever we can do to help, you just let us know," Mark added.

Words clogged in my throat, so I just nodded. This was what I wished Eden had—or what I wished she could see that she already had in her cousin, in me. Unconditional love and support, unwavering loyalty.

Coming from the childhood she'd endured, it might be difficult for her to adapt to those things, but I was determined to help her learn.

For both our sakes.

A S WITH THE BOMB threat, news of the destruction actually brought in more customers than usual the following day. I almost kept the store closed, but I figured it would be easier to maintain an eye on Eden's state of mind if I was nearby. It was also one of Carter's days with me, so I wanted to make sure he knew there was nothing to fear and that everything would be okay.

Unfortunately, the influx of shoppers at both stores meant my contact with Eden was limited to a few quick texts throughout the day. She insisted she was fine, but it was difficult to read her tone via text. Rafael came by to see if I needed any assistance, so I left him in charge of the store and finally got the chance to slip away to check on Eden in person.

Garden of Delights was positively hopping, even on a weekday. A small group of older women eyed me with interest when

I entered the store—gossip moved through Spruce Hill's population at the speed of light, so I wasn't surprised our relationship was public knowledge.

"Ladies," I said with a smile.

"Sorry to hear about your window, Milo. The police will catch the little buggers behind it, I'm sure," one of them replied.

Eden watched both the exchange and my approach with an expression that bordered on trepidation. It reminded me of that day she first walked into Dueling Dragons, like she was bracing herself for impact.

I hated it as much now as I did then, but I had to tread carefully.

For once, I didn't join her behind the counter or greet her with a kiss, just leaned against the other side and swept my gaze over the tiny scabs that weren't hidden by her high-necked blouse. Her left hand was still bandaged with gauze, her beautiful eyes haunted. I wanted to wash it all away, like I could restore her to her usual self with the wave of a magic wand.

"How are you today?" I asked softly.

"Shaken. You?"

"Worried about you, but otherwise fine. The insurance guy is coming this afternoon. Everything is cleaned up. I'm thinking of letting Carter paint the wood over the window. He's a pretty good artist. Maybe when the new glass goes in, I'll hang the wood somewhere to showcase his talent."

Eden blinked at me. "Oh. I mean, that's a good idea."

I stepped aside when one of the women came to make her purchase, then waited until they'd left the shop to prop my elbows on the counter and say, "Eden," in the low, bossy tone that always got through to her.

"Yes?"

"Tell me the truth. How are you doing?"

She sucked in a breath. "Not great."

"I could help you if you'd let me in," I said gently. Even if it *might* work, I wasn't going to order her to open up to me.

Saved by the bell—a customer entered the store. Eden shifted so the woman could see her and offered a friendly greeting before glancing back at my face.

"I just need some time, Milo."

The whispered words were like a blade in my chest, but I tapped my fingers on the countertop for a second before leaning forward. "I don't know what's going on, Eden, but we'll get through this."

When she only nodded, that blade sank a little deeper. I held her gaze for a beat, hoping to convey all the emotions bubbling inside me, then returned to Dueling Dragons in defeat.

No, not defeat. More like a temporary détente for strategizing.

Something had shaken Eden last night even more than the brick through the window, more than the news about her parents leaving the country or the surprise existence of her niece. I didn't know what exactly it was, but my initial concern that she blamed me for her injury seemed unlikely now. There was something deeper at play, and I didn't like it.

As Rafael was leaving, Olivia came into the store, her somber expression a far cry from the contentment that glowed from her since she started seeing Adelaide. She gave the store a slow sweep of her eyes before walking up to the counter.

"Hey," she called.

"Hey. Sorry about your game."

Liv's eyes widened behind her glasses. "Last I checked, some dick throwing a brick through a window doesn't fall under the category of 'Milo's fault.' How's Eden doing?"

"Physically, she's okay. Libby stitched her up and cleaned all the little cuts."

"But emotionally, not so okay?"

I blew out a breath. "Right. I don't know what's going on. Maybe this is how she reacts to extreme situations. It's like she turned off that light inside her. I just don't know how to get it back."

"Do you think Addie could help?" Liv asked gently. "Those two are tight. I get the feeling things are serious between you and Eden, but it hasn't been very long. They have history, and maybe Addie's dealt with this in the past."

"You don't think that's disloyal of me? Circumventing Eden like that?"

"Milo, you're clearly in love with her. If she's shutting you out because of some kind of trauma response, I think you need to work with whatever tools are at your disposal. I'm not saying gossip behind her back, just maybe...call in some reinforce-ments."

"Yeah. I think you're right. Thanks, Liv."

"Any time. I gotta head over to my shift at the library, but I wanted to see if you needed anything first."

I smiled at her and shook my head. "No, I'm good. Carter will be here soon. I'll talk to Adelaide."

Before Olivia was even out the door, Carter came barreling inside, wide-eyed and frantic. Liv steadied him before he tripped over her, squeezed his shoulder, and waved at me as she left.

"Hey, buddy," I said, keeping my tone light.

"Dad told me the store was attacked."

"Attacked? He used that word?"

Carter frowned. "Well, no. Dad wanted to come help board up the window, but we were at pottery night at school. By the time it was over, Grandpa said you guys were all sorted out and that you'd probably need my help today."

I gave a solemn nod. "Yeah, buddy, I do. Here's what I'm thinking."

Chapter Twenty-Six

EDEN

NUMB. THAT WAS THE only word to describe my state of mind in the days that followed. It was like cold had seeped through the cracks until it filled up all the emptiness with frosty, unfeeling ice.

I should have been grateful for the steady stream of customers, but instead, I was annoyed every time I was interrupted from my research into my brother's life.

Not that I'd found much.

His bio on the church's website included that same family photo and pitifully little information. He'd gotten married a month after I left to a woman named Mary Billings—a woman I'd never met, which suggested a quick courtship. Had they even chosen each other, or had the marriage been arranged for them?

Arranged like they'd hoped to do for me, to find some suitable man who didn't mind a young bride who needed a firm hand.

The contents of my stomach roiled and seethed.

Their daughter Eve was born less than a year later, making her almost thirteen now. I thought about Carter, his cheeky grins and fun-loving attitude, and wondered what my niece was like outside of the shadow I'd been raised under. Was she the perfect daughter, as my parents hoped I would be? Did she have hobbies, a life outside the church?

At three years older than me, Isaiah had been treated like a full-on adult well before I finished high school and got the hell out of Dodge. I knew, in a vague sense, that he and my father spent a lot of time at the church, but I hadn't realized Isaiah planned to devote his life to it. Our relationship had been stiff and awkward for as long as I could remember, though now it struck me that when our parents punished me for whatever wrong I'd done—real or imagined—Isaiah always responded the same way.

"I'll pray for you, Eden."

When the next short lull in shoppers came, I opened up the photo of my brother's little family and stared hard at the image, as though it could give me answers. None came, but I thought back to the phone conversation we'd had a few years back.

Our only conversation since I walked out the door of our childhood home fourteen years ago.

A decade had passed and still I recognized his voice the minute I answered the phone.

"Eden, it's time to come home. Forgiveness is yours. This has gone on long enough, don't you think?"

As shocked as I was bitter, I'd replied, "Yes, brother, I think the shame and subjugation of women has been going on far too long. Thanks for the offer, but I won't be coming back. Not now, not ever."

"I'll pray for you, Eden."

Then he'd sighed—not like he was disappointed in me, not an echo of the countless sighs I'd inspired in my parents throughout my life, but like he was disappointed in himself.

How had I forgotten that? What did it mean?

The internet held no further information for me to find, not about Isaiah or about his little family, except that he was still listed as the minister at the Church of Eternal Light in Binghamton.

For half a second, I debated calling him, then shook the urge away with a shudder. I wasn't willing to embroil myself with anyone from that church, not even my brother, without good reason.

And I still wasn't convinced my brother himself would seek to hurt me. He hadn't *helped* when I was constantly in trouble as a child, but he had never ratted me out, either.

Even when he'd had plenty of opportunities to do so.

A pair of giggling twenty-somethings entered the store and I forced a bright smile even as I stuck my bandaged hand in my pocket behind the counter. Detective Hanson was right—I should leave the investigation to them.

I just...wasn't sure I could.

With the flow of customers never truly dying off, I lost all track of time, each day blending into the next. In my free moments, I continued scouring the internet for information about Isaiah, Mary, and Eve, but there was no trace of them on social media.

It was like they were ghosts.

Addie hovered around the store as much as possible, during her work hours and beyond. It was obvious she'd been tasked with making sure I was okay, since Milo hadn't even tried to cross that line I'd drawn in the sand.

A line I wished he'd just swept away, but this distance between us was on me, not him.

"When do your stitches come out?" she asked as she unnecessarily refolded a pajama set beside me.

"Soon. What day is it?"

"Tuesday," Addie answered.

My entire body turned to ice.

"Eden, it's okay. Olivia's taking a couple weeks off from gaming, at least until Milo's new window goes in. I think that's happening this week. Breathe, babe."

I didn't realize I wasn't until I heard the harsh wheezing coming through my own lips. Addie made some cheery excuse to a customer as she guided me into the break room and nudged me down into a chair. Once I was seated, she crouched in front of me and clasped my hands.

"Breathe," she urged again, pressing our joined hands to my chest. "I want to feel your lungs filling with air. You can do it."

With effort, I managed to suck in enough oxygen to lift our hands. Addie murmured soothingly until each breath came more easily than the last.

"Is Milo okay?" I whispered.

"Oh, honey. He's fine, just worried about you. I wish you'd talk to him."

I nodded, but we both knew I was lying. Eventually, Addie had to leave for her shift at the crisis center. Even though I promised her I was fine on my own, now that the initial panic had subsided, this past week had taught me that I wouldn't be alone for long.

If Addie wasn't at the shop, then Olivia found excuses to drop by, along with Monique, Libby, or Terry. It was like a not-at-all covert girl squad had taken responsibility for my well-being.

It didn't feel all that great, honestly, not in these circumstances.

They were worried about me and I appreciated that, but instead of working through my thoughts or sorting out my emotions, I spent all of my time reassuring them I was fine. Every one of them recognized it for the lie that it was, but if I didn't understand what was happening in my head, how was I supposed to explain it to them?

Then again, maybe I didn't need to. When Libby took out the stitches a few days later, she took one look at my face and I knew she saw far deeper than I wanted anyone to dig at that moment.

"Busy place today," I said lightly, hoping I could direct the conversation away from myself long enough to get through this appointment.

"Practically every day, lately. I'm hoping to bring on another doctor in the next few months. It's getting to be too much to handle on my own."

"Good for business, but maybe not for stress levels."

"Speaking of stress levels, how've you been feeling?" she asked, head bent over my hand as she snipped the loose threads.

Shit. I walked right into that one.

I kept my gaze averted, both from what she was doing and from her keen eyes. "Fine."

A disbelieving snort snapped my attention back to her face. "Eden, I've been a member of the Davies family for a long time, and an unofficial member even longer. I know what stubborn looks like from every possible angle."

"I'm not stubborn," I protested.

"You know," she mused, somehow changing the subject and throwing me completely off my defensive position in the same breath, "the mind is a very powerful thing. Some people are lucky enough to feel their feelings and recognize each one for what it is so they can process and move forward."

I stared at the curls bunched at the back of her head. "What about the unlucky ones?"

Without glancing up, she said, "Sometimes, we can't really tell what we're feeling. We go numb, we shut down. We push people away in an attempt at self-preservation."

Tears stung the back of my eyes, but I couldn't respond, not without setting them free.

"There we go, all done. It's healing nicely, but it'll take some time for the scar to fade. Here, I want you to take this." She reached into her pocket and handed me a folded pamphlet with three names and phone numbers on it. "Sometimes it's easier to talk to someone who's not tangled up in a situation. I think you should consider it."

As much as I didn't want to consider it, I took the card, offered the same wooden smile I'd been giving everyone for over a week, and went back to the store.

In the end, Milo's mom was the one who broke through. I was in one of the back rooms on Saturday, sorting through some Valentine's Day stock that had just come in, when Addie sent Terry to join me.

"Hey there, what's all this?"

On my knees in a circle of red and pink, lavender and silver, I gave her the first real smile that had graced my lips in almost a week. "Getting in the holiday spirit. I'll put this stuff out soon, but I wanted to look through it all now so I can design a window display."

"You do all of that yourself?" Terry asked as she eased herself down to the floor at my side.

"Yeah, it's one of my favorite aspects of owning the store, actually. It gives me a chance to showcase my favorite pieces and get creative. I love this one," I said, holding up a pink satin robe with silver hearts embroidered along the edges.

"Hoo-ey, that's lovely," she breathed. "I haven't bought lingerie in almost a decade. Any chance you'd give family some early access?"

Family. I rocked back slightly, staring down at the embroidery that had gone blurry as tears hit my eyes.

"Eden, sweetheart, look at me," Terry whispered.

I lifted my head as a tear rolled down my cheek. Terry, who was everything my mother was not—soft and maternal, warm and welcoming—wrapped her arms around me. With one hand, she guided my head to her shoulder and cooed gently in my ear.

"There, now, let it out, darling girl."

These were not the wracking sobs I'd let consume me that night when I walked away from Milo, just a silent stream of tears that dampened my cheeks as well as Terry's shirt. When I tried to pull away, her gentle grip kept me clasped against her.

"We haven't known each other long, Eden, but you're family now. Once the Davies clan has claimed you, I'm afraid there's no turning back. Why don't you tell me what's been on your mind lately, darling?"

I didn't mean to speak—in truth, I meant to give her the same bullshit response I'd been giving everyone else. Instead, I whispered, "It's my fault."

That was when she drew back, frowning at me. "What's your fault, Eden?"

The words poured like a tidal wave, inevitable and destructive, as I told her about my childhood, the stifling religion I'd finally escaped when I turned eighteen, the dread I'd carried with me since the moment I started planning to open Garden of Delights. I told her about the hate mail we'd received and the note tied to the brick that vandalized Milo's store.

Then I told her about my parents leaving the country without a goodbye, my brother getting married and having a daughter I'd never met, my fear that the kid was living out my miserable childhood all over again.

Terry was silent long enough that I thought she was going to shove me away and tell me to stay away from her son. I even started to flinch away, but she caught my face in her hands and locked eyes with me, that slate gray going soft as kitten fur in the same way Milo's sometimes did.

"You think you're responsible for some vandal's behavior because you grew up in an environment like that?"

My mouth opened and closed twice before I nodded. "Well...yeah. I'm the target. If I hadn't been in Milo's store, they would have thrown that brick here."

"And you know that," Terry said gently, "as fact?"

"I—well. It makes sense, doesn't it?"

She smiled as she brushed her thumbs across my wet cheeks. "A lot of things make sense, Eden, but that doesn't make them all true. Was your name on either note?"

"No," I admitted.

"So whoever did those things might not know a single thing about you, wouldn't you say?"

Good god, was this what it was like having a mother who *cared?* I blinked back at Terry, frowning, even as her lips curved into a smile.

"And do you think, even if that person *was* targeting you, that a man I raised would blame the victim of these acts? A victim he clearly loves?"

"No," I whispered.

"Do you think if you talked to him about it, that he'd want to be away from you while you're hurting like this? That he doesn't deserve to be part of the conversation, to have the chance to keep *you* safe, too?"

"No." I closed my eyes against the ache in my chest.

"Good, because if you thought that of him, I'd tell you he deserves better, Eden. But he loves you, and if I'm not mistaken, you love him, too."

"I do. I'm in love with him."

Her smile widened until it was glowing, radiant. "Good. Eden, darling, you have no control over what other people do. Milo knows that the people we love are always more important than the things we have. His new window is being installed right now, and this incident gave Carter an opportunity to share his talents with the world. There's always a bright side."

A trembling breath slipped past my lips. "You're very wise."

"I've had a lot of practice. Now, what do you say about that early access sale, hmm? I think Tucker would love this little red number, and if Milo is anything like his father—though please don't tell me, I don't need to know—I think you'd look absolutely stunning in this sweet silver nightie."

The laugh that burst from my throat sounded as rusty as it felt, but I gestured toward the piles and said, "Please, be my guest. And I think you're right about the silver."

Terry's smile turned soft. "What he sees in you is what you should see in yourself, Eden. That's not easy, but if you let him show you, you'll find out that he's got impeccable taste. Gets it from his father."

This time, the laughter came more easily. When Terry pulled me in for another hug, I hugged her back. My own mom might have been cold, stern, and strict, but she was out of my life, as far as I was concerned.

Family didn't require shared DNA. The Davies clan was proof of that.

And it was about time I let myself believe it.

T EMPTED AS I WAS to close the shop early and go straight over to Milo, I went home, washed my face until there was no trace of tears, and packed a bag for the night.

The silver nightie was at the top of the pile. I couldn't fix this with sex, but it felt like a peace offering, a little treat for us both after he accepted my apology.

Driving to Milo's house was nerve-wracking, especially when I wondered if I should have texted to be sure he was home—it would have ruined the surprise, but at least I wouldn't be freaking out during those seven minutes in the car. When I pulled into the driveway, his car was there and plenty of lights shone through the windows.

I'd put on the heels that made his gray eyes turn to molten steel, but otherwise, I was wearing the dress I'd worn to work. Though I was prepared to ring the doorbell, Milo swung the door open as soon as I stepped onto the front porch.

"Eden," he said softly, eyes caught on my face. "Is everything okay?"

"No. I screwed up. Big time. I was hoping you'd give me the chance to apologize."

Milo reached out to clasp my free hand and pulled me into the house. I thought he might yank me straight into his arms, but he paused, his eyes searching. Whatever he saw there must have reassured him, because he let his gaze slide slowly down, following the way the dress clung to my breasts, waist, and hips. The moment he reached my shoes, he drew a tight breath as a groan rumbled in his chest.

"You don't need to apologize for anything, Eden, but I have to admit that this giving you space thing is not my favorite."

"I hated every second of it," I confessed. "I just wanted you to be safe."

"Eden," he began, but I shook my head.

"My head was all mixed up, because I feel responsible for what happened. If someone from my parents' church is behind this, I brought that into your life. It's my fault."

"No, it isn't. If I'd known this is what you were battling, I would never have let you shut me out."

I drew a tight breath. "I just thought it wasn't fair to make you suffer through it with me."

Now his hands went to my waist, then eased around to the small of my back. I let my tote bag fall to the floor and tangled my arms around his shoulders. His head dipped so he could brush his nose along my jaw, nuzzling the space under my ear until I shivered.

"I suffered through it without you anyway. Next time, can we agree to suffer together?"

"Yes," I whispered when his lips touched my throat.

"Did you wear those shoes just for me?"

"Yes."

"Eden," he growled. "I hope to hell that bag means you're planning to spend the night. I'm tired of sleeping without you."

"It does," I murmured, "but I have a surprise for you, so you can't just tear my dress off and have your wicked way with me."

Milo drew back to lift a brow. "A surprise? Will I like it as much as your last surprise?"

I smiled at him as every bit of the pain from our time apart melted away under the intensity of his expression. His gaze dipped, following the curve of my lips. The heat in his eyes remained, but it was tempered now by something soft and tender.

"Well, I'm not sure about that, but I wanted to do something special for you," I hedged.

His arms tightened around me. "You, Eden, are the most special thing in the world to me. All I need is you, right here with me, yeah?"

"Yeah," I breathed, just before his lips descended to capture mine.

And for the first time in my life, I believed it, because all I needed in that moment was the sweet warmth of his love wrapping around me as snugly as his arms.

This, I realized, was paradise—and we found it together.

Chapter Twenty-Seven

MILO

Late that night, Eden finally explained what had been driving her reaction after Libby stitched her up. In hushed tones, she confessed the worry weighing on her heart, her fear for my safety, her guilt over bringing me into what she considered her mess.

My heart broke for her even as hope flared blindingly bright inside me.

If she was willing to suffer that misery to keep me safe, then I wasn't wrong to believe she was in love with me, whether she said the words or not.

"I should have told you about the note on the brick," I murmured against the top of her hair.

"Even if you had, I think I still would have reacted the same way. I can't bear the thought of you getting hurt, especially not if it's because of me."

Carefully rolling over so I could study her expressive face, I shook my head. "None of this is because of you, Eden. You're not responsible for anyone else's behavior, and if some asshole thinks he can get to you through me, we're going to prove him wrong."

"Okay," she whispered.

I slid my hand along the sleek silver nightgown I'd refused to peel off her body before making love to her. "By the way, I fully approve of surprises like this."

Just when I reached the bottom of the fabric, she said, "Your mom helped me pick it out."

I froze. "What?"

"She came to the shop while I was sorting the shipment. She kind of...talked me through what's been going on in my head since that night. And then she bought a red—"

I jerked my hand away from her hip to cover her mouth. "Don't you dare finish that sentence, you little monster."

It hadn't even been two weeks since she asked for space, but the sound of her laughter was the sweetest thing I'd ever heard. Her whole body shook with the force of it as she burrowed into me, trying to muffle the giggles bursting from her lips. I let it wash over me even as I buried my face against her neck and tickled her with my beard.

This—this was what I'd missed. The unfettered joy of having her in my arms.

She fell asleep wearing the nightgown and nothing else, but it was rucked up to her waist, leaving one hip bare for my fingertips to explore. Only through sheer force of will was I able to wipe my mother's involvement from my memory. I refused to think of anything but the way it shimmered as Eden's body moved over and under me.

Those images filled my mind until I finally drifted off with her tucked against my body, and waking up to her in that same position was a slice of heaven I'd been afraid I might never get back.

"Is it morning?" she mumbled into my chest.

"Unfortunately, yes, but it's Sunday, so you can stay right where you are."

"I'm sorry it took me so long to come around, but I'm also not sorry the timing worked out this way. I love Sundays."

I laughed into her hair. "My favorite day of the week."

For a minute, she was quiet, then she asked, "Do you know whether the police have any leads?"

"No, though a guy at the cafe across the street got a partial license plate when the car paused out front. The police are still looking for witnesses, so we just need to sit tight. It wasn't like it was midnight. People were out and about. Someone had to have seen something."

"Okay," Eden whispered.

"Tomorrow, you should come in and see what Carter did with the plywood. I think you'll love it."

"Okay."

The word was stronger this time, more like her usual self. I rolled onto my side, keeping her leg draped over my hip, and kissed the tip of her nose.

"So, what should we do with our day? Stay in bed? Make some cookies? Go out for brunch?"

"Will Jiji murder me in my sleep tonight if we spend the day in bed?" she asked.

As if summoned by the question, a plaintive meow came from beyond the closed door and we both started laughing. Eden curled her body into mine like she was seeking shelter, so I tightened my arms around her until she glanced up at me, still giggling.

"I'll take that as a yes," she said, "but I'd be happy just lounging around today."

"We'll invite him in after breakfast."

If it weren't for Jiji, I probably would've kept Eden right there for as long as humanly possible. With the comforter tucked up around our shoulders, we were encased in a warm cocoon together, shielded from the reality of the world outside this bed. Eden shifted slightly, not to look up at me, but to nuzzle her face into my throat.

"I had an idea," she said softly.

"Lay it on me."

"I know there's a certain ambiance in your shop, but what if Olivia ran her games out of one of the back rooms at mine? None of our meetings or events have been on Tuesdays, so I'll just make sure we don't schedule anything when she's got a game night."

Her lips brushed over my skin as she spoke and sent a zing along my nerve endings, but the words kept me from focusing on that sensation. I wanted to move her up onto the pillows so I could see her eyes, but if she needed that distance to speak without getting anxious, I would happily give her that.

"Eden...that's a really sweet offer, but are you sure? I don't want to intrude on your space."

She drew a shaky breath and whispered, "I don't mind. I don't need that much space most of the time, and..."

"And what, doll?"

"It'd be safer. You'd be safer."

My arms tightened around her. "Eden, we're safe."

"Yeah," she replied, but the word was hesitant.

"If it will give you some peace of mind, then I'll talk to Liv and we'll give it a try this week, okay? Even if it's just until the cops catch the person responsible for smashing the window. Sound good?"

"Yeah," she said again, stronger this time.

"Good, that's settled. Now, I'm going to go feed my cat so it's not me who gets killed in my sleep, then I'm going to bring you breakfast in bed. We'll eat, have some coffee, fool around some more, and have a nice, relaxing day."

I shifted out from under her, tucking the blanket tightly enough that no cold would seep in while I was gone. When Eden smiled up at me, my heart clenched like a fist in my chest before it loosened into something warm and profound. I pulled on a pair of flannel pants and leaned down to drop a soft kiss on her forehead.

"Thank you," she murmured.

"For the kiss? Any time."

"No, for everything. I mean, and the kiss, too. But mostly for being awesome."

Cupping her cheek in my hand, I gazed at her, noting each and every difference that had come over her in our time apart. The little nicks in her skin had faded enough to be almost indistinguishable. Even though her stitches had been removed this week, the gash across her hand was still a vivid pink.

But she was here. She was healing.

"I love you," I said softly, stroking my thumb over her cheek.

Eden didn't return the words, not aloud, but she nuzzled her cheek into my palm. I felt the slow curve of her lips just before she kissed my hand. Her expression was open, those hazel eyes unguarded. It felt like a gift, being trusted with the soft center of her without a single barrier in sight.

I would move heaven and earth for this woman.

"Stay right where you are. I'll be back with coffee," I told her instead.

After all, we had to start somewhere.

WHEN IT CAME TIME for me to head into work on Monday afternoon, I convinced Eden to come in with me. Since our reunion, any mention of Dueling Dragons had garnered a certain reaction that concerned me. She'd go utterly still, her muscles tensed like she was preparing to flee.

We needed to overcome her fear of the store itself, and fast.

I held her hand as I let us in the back door, then slipped my arm around her waist to guide her inside. "Deep breaths, doll," I encouraged as we moved along the hallway.

"I'd settle for any breaths," she muttered.

If she could joke, she could handle this. As I greeted Rafael, Eden's gaze shot straight to the front window, now repaired with a shiny new piece of glass, custom cut to fit the frame and paid for—thankfully—by my insurance. She stared for a good minute as we stood behind the counter, then I squeezed her hip and pointed toward the far wall.

Carter usually painted small canvases, but he'd risen to the challenge of working with the larger surface of the plywood sheet. Two dragons, one blue and one purple, each with metallic accents that made their scales shimmer, curled together around the base of a stone lighthouse, gazing lovingly at one another.

The blue dragon had slate gray eyes with silver edges, while the purple dragon's were the perfect mixture of bronze and gold.

"Oh my god," Eden whispered, moving around the counter to get closer to the painting. "That's us."

"Good catch. I didn't even realize what he was doing until the very end, when he finished the eyes. He modeled it after the Spruce Hill Lighthouse up on the lake. Have you been there yet?"

"No, I haven't. This is incredible. Do you think he'd be up for a job?"

I blinked in surprise. "You want him to paint some naked women for your shop?"

"No, I want my own set of these dragons. Smaller, maybe. I'll pay him," she said, still staring up at them.

"I think he'd be happy to paint something for his Aunt Eden."

She sucked in a breath as she turned to me. "I like that."

Rafael called out that he was leaving, but Eden didn't so much as glance in his direction when I waved to him. With wide eyes, she stared up at me, looking like I'd just gifted her the moon. It was impossible not to close the distance between us and kiss her.

"I love you." The words burst from her lips as soon as I lifted my head.

For a second, I paused, letting them stroke over my skin and settle deep inside my chest, then I yanked her against me and captured her mouth again.

I was still kissing her, exploring her like it was the first time all over again, when Carter flew through the front door.

"Aunt Eden, you're back! Did you see my dragons?"

We broke off, looked at my nephew, and burst out laughing.

Chapter Twenty-Eight

Eden

MILO HADN'T REALLY NEEDED my apology, even if I'd definitely needed to give it. I still owed one to Addie, though—and it wouldn't be as easy as showing up at her door with an overnight bag.

I decided to close the store for an extra-long lunch break, stopped to pick up a gift certificate that would cover a nice meal for Addie and Olivia, and stepped into the small offices of the rape crisis center where my cousin worked.

She spotted me across the room and immediately pulled off her headset. "Eden, are you okay?"

"I'm fine," I said quickly, "and this time I really mean that. I'm sorry to interrupt. I was just going to drop this off for you."

Addie looked at the envelope in my hand, then back at my face. When she didn't reach for the gift certificate, I pushed it into her hand. She slid a crimson-tipped nail under the flap and blinked in surprise.

"What's this for?"

"To thank you, and to say I'm sorry. Really, truly, immensely sorry. I love you and I appreciate every second you've spent being there for me, not just these past couple weeks, but for my entire life."

Addie's lips parted in surprise—Milo wasn't the only one who knew I was no good with expressing things verbally. I thought the spiel sounded ridiculous, personally, but then my cousin's eyes filled with tears and she threw her arms around me.

"I love you, babe. Always and forever," she whispered against my ear.

"Ditto," I mumbled, squeezing her tight.

Abruptly, she drew back, her dark eyes opening wide. "Oh, while you're here, come with me!"

Addie dragged me through a honeycomb of cubicles that I'd never find my way out of on my own, then rocked to a halt next to Monique's desk. A slender Black man was seated in front of her with an array of fliers spread across the desk.

"Eden, have you met Arnaud?"

My eyes flew wide, seeing him out of his element. "Oh, yes. Hi. How are you?"

Arnaud was the owner of the martial arts school I attended, up at the other end of Main Street. All of the women's self-defense classes were taught by female instructors, so I hadn't had him as a teacher yet, though I'd seen him around while I was working at the front desk. He was almost always wearing track pants and a black t-shirt with the school's logo on it, but today he was dressed in dark jeans, a trim lavender button-down, and a perfectly tailored blazer.

"Eden, lovely to see you. How are your classes going?"

"They're amazing. I'm taking a little break while we get the store up and running, but I'll be back as soon as I get into the swing of things."

"Excellent. I'm glad you're here—we've been brainstorming some women's and LGBTQ+ self-defense seminars, but we've gotten some feedback from clients who are hesitant about walking into a gym that's primarily staffed by men," he told me.

I blinked at Addie, then at Arnaud, who flashed me a killer smile. "Okay."

"So," Addie said pointedly, "I realized we know someone whose shop has established itself as a safe space for anyone who walks in, and who happens to have enough room for a decent sized group to meet in."

"For a self-defense workshop? That's...actually amazing," I mused. "Absolutely. I'd be more than happy to host that kind of thing."

Arnaud rose to his feet. "I would love to work with you on this, Eden. These ladies saved my little sister's life after she was assaulted, and I've been trying to find a way to pay it forward. We're actively working toward making the school a more welcoming place, but the instructor I took over from was not very open-minded. There's still work to be done in shifting our legacy."

"That sounds like a wonderful goal," I replied. "My classes have been incredibly empowering, and I'd love to share that with a wider audience. Addie and Monique can coordinate a schedule with you, since they're involved in all of our other events. Tuesday is the only weeknight that's booked."

My cousin squeezed my elbow; Olivia had been hesitant to impose, but between Addie and Milo, they talked her around. Game nights were officially taking place at Garden of Delights, starting that very night.

Arnaud shook my hand and thanked me for being open to the idea, Monique kissed my cheek, then Addie walked me back out through the maze of cubicles and out to my car.

"I always knew you'd do amazing things, Eden," she said softly.

"You guys are the ones making a real difference."

"Babe, if you can't see the difference you're making, you need to open your eyes. We're a team, and we're all kicking ass here."

I laughed and hugged her. "Okay, *that* I will accept, but only if we get some cool team shirts."

"Oh, I'm so on it," Addie said, grinning at me. "I'll see you tonight for gaming?"

The flinch almost caught me unawares, but Addie saw it. She grabbed my shoulders and stared into my eyes for so long, I thought she was practicing telepathy.

"Everything is going to be fine, babe. I promise."

I managed a small but honest smile and nodded. "Everything is going to be fine. See you tonight."

MILO SHOWED UP EVEN before Dueling Dragons' closing time that afternoon. I was in the middle of tidying up the floor, trying to keep myself occupied so the anxiety couldn't settle in.

"What are you doing here already?" I asked.

Instead of answering, he strolled up to me and dropped a kiss on the side of my neck, then rubbed his chin back and forth to tickle me with his beard. I couldn't fight the low hum of pleasure rising in my throat, but I felt his lips curve and wondered if that had been his goal all along.

"I wanted to be here when Liv showed up so I could help her set up. You're giving us a free space to use on a weekly basis. I don't want you to feel like your business is suffering because you're trying to do two things at once."

"Hmm. You're incredibly thoughtful, did you know that?"

He laughed and turned me in his arms so he could kiss me properly. When he drew back, he said, "It's come up once or twice. Besides, I had an ulterior motive."

I raised a brow and replied, "Oh?"

"I wanted to take a look at the new merchandise, see if there's anything else to add to my Valentine's Day list," he murmured.

Heat rose in my face—the man certainly did enjoy the lingerie sets I'd worn for him so far. "Right. Well then, be sure to note down any favorites."

Milo grinned, kissed the pink spots on my cheeks, and disappeared into the back room where the table was waiting to be unfolded. I turned to survey the store, playing a guessing game with myself to figure out which items he would pick.

And which ones I would surprise him with even before Valentine's Day rolled around.

Addie and Olivia came through the front door just before I locked it, but they'd told the rest of the players to come around the back. While none of the others minded missing out on the nerdy setting of Dueling Dragons in order to play here, a few of them were intensely shy, especially about walking through a shop full of underwear. Addie told me she'd never seen so many blushing dudes in one place when Liv presented the proposed change of location.

After I finished up out front, I hit the lights and joined the group in the back room. Milo snagged my hand and tugged me into his arms.

"So, how will we entertain ourselves? Should we stay in here and listen, or would you like to join me in the breakroom? I seem to recall seeing a cozy chair in there that should fit both of us."

"Oh? What would we do, all alone in there?"

He leaned down until his lips brushed my earlobe. "I have almost two weeks of missing you to catch up on. I'm sure I could come up with something."

Laughing, I gave Addie a wave and pulled Milo into the breakroom. It wasn't much, just a mini fridge, a tiny microwave, and a couple of thrift store armchairs, but it was private. I took Milo's statement at face value, but after he positioned me on his lap and spent fifteen minutes kissing me, I finally saw through his plan.

"You brought me in here as a distraction, didn't you?" I demanded.

His smile was too sweet for me to hold onto any irritation. "I thought it might be a good idea to take your mind off things. Just for a bit."

I shifted to look him in the eye. We'd come this far—time to get the rest out. After a deep breath, I forged ahead.

"There's not some tiny part of you that says, 'If only I were dating someone else, my shop wouldn't have been vandalized?' Buried deep down in a place where you might not think it's a big deal right now, but in five or ten years down the road, you resent me for it?"

"Eden," he said gently, "we need to unpack a few things here. First off, no. Hell no. There is no part of me, at any depth, that blames you for any of this. Second, I love that you're thinking about five or ten years down the road, but I wish you saw it in a better light."

I blinked at him. "A better light?"

"Yeah, like us living together for real and carpooling to work so you don't have to worry about stealing my parking spot. You officially accepting the role of Jiji's mama. Our stores both thriving so we can hire people to help out while we take a vacation somewhere. Maybe, eventually, marriage and babies if you're interested in that kind of thing."

"Oh," I breathed, overwhelmed by how much I *wanted* that.

"Right. So, there's that, all of which warrants a discussion when you're in the right mindset, okay? But third, Eden, we need to talk about your parents."

My head jerked. "My parents?"

Milo stroked my cheek with one finger and said, "Yes. Is that something they did, sit on a grievance and throw it back in your face years later?"

For a solid minute, I sat frozen, staring at him. Milo was patient, giving me the time and space to process. Even when my gaze grew unfocused and my lips parted, he stayed quiet.

"Those *assholes*," I hissed.

"Eden," Milo began, but I surged to my feet and started pacing the tiny room.

"I can't believe I never saw that. When I was younger, I felt like everything they said to me, all the strict religious crap and hellfire threats, trickled right off my back. I'd come out here and vent to Addie about some of it, then I'd let it go and feel better. I didn't realize how much stuck inside me."

Milo stood, watching me carefully. "I don't know how you could grow up in that environment and *not* internalize some things."

I spun to face him. "Libby was right. I need a therapist. Oh my god, Milo. Their bullshit cost us almost two whole weeks!"

"Two weeks where you learned how many people have your back, Eden," he replied. "And you're right here with me now. That's all that matters."

"Yeah," I mumbled, face-planting against his chest.

His arms wrapped around me without hesitation, enfolding me in his warmth. The rapid shift of emotion inside me made me dizzy, but all of it was underscored by how very grateful I was to have found the man before me.

Eventually, I tipped my head back to meet his gaze while rewinding and replaying the conversation in my mind. While the past had cluttered my head until I couldn't see clearly, Milo had been looking ahead to the future.

Our future. Together.

I let a new sensation curl its way through my chest, forcing out all of the guilt and fear until the only thing left was my blossoming love for this man.

"So," I ventured, "you've been dreaming of marriage and babies?"

Milo grinned sheepishly. "I was really hoping you'd focus on the vacation part first."

"I think I could get on board with that."

All of it, really, but that was a conversation for another time—when whatever threat loomed over us had been vanquished.

Chapter Twenty-Nine

MILO

FOR THE NEXT FEW weeks, life was blissfully beautiful. Eden caught a cancellation with one of the therapists Libby had recommended and seemed to be finally working through some of the baggage her parents had saddled her with.

She'd also been spending practically every night at my house and had agreed to move in for good once her lease was up in March.

It was the first time I'd been in a relationship as Valentine's Day rolled around since high school, when Amy McIntire and I dated for exactly four days. I learned when she dumped me on February sixteenth that she just wanted to see what it was like to have a boyfriend for the big day.

Apparently the experience was disappointing, but I was only fifteen and a much bigger idiot than I was now.

While Eden was working expanded hours leading up to the holiday to take advantage of Valentine's shoppers—she'd been teasing me with a variety of sexy as fuck lingerie for weeks now—I tried to plan something that wouldn't make her uncomfortable but *would* show her just how much I appreciated having her in my life. We'd taken both cars to work, so I had two hours to get everything ready before she got home.

But shit, I was trapped between feeling like it was too much and not enough.

Jiji watched, blatantly critical, from the back of the couch while I baked cookies and turned on the lo-fi music Eden loved to relax to.

The delivery from Thai Me Down showed up about two minutes before she walked in the door to find me serving up her favorites at the candlelit kitchen table.

"Milo," she breathed. "What is all this?"

"I know we said no gifts, but you deserve a break after how hard you've been working recently. I've got dinner, dessert, and some bath stuff I bought from Mark's shop so you can soak after we eat."

She bit her lip and the flickering light of the candle danced in the tears filling her beautiful eyes. "I don't know what to say."

"Come here," I said, but I was already moving toward her, tucking her against my chest when a hiccuping laugh escaped her lips.

"Thank you. This is...perfect."

Her fingers twisted in the sides of my shirt as she fought back those tears, so I didn't take my arms from around her until she let go. Then she lifted up on her toes and kissed me, the sweetness of it voicing everything she'd told me she had difficulty speaking aloud.

And when she insisted I join her in the tub, which was definitely not built for two, I couldn't refuse. We soaked, we laughed, we cuddled—not a barrier in sight between her heart and mine. That closeness lasted even when we went to bed, tangled together under the covers.

In the middle of the night, my phone rang.

Eden groaned as I shifted her off my chest to grab it from the nightstand, then the source of the ringing registered and she shot upright beside me. The number on the screen was local but unfamiliar—not a family emergency, thank fuck.

"Hello?"

"You're next." The voice sounded computerized, like one of those robotic voice-changers Carter got for Christmas a few years ago.

The call disconnected and I stared down at my phone in confusion. Eden frowned, leaning over to look at the screen.

"Who was it?" she asked.

"I have no idea. They just said I was next. I don't even know what that means."

The phone rang again, startling us both half to death. I fumbled it so badly, I was afraid I'd miss the call completely before I managed to pick up, but this time the caller was already in my contacts.

Detective Rose Hanson.

"Hello?"

"Milo, Rose here. Sorry to wake you."

"You didn't, actually. Someone called just a minute before you, told me I was next, whatever that meant, and hung up."

Rose went silent for a beat. "Right. We have a situation on the street outside the stores. This might be presumptuous, but is Eden with you?"

"Yes, she's here," I replied, glancing down at Eden's wide-eyed expression.

"If both of you can come over as soon as possible, we'd appreciate it. The stores are fine. Just...something we need you to see. And bring your phone. I want to take a look at it."

I told her we'd be right there, scrambled to get dressed, and grabbed Eden's hand. The streets were silent and empty at this time of night, but an odd chemical smell hit us the minute we turned onto Main Street. Then, as we got closer, the flashing lights of emergency vehicles illuminated the area outside our stores.

"What the hell?" Eden whispered.

Right outside our front doors sat the charred husk of a car. Barriers blocked off the street again, though there was no traffic at this time of night, so I pulled into a parking spot on the next block and we moved toward Rose, both of us staring at the burnt car.

"Milo. Eden, this is Chief Roberts," Rose said, introducing Spruce Hill's police chief.

Eden murmured a polite greeting as the chief shook her hand. Though Roberts was originally from Oakville, the next town over, he'd been part of our community for a long time, coaching Little League and volunteering at school events. In all my life, I'd never seen him look the way he looked now.

Completely and utterly furious.

He schooled his expression as he spoke to Eden, but when we all looked toward the car, I caught his scowl out of the corner of my eye. Whatever this was, he was *not* happy about it.

"I know it's hard to tell," Roberts said in a low voice, "but that car was originally pale gold. Plate matches the partial we got from a witness at the coffee shop."

Eden jerked at my side, her hand clenching tight around mine. I turned her into my arms and met Roberts' gaze over her head.

"If you were going to destroy evidence of a drive-by, wouldn't you do it somewhere not associated with the crime?" I asked.

"You might, unless you wanted to send a message." Roberts gestured for us to move to the sidewalk in front of the stores. "Hanson said you got a phone call tonight?"

"Yes. The caller said, 'You're next,' and hung up."

"Man? Woman? Any indication?"

I frowned. "No. It was quiet and hoarse, like they were disguising their voice."

"Phone number?" Rose asked.

"Local," I told her, "but I didn't recognize it. I would've tried a reverse look-up, but you called right after."

She held out a hand, so I passed her the phone. Roberts led me and Eden closer to the wreckage of the vehicle while Rose jogged toward a police cruiser parked down the block. When Eden shivered, I tucked her back under my arm, then we caught sight of the side of the burnt car and my body locked solid.

PURIFY.

The word was gouged deep into the metal, showing starkly silver against the blackened skeleton of the vehicle.

Eden let out a strangled sob before burying her face against my chest. For a long moment, I stared at the car, then I looked at Chief Roberts. My blood had frozen, like ice water now ran through my veins.

"Who owns the car?" I asked.

Roberts glanced at Eden, then said, "It's registered to the Church of Eternal Light, out in Cortland. Do you know anything about that location?"

"That's the church my parents belong to," Eden replied, "but they were in Binghamton. My brother is the minister there now. I didn't even know there was a congregation in Cortland."

"Only name associated with that location is Pastor Simon Baumgartner, who reported the car stolen three weeks ago. His name ring any bells?"

Eden shook her head. "No, I don't think so. I stopped attending services with my parents when I was twelve. I haven't heard from them since I left home at eighteen, and I only know about my brother because Addie found an article about him."

"We'll be taking a closer look, don't you worry. Cortland's only an hour and a half away, but that's a trek for random acts of malice."

That was true—which meant there was probably a resident of Spruce Hill with some connection to the church, maybe a connection to Eden's past. I wanted to sweep her in my arms and take her away from here until the culprit was caught, but the chances of getting her to agree to that seemed slim.

"Are we in danger? Is Milo in danger? That phone call has to be related to this," Eden said quietly.

I opened my mouth to brush it off, but Roberts sent me a stern look. "I'd certainly like to know why he received that call. We don't have a whole lot of manpower, but I'll have officers driving by your house, Milo, Eden's apartment, and the stores. If you see anything even remotely suspicious, I want you to call us immediately."

"Of course," I murmured.

"Look, this might be overkill, but an old buddy of mine jumps in as a security guard at the mall around the holidays. With so many stores closed down there, they don't need him as much and the stretch after New Year's dies down. If you two are interested, I think he'd be willing to cut you a deal, keep an eye on both shops."

If it had just been me, I probably would have refused the offer. With Eden shivering against me in the cold, dark night,

I couldn't deny that I'd feel a whole hell of a lot better with someone else looking out for her.

"I'll take his info, if you don't mind," I replied.

Rose came back over to our little huddle and passed my phone over. "Number is local, monthly no-contract type situation. I got what I need to keep digging, but let me know if you get any more calls."

"This will all be cleaned up by morning," Roberts said, pressing a card into my hand. "That's Leonard's number. Tell him I sent you. Sorry to bring you out here like this."

"Thanks, Chief. Rose."

I tipped my head to them each in turn, then hustled Eden back to the warmth of my car. Even once the engine was running and the heat kicked in, I could hear Eden's teeth chattering beside me.

"Eden, baby, come here," I murmured.

She didn't hesitate, just scooted as close as she could get and let me hold her until the trembling stopped.

"You with me?" I asked.

"Yes."

The word was barely more than a puff of breath against my throat, so I squeezed her tight. "We're going to get through this, Eden. Together. Yes?"

This time, she tipped her head to look at me and managed a tiny smile. "Yes, Milo. Together."

I couldn't hold back the rush of relief at her confirmation. "That's my girl."

Chapter Thirty

EDEN

DESPITE THE LACK OF personal profiles for my brother or his wife, the Church of Eternal Light itself was all over social media these days.

I stared at the website, with links to multiple platforms for each of their half dozen churches throughout the state of New York. Though I hoped to recognize even a single person in any of the dozens of photos plastered across the different pages, aside from my parents and my brother, no one looked familiar.

"Why are you in Spruce Hill?" I whispered at my laptop screen.

Simon Baumgartner was probably close to my father's age, but he appeared to be the youngest of the pastors from the various branches, aside from Isaiah.

And not a single one of them looked particularly capable of throwing a brick through a plate glass window, nevermind setting a car on fire in the street. Old, older, frail, frailer. It was like a lineup of grandfathers with age spots and wrinkles. They could have managed the envelope left in the mailbox, sure, if one of them happened to be in town, but the rest? It seemed unlikely, at best.

But if that was the case, who the hell was behind these things?

"Eden? Babe, you here?"

Addie poked her head through the doorway just as I closed the laptop. Her eyes narrowed on my face.

"Watching porn?"

"No, I am not," I muttered.

"Researching romantic getaways?"

I glared and asked, "Do you need something, Adelaide?"

"Yes, actually. Arnaud is here to see the room, but there's a couple shoppers out front ogling the remaining Valentine's collection. Which do you want to take?"

"Oh, right." I stood and slid my laptop back into the messenger bag on the table. "I'll show Arnaud around. Thanks, Addie."

I followed her out of the breakroom to where Arnaud stood at the counter, looking completely at ease as he studied a rack of nightgowns. However I'd expected a martial arts instructor to dress outside of classes, it wasn't anything like Arnaud's wardrobe. Today he was in a slim-cut suit made out of a purple fabric so dark it was almost black. Only a faint shimmer when the light hit him betrayed the color.

"Arnaud, hi. Thanks for coming by," I said, offering my hand.

He clasped it, flashed a brilliant white smile, and replied, "The pleasure is mine. Do you gift wrap?"

"Theoretically, yes. I'm not amazing at it, but if you catch us while Addie is here, she can take care of you with a bit more style."

We reached the back of the store and I showed him both room options. "This one has more square footage, but it's narrower. The other is smaller overall but more square in shape. I don't know what will work best for you, but both rooms will be available."

"Perfect. Adelaide said the roster is almost full for this month already. And you don't mind us signing participants up for our regular program, if any are interested?"

I grinned at him. "Not at all. I'd love to see a few new faces in my class."

"The seminar will be a good introduction to our style of teaching, I think. Our female instructors will be there to help with the workshop, but if you're willing and comfortable with it, I'd love to have another person to demonstrate as we go through the moves."

"Oh," I said, surprised by the invitation. "I'm not sure how graceful I'll be, especially in front of an audience. I haven't been doing it very long."

"You're clever, Eden, and fierce. My wife would call you a spitfire," he teased. "Besides, your teachers speak very highly of you."

Flattered by both assessments, I replied, "Well, then. I'm in."

Once Arnaud decided on a room for the class, he left the store. Addie, the customers, and I all stared after him as he strolled down the sidewalk, admiring the way his suit gleamed in the sunlight.

"There's this meme that says, 'I'm bi, which means I'm attracted to all women and one man,'" Addie muttered under her breath. "I think he's that one man."

I snorted a laugh. "He's married, Addie."

"Yeah. And I've got a hot date tonight with Olivia."

"I love you," I said out of the blue.

Addie turned to look at me, moving cautiously, like she was afraid I might burst into tears or something. "And I love you, babe. Always."

I tossed one arm around her shoulders. "Right, that's settled. Now, tell me about your plans for tonight."

THOUGH I DIDN'T WANT Addie to know I was looking further into my brother's church, it wasn't something I could keep from Milo. We talked it over that night on his couch, with him lying on his back, me draped over him, and Jiji curled up behind my knees.

"I looked at their website, too," he admitted, fingers toying with my hair. "I didn't see anyone in any of their photos that I recognized from town, though."

"Why you? Why would you get that phone call? My number hasn't changed since my brother called me years ago, not that my parents ever used it—but what was the point of calling your phone with the warning? Why not me?"

Milo's hand stopped moving for a second, then he said, "I don't know. We're living in sin, basically, right? Maybe they shifted their sights to me because I let you lead me astray?"

His tone was teasing, but the words hit me like a blow. I knew the instant he felt my reaction, because he shifted suddenly and cupped my jaw with one hand.

"No," he said sharply. "No way, Eden. I was just kidding. I'm sorry."

"It's okay," I said quickly, but my muscles remained tense.

"You are not taking responsibility for this. No matter what messed up rhetoric somebody is using to justify any of what's happened, it is not your fault. Not. Your. Fault."

My body relaxed again, melting into him. "I know."

"Good. What do you think about the Chief's suggestion that we hire a security guard to keep an eye on the stores?"

"No."

He grimaced. "That was very definitive."

Sighing, I propped my hands under my chin. "I want you to be safe, so if you want to call him and have him over at Dueling Dragons, I'm in full support."

"But?"

"But Garden of Delights is a safe space for people. The thought of some guy hovering, even if he stays outside the store, makes me uncomfortable. And if I feel that way, I imagine a lot of my customers might also feel the same, and then I'm setting myself up to lose business right as I'm just getting into a groove."

"I hadn't thought of it like that," he admitted, "but I see your point. Okay, we'll hold off on that. Can we agree to leave the stores together when it's dark out? I'll come over after I close up and walk you out?"

"That I can absolutely agree to," I said, smiling down at him.

"So, tell me what's on tap this week."

I rattled off the schedule—game night on Tuesday, Addie's support group Wednesday, self-defense seminar on Thursday evening. Though I didn't sit in on Addie's groups, Milo felt uncomfortable even being in the store to keep me company in the break room, given the nature of the meetings. For this week, the same would go for self-defense, though I wished he could be there to see me do some ass-kicking.

"I might have to show you my moves at home," I warned him.

Milo laughed. "I look forward to seeing what you know. I'll stay over at Dueling Dragons until you're done, but text me so I can come walk out with you."

It wasn't strictly necessary, but as February wore on, it was still pitch black outside by the time I closed up even on a regular day. The reminder that it might not be safe for either of us to wander around alone after dark was sobering.

"Hey," he whispered against my ear. "Everything is okay. We're taking care of each other. Besides, you're a certified badass, so we'll be even safer, right?"

"Certified, huh?"

"Absolutely. The baddest badass in town by my side, what could go wrong?"

A lot.

I didn't speak the words aloud, just burrowed deeper into Milo's chest. Neither of us paid any attention to the movie playing across the room. Between the slow stroke of his fingertips through my hair and Jiji purring against my spine, my body relaxed, but my mind kept going back to that one question.

Why was that warning directed at Milo?

Chapter Thirty-One

MILO

"Am I codependent?" I asked my brother on Wednesday evening when he came to pick up Carter. He'd needed to work late, so Carter and I had closed up the store and eaten pizza while we debated the relative strength of Superman and the Hulk.

Maverick lifted his hands up and down like he was weighing the possibility. "I don't think it's codependent to miss your girl when you've been apart all day, bro."

Carter finished his final slice of pizza and chimed in, "Besides, Aunt Eden misses you when you're apart. I can tell."

"You can? How?" I demanded.

"When she comes over, her eyes light up. Instead of brownish, they turn gold like in the dragon painting. Yours don't really turn silver, though. They look darker, like...wet stone."

Maverick and I stared at his son for a beat before I said, "Thanks, buddy."

Carter grinned. "So are you two going to get married?"

"Right, time for you to go home," I replied.

They both laughed as Carter grabbed his backpack and stuck his paper plate in the trash can under the counter. Before they left, though, Maverick grabbed me by the back of my neck and dropped his forehead to mine.

"So happy for you, baby brother."

I inhaled sharply at the emotion thickening his voice. "Thanks, man."

He gave me a squeeze before letting go, then waited for Carter to reach him. That was when he turned and added, "I've seen the way she lights up around you, too. You got this, Milo."

Even as I stared out into the dark after them, that assurance glowed inside me, a physical warmth that spread slowly from the center of my chest outward until my limbs were lit with it. If Eden had been there, I'd have poured it into a kiss, watching for that light even my cynical oldest brother could see.

The reason for leaving the stores together each evening didn't thrill me, but having that opportunity to reunite was definitely a sweet moment no matter how boring or hectic our days had been.

And when Addie and Monique walked Eden to my door that night, I saw it happen firsthand.

Eden hugged them both and bid them goodnight, then turned to me. Her expression grew soft, lips curving slightly upward as she reached out to slip her arms around my waist. In the darkness, her eyes were almost black, but the street lamp in front of the building made them twinkle with golden sparks, just like Carter said.

"Hi," she murmured.

I dipped my head to kiss one corner of her mouth, then the other. "Hi. How'd it go?"

"Good, I think. Everyone seems to be happy with the arrangement, so I think Addie will keep it going. Someone bought my last Valentine's robe." She practically purred as she snuggled into my chest. "You're always so warm."

"Let's get out of the cold then," I replied, bundling her away from the building to get to my car.

"What a great parking spot," she murmured as she buckled her seatbelt.

I leveled a stern look in her direction. "Isn't it?"

Her laughter rang out as we pulled away from the curb, and I soaked in the sound. Carter's earnest reassurance echoed in my head, followed by Maverick's sincere confirmation.

She lights up around you.

Hell, yes, she did.

T HURSDAY WAS MORE OF the same, though Rafael came in for the afternoon to help with inventory. I stayed open an extra hour as a test run, a joint effort to keep myself busy during Eden's event and to see if any after-work shoppers might take advantage, but the store stayed pretty empty after sunset.

Just as I crossed the store to lock up, though, a middle-aged woman waved frantically at me through the glass. She was wearing a long skirt and carrying one of those huge purses that made me think of Mary Poppins.

"Please, could you just give me five minutes? I need a gift for a birthday this weekend," she begged when I opened the door for her.

"Sure, take your time. Is there anything I can help you find?"

"Oh, no, I'll just take a look around. Please do whatever you need to do. I'll be as quick as I can."

I smiled at her and moved to the other side of the store to tidy the displays while she browsed. Eden's self-defense seminar wouldn't be over for another hour, so all I had waiting for me after this shopper finished up was the book I'd left on the counter.

"Pardon me," the woman called, "would you take a look at this for me? I think there's a scratch on his face."

"Of course." When I reached her side, I peered down at the action figures in front of her. "I think that's part of the design, but I can look in back for another—"

Something heavy bashed against the side of my head and pain exploded outward until I felt myself falling behind the display of Star Wars characters she'd been looking at. My vision went hazy for a minute before the woman's shoes came into focus, and all I could think was that they looked like the kind of old lady sneakers my first grade teacher always wore.

A thunk sounded as she dropped the weapon she'd used to strike me, one of the pewter dragon statues Eden had admired the day of the window incident. It landed on the carpet close enough to my head to make me flinch, especially when I saw one of its folded wings smeared with blood.

"Why..." I whispered, blinking hard at the dragon beside me.

It fizzled in and out of focus. My limbs had turned heavy and uncoordinated, like lead weights were keeping me there on the floor. Even if I could get them to cooperate, I doubted I'd be able to sit up without dizziness overwhelming me.

"Because you're peddling the Devil's goods, Mr. Davies. This place must be purified."

The words wormed their way through my fuzzy thoughts. "Purified."

"Yes," she said harshly, her feet moving out of sight for a moment before she returned with that enormous purse, which she set down beside me.

A carpet bag. That was what they were called.

From inside, she withdrew a red can, then she moved away again. "You think these are innocent games, but you're opening up young minds to the darkness, Mr. Davies. Ruining families. Offering a game like *that*, hosting demon playtime for teenagers."

"Game like what?" I rasped, trying to follow her words.

"Wizards and demons, Mr. Davies. Trying to lure children into Satan's trap. Innocent children. This town has no idea the evils you're unleashed. I tried to stop you, again and again, but you just wouldn't listen."

None of it made any sense, but the smell of gasoline abruptly halted my attempt to follow her thought processes. If she set fire to the store, it would spread straight toward Eden's shop.

I'd never make it to her in time, not if I couldn't get my ass up off the floor.

"No, please. You don't have to do this," I begged.

The words sounded clumsy and thick, my voice weak under the steady glug of the gas can. Wetness dripped from my temple toward my ear. With an enormous effort, I managed to roll from my side to my back, then my muscles rebelled and I lay there, staring up at the dirty ceiling tiles overhead and wondering, if I lived through this, would there even be enough of them left to be cleaned.

"Of course, I have to. Someone has to. 'Let us purify ourselves from everything that contaminates body and spirit, perfecting holiness,'" she intoned.

I opened my mouth to argue that *thou shalt not kill* seemed a little higher on the biblical priority list, but before I could force the words past my lips, the room started to spin before my eyes.

Then, slowly, everything faded to black.

Chapter Thirty-Two

EDEN

THE CLASS WAS NEARLY over when a frantic pounding rang out against the steel door at the back of the shop. At first, I thought it was the bass from the music playing over Arnaud's bluetooth speaker as we practiced elbow strikes, but the song ended and the beat continued.

"I'll go see what that is," I murmured, stepping away from Simone, who was my partner for this section of the workshop. We'd spent each short water break making plans for the boudoir photo offerings.

Arnaud caught my arm gently before I made it out of the room. "I'm coming with you."

My mouth opened, then I snapped it shut and simply nodded at him as we made our way to the door. Arnaud, dressed today in his school's t-shirt and a pair of track pants, tipped his head to indicate I should move behind him.

Since my pulse had skyrocketed the second we stepped into the hallway, I did so without argument.

Arnaud pulled the door open, stepping toward the threshold so no one could shove past him to get to me, then said, "Whoa, hey, what's going on?"

I peered around him to see a young teenage girl, her face red and tear-streaked. She wasn't dressed for the cold, wearing just short sleeves and leggings. It looked like she had slippers on her feet. Her hair, bleached blonde with pink tips, was pulled into a messy ponytail that had come halfway undone.

"Come in," I said immediately, reaching toward the girl.

She jerked away like I was going to pinch her. "No! No, please, you have to hurry. I tried to stop her, I swear!"

Arnaud held up his hands in a pacifying gesture as he murmured, "It's cold out, sweetheart, why don't you come inside?"

"You have to get him out. You have to get everyone out," the girl cried.

My heart turned to lead. "Get who out?"

"That guy next door. She's lost it. I think she's going to hurt him. Please, you have to get them all out of the building. I don't know what she's going to do!"

Addie came up behind us at that moment and wrapped her arm around the girl, drawing her out of the doorway. I jerked my head to meet Arnaud's eyes, panic threatening to overcome me.

"I'm going to check on Milo," I said, brushing past him.

"Not alone, you're not. Adelaide, get the rest of the students out of the building and call 911. If she'll tell you anything more, relay that to the police."

Arnaud wrapped his hand around mine as we ran toward the back door of Dueling Dragons. It was locked, but Milo had given me a key. My hands shook so hard I couldn't get the key in the lock, so Arnaud reached out to turn it.

Even unlocked, the door wouldn't budge.

"We have to go around front," I called, grabbing his arm as I started running around the side of the building.

The sight that greeted us was the stuff of nightmares.

Inside Dueling Dragons, the lights were off, but the store was lit by the eerie glow of flames licking their way up toward the ceiling, devouring shelves of books and comics. We froze on the sidewalk, then I heard Arnaud talking into his cell, requesting immediate assistance from the fire department.

I knew he'd never let me through that door unless he was distracted, so I took advantage of him reading off the address to the emergency operator and ran for the door.

It was unlocked, but the wall of heat nearly knocked me backwards onto my ass.

"Milo!" I screamed, frantically searching for any sign of him. "Milo, where are you?"

The roar of the fire drowned out everything else, but I saw movement out of the corner of my eye and darted toward one of the display tables. Relief brought me to my knees beside Milo's body, then I spotted the blood darkening one side of his head.

We had to get out of there. The fire couldn't have been burning for long, but the entire shop smelled like gasoline.

"Milo, we have to go. C'mon, please, I need you to help me here," I pleaded, trying to tug him into a seated position.

"Eden," he whispered.

"I'm right here. We're getting you out of here."

His body tilted to the side and I almost lost my grip, but I managed to tuck my shoulder under his arm. He felt like dead weight—shit, we'd both be dead weight in a few minutes. A hysterical laugh bubbled up in my throat, but when it burst from my lips, it emerged as a broken sob.

"Love you," Milo said hoarsely. "You have...to go."

"Not. A. Chance," I grunted, hauling us to our knees.

"Fierce," Arnaud muttered as he joined us.

I heard the word, half praise and half admonishment, but I couldn't turn my head far enough to see him until he rounded Milo's other side. Together, we managed to get Milo to his feet, though he stumbled along like he was drunk off his ass.

"Not," Arnaud added with a grunt, "that I approve of you running into a burning building alone."

The laugh that escaped me was breathless and strained, but it was an actual laugh, at least. "I'll keep that in mind for the future."

Just as we made it out the front door, a whooshing sound roared up behind us and the windows on either side of the door exploded outward onto the sidewalk. Arnaud cupped the back of my head and bent us both forward over Milo, shielding our little huddle from the shards.

We stumbled into the street as a firetruck barreled to a halt outside the building. The flashing lights glittered off the broken glass, striping Milo's pale, blood-streaked face in red and blue. Before I could ask Arnaud if we should lower him to the ground, an ambulance pulled up a few yards away and the paramedics immediately began unpacking a stretcher.

With Arnaud supporting most of Milo's weight, I turned my face into his soot-covered shirt and tried to keep the sobs from erupting out of my chest.

"Eden," Milo murmured as two uniformed EMTs joined us and guided him down to the stretcher.

"I'm right here."

"Safe." The word was barely a breath past his lips.

"We're safe, Milo," I whispered, squeezing his hand, but I was forced to let go when they wheeled him back toward the ambulance.

One of the paramedics returned to my side, a woman with hair a brighter red than the fire engine nearby. "You must be Eden," she said gently. "I'm Casey. Looks like the chief wants to talk to you. We'll take good care of Milo and I'll make sure you know where to find him when you're ready, okay?"

Maybe I nodded, or else she couldn't wait for my response, because the woman hopped into the back of the ambulance as the driver closed the doors after her. I didn't even feel myself shivering until Chief Roberts wrapped a thick fleece blanket around my shoulders.

"We'll do this quick, Eden, and then get you back to his side."

The story came out in disjointed fragments, as broken as the front window of Milo's shop—again. At one point, I trailed off, staring at it, until Chief Roberts gently called my name. I blinked back in his direction, realizing he must have repeated it more than once.

"His insurance is going to be pissed," I whispered.

The chief smiled at me reassuringly. "I'll put in a good word for him. We're all set here for now, Eden. I think your ride to the hospital just showed up."

I glanced up to see Maverick and Carter waiting for me at the far end of the barricades blocking the street. Carter lifted his hand in a little wave, looking on the verge of tears, but his father's eyes were on the scene of destruction that was Dueling Dragons.

Sometime during the mayhem, the girl who'd come to my back door disappeared. Addie said she had her arm around the kid one minute, then they heard the sirens and suddenly she was gone. Nobody in the group from Garden of Delights had recognized the girl.

Rafael, who lived a block away and jogged over when he saw the smoke, volunteered to stay there with Addie until every-thing was situated so I could head straight to see Milo. Libby had already texted an update that he was in stable condition and his vitals were good, but I kept seeing those strobing lights across his face, the blood darkening his hair.

Maverick guided me to the back seat of his car so I could keep hold of Carter's hand during the drive to the hospital outside of town. Though Chief Roberts wanted me to get checked out, I'd refused to sit long enough for another set of paramedics to look me over. There were a few stinging spots on my arms where sparks had landed, another on the back of my neck that had singed a bit of hair at my nape, but I barely noticed any of it until the chief pointed out the burns.

The ride was silent as Carter and I huddled together. When we reached the hospital, Maverick pulled up to the entrance, where Mark waited for our arrival. He leaned in, unbuckled me, and tucked me under his arm as we entered the hospital.

"They'll go find a parking spot and meet us inside," he said quietly, like he was trying to hold me together. "Mom and Dad are up in the waiting room on his floor with Libby while he talks to the police. He's okay, Eden."

"He's okay," I repeated.

"You're shaking, sweetheart. Do you need a minute before we go up?"

In response, I sucked in a shuddering breath and abruptly stopped walking. Mark shifted so he could wrap his arms around me. It wasn't the same as an embrace from Milo, but it was close enough that Mark's steady strength seeped into me.

"He's okay, I promise. Miraculously, there's no skull fracture, just a concussion and a nasty ass cut. He's awake, he's coherent. I need you to brace yourself, because he looks like shit. He's a little uglier than usual."

A hiccuping laugh escaped from my lips. "Brace. Okay."

"There's a bandage over the stitches, but the bruising is spreading a bit."

I nodded, trying not to picture it in my mind. We stopped for my visitor pass at security, then Mark hit the button for the elevator and slung his arm around my shoulders. Once the doors closed behind us, he gave me a squeeze.

"I know there's been a lot going on, Eden, but I'm really pleased for you and Milo. I can't remember ever seeing him this happy."

"Happy lying in a hospital bed? Happy with his store in ashes?" I whispered.

Mark frowned as he turned me, his hands tightening on my shoulders. "Eden, none of that is your fault."

"If it weren't for me—"

"No," he said, his tone sharp enough that my gaze jerked to meet his. "None of it. Did you hit him over the head?"

"No, of course not."

"Did you pour gas around his barely conscious body? Did you light the match?"

"Oh god," I whispered.

Suddenly, my limbs were trembling again, vibrating so hard that I wasn't sure I could stay standing. Mark pulled me against his chest, cupping the back of my head. I couldn't have pulled free if I'd tried—but I didn't bother. I dropped my forehead to his sternum and continued shaking like a leaf in his arms until the elevator doors opened.

Libby stood there, looking distinctly un-doctor-like in yoga pants and a black sweater. Her dark eyes traveled over the two of us, then she opened her arms and I found myself passed from one family member to another.

"Let it out, sweetheart," Libby cooed, stroking my hair like I was a child with a skinned knee. "Everything is going to be fine, I promise. Milo's doing much better than expected. He should be ready for you by the time we get to his room, okay?"

I sniffled miserably but nodded, then Mark pressed a wad of tissues into my hand and I managed a watery smile.

Libby rubbed my back, her touch gentle despite her brisk tone. "Good. Now, will you let me check out your burns, or does Milo have to bully you into accepting medical treatment from a doctor on staff?"

Chapter Thirty-Three

MILO

As long as I stayed perfectly still, I could pretend my brain wasn't jumbled inside my skull, though I still had the headache from hell throbbing with every beat of my pulse. When Libby ushered Eden into the room, however, I sat up so quickly I burst into a coughing fit from the smoke inhalation. As soon as it subsided, I pulled off the oxygen mask.

"In case you wondered, he's a terrible patient," Libby muttered under her breath.

"I heard that," I replied, bracing my hands on either side of my body as Eden hesitated just inside the doorway.

Whether it was the concussion or my relief that she was unharmed after rushing into a burning building to save my ass, a fresh wave of dizziness hit me at the sight of her.

I held out one hand. "Come here, beautiful."

She approached slowly, like she was afraid I'd change my mind. I caught the look Libby and Mark shared behind her and understood immediately—she'd been a wreck after the store was vandalized, and now I was lying in a hospital bed. My determination to get her in my arms ballooned. As soon as she was within reach, dizziness be damned, I reached out and tugged her onto the bed beside me.

My mother made a choked sound, then suddenly there was an exodus of family members from the room, leaving me alone with Eden.

"Look at me," I said quietly.

When she did, her eyes flitted across the bandage and the bruising. Under the harsh fluorescent lights, those sweet golden depths filled with tears.

"I love you," she said, choking on a sob as she face-planted against my chest.

Careful of the IV in my left arm, I clasped her against me. "I love you right back. It's going to be okay."

"Your store," she whimpered.

"Yeah. It sucks, but we're okay. You're okay, even if you ran into a burning building to drag me out on your own, you reckless, incredible woman. Next time, though I sincerely hope there will never be a next time, there's a fire extinguisher behind the checkout counter."

She sniffled against my shoulder, shoving a palmful of tissues against her face, then lifted her head to glare at me. "Are you serious?"

Though I burst out laughing at her expression, I took a moment to appreciate all of it—the scowl, the adorable pout on her lips, the solid, reassuring feel of her cradled against my body. This night could have ended very differently for us both.

"You are precious to me," I whispered, kissing her lightly on the mouth. "The most precious thing in the world. You could have been hurt."

"You *were* hurt," she shot back as she scowled at me. "What the hell happened?"

"Remember that statue you were admiring the night the window broke? Let's just say I regret stocking those suckers."

She blinked. "That's what you got hit with?"

"Yeah. They said there's no fracture, but I already have a real bastard of a headache."

"I'll take care of you," she whispered, dropping her head back to my shoulder.

"Eden, I need you to listen to me, because this is important—none of those things were meant for you."

She jerked in my arms. "What?"

"None of it was directed at you. Not the flier, not the brick, not the phone call. I was the target the whole time. The woman who hit me was ranting about my game nights corrupting innocent minds. She didn't so much as mention you or your shop."

Eden drew back slightly, frowning again. I reached up my free hand to rub a finger between her eyebrows. For a long minute, we just stared at one another, then she slumped against me again.

"Do you know who she was?"

"Not a clue," I replied. "She looked vaguely familiar, but not enough for me to identify. She posed as a customer, asked me to look at an action figure, then she clocked me with the dragon statue."

"A girl came to the back door of my shop to warn us. I wonder if it was her daughter?"

I pressed my lips to the top of her head. "Maybe. If so, she saved my life."

A shiver ran through Eden as her fingers tightened in the cotton hospital gown I'd been forced to don upon admission. It was another moment before her breath hitched and she curled in on herself, even though she was already half on my lap.

"Shh, we're safe now," I murmured into her ear.

"What if she comes back to finish it?"

Her tortured whisper struck an even harder blow than the dragon statue. Ignoring the IV line, I captured her face in my hands, ready to tell her we were leaving on vacation first thing in the morning, but she flinched when my finger brushed the back of her neck.

"Eden," I growled, tipping her head forward so I could look at the burn on her nape.

"It doesn't hurt."

"Libby? You all still hovering out there?" I called. "Eden needs this burn checked out."

My sister-in-law popped her head in quickly enough to confirm my suspicion. "Ready when you are, Eden. Unless you want me to flag down Dr. Thorne. I'm sure he'd be willing to add you to his roster next time he comes to check on Milo."

Unsurprisingly, Eden's scowl didn't fade, but she flopped back against the raised head of the bed and muttered, "Fine, go ahead."

"Who's the terrible patient now?" I teased.

Eden tilted her head and held out her arms one at a time while Libby assessed the damage. After dabbing some kind of burn cream on Eden's neck and carefully placing a gauze bandage over it, she leaned in to kiss my cheek, then Eden's forehead.

"You're both terrible patients and you deserve each other. Visiting hours end soon, so I'm going to send the family in and go arrange for Eden to stay with you tonight."

I felt Eden's relief as clearly as my own. Her grip on the hospital gown eased and her body relaxed against my side.

"You're stuck with me," I whispered in her ear.

"Oh no, anything but that."

I was still grinning when my parents, Maverick, Carter, and Mark all spilled into the room. Carter's eyes, big as saucers, landed on my bandages and the poor kid flinched. Then he looked at Eden and his lip quivered.

"I'll make you a new dragon painting," he vowed. "Better than the other one."

Eden held out her hand and my nephew immediately moved toward the bed. With her arms around him, Eden murmured in his ear until Carter nodded, straightened his shoulders, and smiled at her. Not even a teenager yet and the kid was already a charmer.

Mark and Maverick came to my side as my parents spoke to Eden. For a second, the two of them just looked at me, but I knew what they saw on my face.

Relief. Comfort. Peace.

I had been a mess from the minute I was closed in the ambulance until Eden finally came through that door. Everything felt easier now that she was at my side, from breathing to keeping my eyes open again.

"Holding up okay, bro?" Mark asked.

"Yeah. Better now that she's here."

Maverick smirked. "Not surprised. She have any hot nurse outfits in that shop of hers?"

I narrowed my eyes at him, but of course Eden had overheard. She tried to muffle a laugh, which turned into a snort, which sent both her and Carter dissolving into giggles. My mom held out another half second before joining in, then my dad started chuckling.

My brothers and I stared at the lot of them—not with irritation or surprise, but with warmth.

With love.

I'd never been so grateful to have my family nearby, to see them open their arms and their hearts to the woman who meant everything to me. Though Eden had slapped one hand over her mouth, the other rested on my knee. I laced my fingers through hers and she squeezed them so tightly, I knew she was grateful, too.

The situation wasn't amazing, but we'd get through it, just as we'd gotten through everything else. Even if Eden had seemed afraid I was going to blame her when she first got to the hospital, at least she wasn't bolting.

Hopefully, I'd finally convinced her of what she had in me, showed her that she'd found exactly what she'd been searching for.

Family.

Chapter Thirty-Four

EDEN

SINCE THE STRINGS LIBBY pulled to get permission for me to stay didn't extend to sharing the tiny hospital bed, I spent the night on the pullout hidden in one of the room's hideous green vinyl chairs. Weirdly, I slept like a rock, knowing Milo was safe and sound barely an arm span away.

Before he was released to go home, however, Chief Roberts and Detective Hanson came to talk to us again—together this time.

"Milo, I'd like you to take a look at a couple photos for me," the chief said as he pulled up a chair.

"Okay," he said, pulling himself upright.

Hanson laid out a few photos on the edge of the bed, each showing a woman in her fifties or sixties. Milo shook his head once they were all in front of him.

"No. None of these are her."

The chief tapped the top photo. "This is Martha Baranski. She's the woman who applied to move into Eden's store. Definitely not the woman who attacked you?"

"No. I'm sure of it," Milo replied, shaking his head.

"Okay. Then we've got good news and bad news. Traffic cams caught some video of the woman leaving the store after she set the fire, Milo, and we got prints off the statue she hit you with."

"Those both sound like good news," Milo said hopefully.

"The bad news is we still haven't identified her. Prints aren't in our system. However, on the chance that the girl who showed up to warn Eden was this woman's daughter, we hoped maybe you would be willing to take a look at the most recent high school yearbook. If we can pin down the kid, we can track down the mom."

My eyebrows lifted. "Oh. Sure."

Hanson passed me a heavy book with a gold embossed pirate on the cover. When I smirked at Milo, he grinned and said, "Spruce Hill Scallywags for life."

"You're kidding."

He shook his head. "Nope. Did you know there were pirates along the Erie Canal? That's where the mascot came from."

"I did not. Learn something new every day," I muttered, flipping open the hard cover.

My parents had refused to pay for my own yearbooks back in high school—hell, they'd only allowed me to attend public school after I got myself kicked out of the tiny Christian school they'd forced me to attend until I decided I was done following orders—but I'd managed to save up enough from my after-school job to get one my senior year. Looking through the pages of strangers threw me right back to my teenage years, an outsider watching everyone else laughing in the quad, joining clubs, signing the blank pages at the back with inside jokes and sentimental musings about unending friendship.

Milo seemed to sense my disquiet, because he squeezed my hip and rested his chin on my shoulder as we bent over the book. The sections of official school photos were sorted by grade, and I flipped the pages slowly, scanning each and every face for any sign of the girl who'd saved Milo's life.

"These kids look way too cool," Milo complained. "Where's the bad hair and goofy smiles? I don't think a single school picture day in our family resulted in anything half as nice as these."

I huffed a laugh, thinking about every blank order form I'd reluctantly handed back to the photographer throughout my years in school, about every teacher who wondered if I'd forgotten to give it to my parents before picture day. Thankfully, most of them knew me well enough by then to understand the situation at home.

"She was terrified last night," I whispered, images of my childhood and this girl overlapping in my head. "If her mom finds out she warned me..."

Roberts shook his head. "If we find her, we'll tread lightly, Eden, don't worry about that. She's wanted for attempted murder. We won't give her the chance to take anything out on the kid, all right?"

I nodded. "Okay."

"Word is they'll be discharging you soon, Milo. I'm leaving Officer Ford outside your door, and when you head home, he's on duty outside your place. You need to go anywhere, he tails you."

Milo grimaced, but acquiesced. "Understood."

"I don't see her," I said, frowning as I reached the final page of the yearbook.

Roberts nodded slowly. "I was afraid of that. She could be homeschooled, or it's possible she's still in middle school, but they don't do yearbooks like the high school does. If we can find any class photos, we'll get in touch. Thanks for looking, Eden. We got descriptions of her, but is there anything else you remember?"

I thought about it and started to shake my head, then something niggled at the back of my brain as Milo's words about the woman came back to me. "The kid looked a little familiar, but I don't know why. I occasionally get curious teenagers in the shop, but I'm positive I hadn't seen this girl there before."

"We'll do what we can to track them both down, but if anything comes to mind, you let me know. In the meantime, you two focus on healing, got it?"

After Roberts and Hanson left, Milo leaned in close and whispered, "Ford's got the hots for you. Maybe we should make out for a bit, just in case he peeks in here."

"Don't be ridiculous."

"Mm-hmm. The day of the bomb threat, I thought he was going to ask for your number right in front of me."

I rolled my eyes and cuddled back against him. "Unfortunately for him, I'm pretty into this guy I'm seeing. Maybe you know him. Tall, broad shoulders, amazing in bed..."

Milo's arms, warm and snug around me, tightened ever so slightly, then I felt his lips brush my temple. I could deal with the narrow hospital bed and the constant checks from nurses, because this, right here, was exactly where I wanted to be.

B Y THAT AFTERNOON, WE were settled back at Milo's house. His brothers had parked his car back in the driveway and his parents chauffeured us home—after completely restocking his kitchen full of more groceries than we would need for a month.

"Snow's coming next week," Tucker said when Milo looked at them in question.

Terry squeezed us both tight. "Better safe than sorry, right? Besides, now you won't have to go out anytime soon."

We stood at the door and waved as they left, though I ended up crouched beside Milo so I could give Jiji some love after our absence. The family had been by to take care of him, but he seemed overjoyed at having us back.

"Aren't cats supposed to hold grudges?" I asked, rubbing his soft cheeks.

"Not this one," Milo muttered. He helped me to my feet and lifted the cat into his arms. "Jiji would never be so cruel."

Both stores were officially closed until Tuesday at the earliest, and I wasn't sure the impending snowstorm was a bad thing. Staying holed up with Milo at his house while he recovered sounded kind of ideal. He needed to rest, and I needed to remind myself that he was okay after this ordeal.

Eventually, I'd also have to process my intense relief at the fact that nothing from my past was responsible for his injuries. I still couldn't quite believe it, but after hearing his full account of what transpired at Dueling Dragons, I was unable to cling to the guilt that had plagued me for weeks.

"C'mon, let's get you into bed."

His eyes danced behind the glasses his parents had brought to the hospital. "Okay, but you'll have to do all the work."

"No one is doing any work, Casanova. You're supposed to avoid all physical exertion for another twenty-four hours."

Milo groaned. "Fine, but I'm only staying in bed if you're there with me."

"I think I can tolerate that."

A slow smile lit his face as he set Jiji on the back of the couch and slid his arms around my waist. Despite my warning glare, he lowered his face so our lips were barely a millimeter apart. It took an enormous amount of effort not to close the distance.

"I'm not sure I thanked you yet for saving my life," he whispered.

My body jolted. "You don't have to—"

"I absolutely fucking do. Thank you, Eden."

My response caught in my throat, wedged there like marbles, so all I could manage was a tight nod. Milo understood, though. He dropped his mouth to mine, coaxing and sweet, like he could pull the words free. By the time he lifted his head, I was pretty sure he'd succeeded.

"Are you hungry?" he asked out of the blue.

I blinked away the daze of his kisses. "I am, yes."

"Good, Mom said there's a couple plates of cold chicken and potato salad in the fridge. Let's eat and then we'll both get into bed."

Jiji sat on the table beside our plates, waiting for one of us to offer him tiny shreds of chicken as penance for being gone all night. Aside from the bruising on his face, Milo looked better now that he was home—less wan, more alert. I tried very hard not to think about the impact of one of those hefty statues against his head, but every so often, my imagination betrayed me.

I must have flinched at the thought, because he reached over and grasped my hand across the table.

"Look at me. I'm alive. We're safe. No one else got hurt. The fire was contained before it spread into Garden of Delights, though Maverick said the inner wall had a bit of damage on my side. It'll all be taken care of."

"I know," I whispered, blinking back tears. "It's just...that woman, she might be that girl's mother. What the hell kind of life is that kid living with her? I hate to even think of it."

"Because it hits too close to home?" Milo asked gently.

My breath stalled for a few beats, then I gave a gasping laugh. "Probably. I hadn't thought of that."

We both fell silent, turning back to our food with significantly less gusto. When we rose to clear the table, Milo paused before heading toward the kitchen.

"Your birthday is next week," he began, sounding almost hesitant. "Did you have plans with Addie, or your aunt and uncle?"

I hadn't even realized we were so close to the end of February, especially after the time we'd lost to my numbness after the brick incident. My birthday was one of my least favorite celebrations, anyway, but I couldn't remember the last time I'd been in a relationship when it came around. My parents had treated it as a day of prayer, spending the entire day in church, like maybe they would finally get the obedient daughter they wanted if they just begged for it hard enough.

Even though Addie tried to make it special in the years we'd lived together, I still hadn't quite gotten used to being celebrated.

"No. No plans."

He drew a breath and continued, "My mom asked if they could host a birthday dinner for you. All of us—my brothers, your cousins, your aunt and uncle. The Davies clan goes big for family birthdays. If you'd rather stay home and keep it low-key, though, we can do that instead."

"But I'm not family," I said, confused.

"Yes, Eden, you are."

The words were quiet but firm, leaving no opening for argument. I blinked at him as that settled into my chest. Would it ever cease to be a surprise? Even struck silent, yet again, I knew Milo needed an answer.

"Yes. We should go," I said hoarsely. "I want to go."

That smile, the one I fell in love with at a hotel bar, the one I continued to fall in love with over and over again every time I saw it, crept across his face like a gift from the heavens. His gray eyes went velvet soft, crinkling at the corners as he smiled down at me.

He didn't say anything, just leaned down to press his lips to my forehead, and one thing became perfectly clear as my resolve hardened into something fierce and protective.

If Milo was that woman's true target, it was up to me to do everything in my power to keep him safe.

Chapter Thirty-Five

MILO

NOT ONLY DID EDEN *not* favor me with a sexy nurse costume, she was a complete and total hardass when it came to my recovery. I never imagined being sentenced to spend day after day in bed with my gorgeous girlfriend as my jailer would be so boring.

So. Very. Boring.

As soon as screens stopped giving me a headache after five minutes of watching, we binged our way through what felt like every nerd series known to man. By the time she returned to work on Tuesday, I was jumping for joy—figuratively, because somehow she'd know that my brain had been jostled and the consequences would be dire—at the prospect of wandering the house at will.

Fortunately, my sister-in-law was willing to make a house call so she could assess my progress and hopefully lift all remaining restrictions. I had work to do, not only at the store, but also in catching up on lost time with Eden.

I had more than a few ideas of how to exact retribution for her strict no-fooling-around rule these last several days. Those revenge efforts would be immensely pleasurable for us both.

Libby arrived at the house promptly at noon. Her gaze swept over me, apparently evaluating my health with her laser eyes, then she beamed at me. "You look good, Milo. I see Eden's been taking good care of you. How's the noggin feeling?"

"Headaches are pretty much gone," I said, gesturing for her to come in, "and Eden has been an absolute tyrant."

Libby choked on a laugh, then shrugged. "Whatever works on you stubborn Davies boys. Why don't we sit in the kitchen, I'll check you out, and then you can get your ass in gear to make my favorite chocolate peanut butter pie for Eden's birthday dinner at your parents' house? That's still the plan, right?"

"Yeah, we'll be there." I couldn't hide a tiny smile at that admission, because I was so happy Eden had agreed.

Eagle-eyed Libby didn't miss it. Her expression softened. "Good."

After a more thorough examination, Libby declared me well on the road to recovery. I probably should have seen it coming, but her dark eyes took on a mischievous glint when she looked back over her shoulder at me on her way to the door.

"You can resume physical exertions, just listen to your body. From the neck up, that is. I don't care what the rest of your body tells you. If it hurts your head, don't do it."

I snorted. "Thanks, Doc."

Libby winked at me, called, "See you Thursday," and blew a kiss before getting in her car to head back to the clinic.

From the doorway, I waved and watched until she had pulled down the street. My first order of business would be making sure I had all the ingredients required for the pie—knowing that my parents had stocked the fridge and cupboards, I was reasonably sure I did.

Second order of business: planning just how to celebrate the freedom to finally make love to Eden again.

EVERY ONE OF MY plans flew out the window when she got home that evening. She looked exhausted and harried, her usual smile nowhere in sight. It was like the real Eden left the house in the morning and a shadow of her returned just as dinner came out of the oven.

Panic snaked up my spine.

"What's wrong?" I asked immediately, setting the casserole on top of the stove. "What happened?"

Eden dropped her purse to the table by the door and slipped off her shoes with a grateful sigh. I moved toward her, opening my arms as she walked straight into them and face-planted against my chest.

"I think I underestimated the power of small town gossip. We were swamped all day long, which is great for business so I'm not complaining, but if I have to smile while fielding any further questions about whether you have brain damage from the incident, I'm going to scream."

"Ahh, yes. The Spruce Hill rumor mill is legendary, as you've unfortunately learned, but my mom said it's been an absolute circus this time around."

"It is, and I hate it."

"I wish I could say it'll get better soon, but all we can do is give it time to die down."

She sagged against me. "I could go to sleep right now and not wake up before morning. Dinner smells delicious, though, so I'll try to rally. How are you feeling?"

"I'm good, baby."

Peeking up at me, a tiny smile tugged at one side of her mouth. "Good."

My seduction plans could wait; Eden clearly needed a quiet night to recover. I rubbed my hands up and down over her back, then pressed a kiss to the top of her head.

"Go get some jammies on. We'll eat on the couch, watch a movie, and go to bed early. If you're up for it, I'll give you a backrub before you fall asleep."

"How was your appointment with Libby?" she mumbled into my chest.

"She said everything looks good and I'll be right as rain in no time. Go on, jammies."

I had to physically shift her body away from mine before nudging her toward the bedroom. For a moment, I watched her go—the slump to her shoulders was mostly gone, and though she didn't have the usual spring in her step, she no longer looked like she was wearing a leaden backpack.

By the time she returned in a pair of fleece pajama pants and one of my hoodies, I had dinner laid out on the coffee table and was in the midst of actively defending our food from Jiji's curiosity. Eden lifted the cat for a quick cuddle, resulting in a purr so loud its rattle echoed in my own chest, vibrating with contentment.

Though maybe that was just from watching the woman I loved slowly come back to herself.

Eden set Jiji on the floor and ignored her plate to flop onto the couch, snuggling into my side as she mumbled, "I missed you today."

"I missed you, too. Once I get my next steps sorted with Dueling Dragons, I could help you at the shop, if there's anything I can do. I'll go stir crazy staying home much longer."

Her eyes brightened. "You'd do that?"

"Not sure I'll have much else to do until the shop is repaired. I'm meeting your cousin Rob over there tomorrow to get an estimate on whatever work needs to be done. I'll get any undamaged stock listed online, make sure the website is ready for the added traffic."

"That's a great idea," she replied, smiling. Then she cocked her head at me. "I had a thought."

I waited for her to continue, but her expression went pensive and she remained silent. "Are you going to tell me what it was, or should I guess?"

"The back rooms. If your place needs almost total rebuilding, which is what it looks like to me, then maybe...maybe Rob could find a way to cut through so you could have access to the back room on that side. I do need space for meetings and events, but we really don't use both rooms at once. The participants at most of my events overlap quite a bit, so it makes no sense to run two things on the same night."

I stared at her while a slideshow of ideas tumbled through my bruised brain. The back of my storage closet shared a wall with one of those rooms—it couldn't be that hard to install a door between them. Warmth seeped through me at her offer.

"You're a genius. You'd really do that for me?"

"I'd do just about anything for you, Milo," she said softly.

I wrapped my hand around the back of her neck and kissed her, hoping it could convey the depth of my feelings for her. When we drew apart, color had blossomed in her cheeks and those hazel eyes sparked with desire.

Maybe some of my plans for the night would still come into play.

"Let me talk to Rob about it tomorrow to make sure it's even doable, then I'll touch base with the landlord. We can work something out on the rent, either through him or on our own until our leases are up for renewal. You...fuck, Eden, I can't even articulate how much I adore you."

With a sexy little smirk, she settled back into her spot on the couch and let her hand linger on my thigh, just high enough to tease. "Assuming you've been cleared for exercise, I guess you can show me after dinner, then."

Chapter Thirty-Six

EDEN

WEDNESDAY KICKED OFF NEARLY as chaotic as the day before, but the flow of shoppers slowed to a steady trickle after that. In honor of my birthday plans, Addie had insisted she'd be taking over for me halfway through Thursday as part of my gift so I could go home to Milo and relax before dinner with his family that evening.

After Milo ascertained that a bigger crowd wasn't a deal-breaker for me, Terry had invited Addie, Rob, and their parents, who would all be joining us. Needless to say, I'd never experienced any kind of "merging the families" moment in my entire life, and I was nervous as hell.

Only the promise of having Milo by my side the entire night soothed my anxiety.

While Addie and I were rushing around to take care of the continual stream of customers—most of whom had fortunately stopped asking if Milo was going to recover—Terry was scheduled to bring Milo over to Dueling Dragons for his meeting with Rob around lunchtime.

"I hate to look a gift horse in the mouth, but I hope things quiet down soon," I muttered as soon as I had a moment to breathe between customers.

"Why don't you go take a break while we've got a lull, babe? I'll shout if I need you."

Gratefully, I took her up on the offer and retreated to the breakroom for a few minutes of blissful silence, shutting the door behind me.

There was no time to waste.

Flipping open my laptop on the table, I pulled up the website for the Cortland branch of the Church of Eternal Light. Without giving myself the opportunity to chicken out, I dialed the number at the bottom and lifted my phone to my ear.

"You've reached Pastor Baumgartner. How may I help you?"

My stomach bottomed out under the boom of his voice, then I pulled myself together and said, "Right, hi. My name is Eden Campbell. I just wondered if—"

He cut in before I could finish, surprise coloring his voice over the line. "Campbell? Is this Isaiah's sister?"

I froze solid, my blood running ice cold at the realization that he knew who I was. For a second, I couldn't formulate a coherent thought, nevermind a response, but it didn't matter anyway when he continued speaking.

"Eden," he said gently, "I doubt you remember me, but I attended your parents' church in Binghamton briefly, back when I'd just started my training. You were maybe nine or ten at the time."

"Oh."

That was a period of time I'd rather forget. I was aware enough to start recognizing the wrongness of my own experiences without being old enough to do anything about it.

Baumgartner huffed out a humorless laugh. "I'd never seen a child so solemn. I offered you a butterscotch candy and your father stepped in front of you like I was handing you poison. I never forgot that moment."

Memories filtered in, hazy and dim after decades of neglect. Without his reminder, I probably never would have summoned up the recollection of that day, but there it was. A relatively young visiting pastor in his thirties or forties, the golden wrapper in his hand, my father's stern rebuke—telling him I didn't deserve the treat, no doubt.

I tried to remember what was said, if my father had detailed my recent sins to this stranger, but the truth was that it was only one of many such moments.

Eighteen years full of them.

"I tried to keep track of you after I moved," Baumgartner said quietly, "to be sure they weren't hurting you. Bishop Graap refused to consider such a thing and swore they were good, upstanding members of his church, but...I still recall the way you flinched when your father spoke."

After a shuddering breath, I said, "I'd forgotten all about it, but I remember you."

"I should have done more for you, Eden. I hope you'll accept my sincerest apologies that I held my tongue."

"I...thank you. I'm not really sure what more you could've done."

He made a noise of disagreement. "I hoped I'd see you again at your brother's ordination, but your parents shut down any mention of you."

I hesitated, then said, "You know him well, then? Isaiah?"

"We see each other at regional events, church meetings, that kind of thing." After a beat of silence, he said, "He's not like your parents, Eden. He's a good man, a good father."

I sucked in a breath that I was sure he heard over the line. "I'm glad to hear it. That's not why I'm calling, though. I had a couple questions. There's been a situation here."

"Of course. How can I help?"

Biting my lip, I decided to lay it out as quickly and concisely as possible. "Someone is threatening a man who means a great deal to me. She used a car stolen from your church."

"Sandra," he said immediately. "Sandra Billings."

Some memory tried to surface, but I couldn't quite grasp it. "Who is she?"

"She was the church secretary here for several years. I reported the car missing when she disappeared, along with several weeks' worth of offering plate envelopes."

"So she was living in Cortland?" I said, frowning down at the breakroom table.

"Yes. I spoke to the police in Spruce Hill when the car was found. Is that where you are now?"

My thoughts drifted to that photo of my niece, looking as haunted as ten-year-old me must have looked to Pastor Baumgartner. When I didn't reply, Baumgartner called my name, sounding concerned.

"Yes, I'm in Spruce Hill. Does Sandra have any children?"

"No, I don't believe she ever married. Eden, what's going on?"

I wrinkled my nose as I debated the answer. "I don't know. We need to find Sandra Billings as quickly as possible, though. Do you have any idea where she'd go if she needed a place to lay low?"

Baumgartner went silent for a second before saying, "Maybe, but I think I should get that information to the police."

"Yes, you should," I agreed quickly, already typing a search into my laptop as an idea popped into my head.

I held my breath as the results loaded, including an article regarding the church's purchase of an old warehouse along route 104, maybe half an hour east of Spruce Hill. There was no address listed, but a few clicks led me to two potential properties, both sold in the past six months.

Bingo.

"Eden."

The word was a warning, one I ignored even though some deep, hidden part of my psyche warmed at the thought of this stranger's concern for my safety—twenty years ago *and* now. I couldn't leave this to the police. Milo had almost died and might still be in danger, and I knew intimately how twisted some of the church's teachings could get inside someone's head.

I'd learned that well before the first time I met Pastor Baumgartner.

"Thank you for speaking with me, Pastor. I really do appreciate your help."

"Eden, please don't do anything that might put you in harm's way," he pleaded.

"Of course," I agreed, the lie tripping off my tongue with only a tiny twinge of guilt. "Thank you again."

I ended the call before he could push any harder. With my luck, he'd immediately contact Chief Roberts and my advantage would be lost. I needed to hurry if I had any chance to act on the information before someone showed up to stop me.

No one else would be hurt by this. Not if I had anything to say about it.

Shoving my phone in my pocket, I grabbed my coat and peeked out into the shop. There was only a lone shopper browsing the racks.

Addie caught sight of me and lifted her brows. "Going somewhere?"

"I just need to run out. Will you be okay on your own?"

"Sure, things are slow enough now," Addie said easily, but her expression turned suspicious. "Where are you going?"

"I'll explain when I get back. I'll be as quick as I can. Thanks, Addie!"

Snow was just starting to fall as I slipped out the front door and headed to my car. I saw Rob's truck parked around the corner and carefully avoided looking toward Dueling Dragons when I drove past, though they wouldn't be able to see me through the boards now covering the front wall of the store where the windows had blown out.

The rush of finally deciding what to do next kept me going as I drove toward the lake and turned right on Route 104. I could just barely make out the rotating light of the Spruce Hill lighthouse, flashing through the snow, as I followed the road east along Lake Ontario at the northern edge of town.

The two possible warehouse options were only ten minutes from one another. I'd just scope them both out for signs of life, then try to figure out how to talk sense into someone like Sandra Billings.

I was halfway to my first stop when recognition hit me so fast I swerved into the other lane, wrestling against the slick road and my own adrenaline to straighten out the car again.

"Holy shit. Billings," I whispered, my breath a faint plume in the cold inside my car.

Mary Billings was the name of Isaiah's wife. If she'd taken our last name when they got married all those years ago, as the church decreed, Pastor Baumgartner wouldn't have made that connection.

Sisters.

Oh my god.

Over and over, realizations pummeled my chest like hailstones until I was hyperventilating.

The girl at the door that night had to be my niece—no longer the somber, dark-haired child in the photo, but a teenager with access to blonde dye. If she was in town, her mother must have been in on it. Christ, I hoped Isaiah's wife was the passenger who'd thrown the brick through Milo's window and they hadn't made the poor kid do it.

Did Isaiah know what was going on? I'd finally convinced myself he wasn't involved in any of this, especially when it became clear Milo was the target, but now...I couldn't be sure.

No matter who was behind it all, I would do everything in my power to protect those I loved, my niece included.

Milo's life wasn't the only one at stake. Failure was out of the question.

Chapter Thirty-Seven

MILO

ENTERING THE CHARRED REMAINS of my life's work was more painful than I anticipated. As much as I wished Eden were at my side, her cousin Rob was both patient and cheerful, which helped to soothe the ragged, gaping wound inside my soul as we picked our way through the ash-covered rubble.

After dropping me off, my mom headed to pick up Carter from school to make up for him not being able to hang at the shop with me, so at least she didn't have to endure the lingering smell of smoke while Rob and I figured out what needed to be done.

Fortunately—if any aspect of this disaster could be considered fortunate, apart from my unlikely survival—my assailant was not an experienced arsonist. The blaze had been focused on the area between my body and the front corner of the store, since she ran out of gasoline before dousing the rest of the shop.

The smoke and water damage, however, were extensive.

I tried not to cringe at the destruction as we picked our way through the mess of waterlogged books and singed game sets. My family had come in once the fire department gave the green light, but there wasn't much they could do apart from boarding over the shattered windows.

Again.

I still couldn't believe Eden had made it through this experience largely unscathed. The small burns had healed quickly, and more importantly, she hadn't withdrawn emotionally.

That was the biggest success to come out of all this.

"This might be an inappropriate time for this," Rob said as he dusted a layer of soot from the cover of a graphic novel, "but I feel like I should ask your intentions toward my cousin."

A strangled, slightly hysterical laugh erupted from my throat, but Rob looked completely serious, so I answered in kind.

"I intend to make her happy for as long as she'll let me, hopefully for the rest of our lives."

Rob held my gaze for a long moment, then grinned, warmth filling the dark eyes he shared with his sister. "Excellent."

And that was that.

We made our way through the store, Rob pausing here and there to jot down measurements in a little notepad he kept in his back pocket. When I described what Eden and I discussed the night before, a slow smile crept across his face.

"That's Eden for you." His tone was full of affection. "Show me the wall. I'll see what we can do."

While Rob poked around in the storage closet, which was barely big enough for two people—if you didn't count the time I'd dragged Eden in there for a brief makeout session while Carter finished his math homework—I stood in the hallway feeling useless.

"I'll need to take a look at the other side, but this should work," Rob called over his shoulder.

At his words, I sent a silent note of gratitude out into the universe—not for the spare room I might be able to add to my store, but for Eden first coming into my life, then saving it. My existence before I met her had been fine, but now?

It was so beautiful I had to pinch myself at times to be sure it was real.

Rob tucked his notebook away and we headed out the front door toward Garden of Delights. I blinked in surprise at a little blue sedan that was parked where Eden's SUV had been when I arrived. The forecasted snow was falling heavily now, coating the sidewalk, but I took a minute to glance in either direction down the street before following Rob into the shop.

Adelaide was alone behind the counter.

"Hey sis," Rob said, tipping an imaginary hat at her. "Where's Eden?"

"I have no idea. She said she was just running out for a minute, but that was half an hour ago. I texted her twice about picking up coffee on her way back, but she didn't answer."

My heart plummeted straight through the floor. "I'll see if I can reach her."

Addie shot us a worried look as she turned to help the next customer, but Eden's phone went straight to voicemail when I called. I let Rob usher me into the back of the shop, though whether he wanted to get me away from the prying eyes of customers or prevent me from freaking his sister out even further, I wasn't sure.

I paused outside of the breakroom as I tried for a third time to get through to Eden. There on the table was her laptop, still open as if she'd rushed out of there in the middle of something, though the screen had gone blank. It was Rob who broke the silence as we both stared at it.

"I'll look, if you want plausible deniability."

Invading her privacy wasn't something I *wanted* to do, but I wasn't sure it made a difference which of us did the deed. I shook my head, pocketed my phone, and hit the touchpad to activate the laptop screen.

When a map of the area popped up, I frowned, sinking into the chair Eden had abandoned. The search bar showed she was looking for a warehouse along Route 104. Two results were marked with red dots on the map.

"What the hell?" I muttered.

"Look," Rob said, pointing to a second tab open in the browser.

I clicked on it and found the website for the Church of Eternal Light in Cortland. Air rushed from my lungs as I realized she hadn't rushed out to go on some cutesy errand like finding wine to bring to my parents' house tomorrow.

Eden was trying to find the woman who attacked me.

"Shit. We need to go after her," I hissed.

"Snow's getting worse, but my truck has four-wheel drive. She's gotta be heading to one of those locations, right?" Rob snapped a photo of the screen and zoomed in on the two dots.

I rubbed my forehead, wincing when I hit the edge of the remaining bruise. "I would think so."

"Then what are we waiting for?" he demanded.

Nothing, apparently. Maybe the injury had left my decision-making skills sluggish, but at Rob's question, conviction flooded my veins.

We had to find her before she rushed headlong into danger.

I closed the laptop and followed him back out to the shop, where he gave Adelaide some bullshit excuse as we hurried past the front counter—we didn't have time to go into detail, not if we were going to catch up to Eden. Addie didn't look like she believed him for a second, but we somehow managed to get out onto the sidewalk without fully explaining the situation.

"You'll have to teach me that trick," I said under my breath.

Rob threw me a grin as he shifted the truck into gear. "Somehow I don't think it'll work on Eden, but you're welcome to try."

Visibility in the snow wasn't terrible yet, but the roads were getting worse by the minute as we made our way out of town. When Rob passed me his phone, I pulled up the photo and wondered which of these was Eden's destination.

"What was she thinking, going out there alone?"

"Milo, if there's one thing I know about Eden, it's that when she has an idea in her head, she fights like hell to make it happen. She's been like that since she was a toddler. Not impulsive, just...determined."

A memory of the look on her face that night when she approached me in the hotel bar, vulnerable but so beautifully bold, flashed through my mind.

Determined was a good word for it. In this instance, it was hard to appreciate that trait, but I had so little insight into Eden's childhood that I thought a little bit of information might take my mind off the danger she was diving straight into.

I scrubbed a hand over my jaw and muttered, "Determined. Yeah. I've noticed."

"And also stubborn as a mule. Honestly, I'm willing to bet that was why her parents fought so hard to shut her down at every turn. If Eden knew how powerful her own will truly was, she'd have left them in the dust years earlier."

"She was just a kid."

Rob laughed bitterly. "A kid, yeah. A kid who could have moved mountains. I'm thankful every goddamn day that they never managed to crush her spirit. They certainly tried hard enough."

Christ, I hated that. I had to close my eyes against the urge to scream at the injustice of it all. When I finally had a handle on my temper, I forced myself to ask the question I knew I should be asking Eden.

"Did they hurt her?"

After a harsh exhalation, Rob said, "No. Not physically. Our parents considered suing for custody, but there was no evidence of anything they could use in court. Just the religious stuff, the criticisms, cutting her down. My mom knew if they tried and failed, we'd never see Eden again."

"And then she'd have no one," I murmured.

"Exactly. For years, they kept a journal where they wrote down anything Eden mentioned happening at home, in case it came to that, but she was healthy, if not happy. She did well in school, even if she had no real friends besides us."

"What about her brother?"

Rob didn't glance away from the snowy road, but he made a face. "Isaiah stayed in his lane. He wasn't an asshole, not to Eden, but he didn't do a thing to make her life easier."

"She was afraid he had something to do with this," I said quietly. "Do you think he's capable?"

The immediate shake of his head was more of a relief than I anticipated. "No. He had plenty of opportunities to drag her back under their thumb when she was a teenager, and he never did. I think…"

"What?" I prompted when he trailed off.

"I think he wanted to show her it wasn't all bad. Even if their parents took it too far, Isaiah's one of those people who just has that faith, you know? Less fire and brimstone and punishment, more love and forgiveness. I think he was shackled too tight by his dad to be able to share that with Eden back then."

It broke my heart to think of the child she'd been, friendless and alone apart from the occasional visit with her cousins.

Now, though? She had all of those things she'd been missing out on—a life she'd created, friends and family all around her, a home where she was happy. And she'd chosen to run off in a snowstorm to face down a woman who was like a specter from her past.

For me.

My lungs felt too tight to take in enough air as panic crawled up my throat. "Rob, we need to tell the police where she went. I should've thought of that before we even left. I just hoped we'd catch up to her at one of the buildings."

"Call them," he said immediately, peering through the snow that now fell like a curtain over the road in front of us. "Call them now, because we're almost there."

Before I could choke on the threat of what we might find when we arrived, I set Rob's phone in the cradle on the dash so he could see the map, pulled up Rose Hanson's contact on my own phone, and hit the green button.

"Milo, what the hell is going on?" she demanded as soon as she answered the call.

Surprised by her response, I said, "Eden went after the woman who attacked me."

"Where are you now?"

I glanced at the map on Rob's phone. "On 104, heading to the old Juniper Canning warehouse. Eden marked two options on her laptop, but I don't know where she headed first."

"Listen, the woman who came after you is named Sandra Billings. She's Isaiah Campbell's sister-in-law. He called us about ten minutes ago."

"Shit. Are they working together?"

"No. His wife said her sister had been talking about devils and games opening the gates of hell. She thought it was just senseless rambling."

"Jesus," I muttered. "What about the kid?"

I heard muffled talking in the background, then Rose's voice gentled. "It was Eden's niece, Eve. She was spending her school break with a friend in town. They played some Dungeons & Dragons, I guess, and she was curious about your store. She was going to come in, but she saw you closing up and thought she'd missed her chance. That's when she saw her aunt show up and hit you over the head."

Her niece had saved my life just as surely as Eden had. I squeezed my eyes shut for a moment, hoping the two of them would be able to get to know one another when this was done.

Rose murmured some directions to somebody, then said, "Eve just got home today, and when the pastor from Cortland called Isaiah to say he thought Eden was in trouble, Eve told her parents everything. Isaiah called us immediately."

Rob sent me a quick glance with his eyebrows raised. Maybe Isaiah Campbell had some redeeming qualities, after all.

"Look, we're on our way to you. Do *not* do anything stupid, you hear me?" Rose said sharply, but I wasn't going to waste time arguing.

Eden was in trouble, and we might just be the only ones who could reach her in time.

Chapter Thirty-Eight

EDEN

THE FIRST LOCATION WAS a bust. It looked like an old barn, wide open inside and missing at least half of its roof. There was no sign anyone had been there in years. I let adrenaline carry me through most of the trip out to the second warehouse, then doubt began to settle in.

What the hell was I thinking? I didn't have a weapon on me, hadn't told anyone where I was going. A dozen missed calls and even more texts from Adelaide and Milo flashed across my phone screen as I turned down a driveway that was only distinguishable now by the wooden plow spikes lining it.

As I pulled up beside the warehouse, I tried to peer into the hazy windows, searching for signs of life. Between the dark clouds drowning the last of the weak afternoon sunlight and the falling snow, there wasn't much to see. No other cars were parked outside the dingy gray building, no steam rising from a chimney, no lights shining from within.

It looked utterly deserted.

"I'm an idiot," I whispered.

When my phone rang a second later, I answered it. This was a stupid plan, and I was now sitting half an hour from home while the roads got worse and worse.

"Milo, I'm sorry," I rushed, "but I—"

"Eden, where are you?"

"Sitting outside the old Juniper Canning warehouse on 104. I'm going to turn around and head back now."

After some muffled murmurs, Milo said, "No, stay right where you are. We're almost there. The police might beat us to you, though, so don't freak out if they show up first."

I stared blindly at the swirling snow coating the windshield. "The police?"

"They spoke to your brother. Listen, Eden. I want you to stay on the line with me until somebody gets there, okay? Are you warm enough?"

"I'm fine, Milo. Is that Rob I hear?"

The smile in Milo's voice settled the fluttering nerves in my belly. "Yeah, Rob's driving. We'll be there soon."

"Did he have any thoughts on the shop?

"Yes, he thinks you're a genius. He'll work up some plans for joining the rooms and we can take that to Jim."

"Good," I murmured, dropping my gaze to the steering wheel. "That's good. Are you sure I shouldn't head back toward town? There's no one here—"

The phone clattered to the floorboards as my door was thrown open. I was too startled to do anything but shriek as an arm reached across my body to unbuckle the seatbelt, then I was yanked out into the cold.

I fell hard onto my hands and knees. The snow did little to cushion my landing against the frozen asphalt, which bit into my palms and tore through my thin tights. A sharp, cold wind stung the back of my thighs—apparently a jacket wasn't much protection against a snowstorm when you were wearing a dress underneath it.

"Shit," I muttered as I sat back on my heels, wiping my stinging palms against my legs.

As soon as I was partially upright, the dark figure slapped me hard across the face. I reeled back, barely catching myself from falling on my ass in the snow, and blinked past the hot sting of tears to finally bring her into focus.

"Watch your whore mouth," the woman hissed. The resemblance to my sister-in-law was there in the downturned mouth and permanent scowl—this had to be Sandra Billings, though she looked at least ten or fifteen years older than Isaiah's wife.

I hoped, for my brother's sake, that her sister had a kinder heart.

Distantly, I heard Milo yelling from my phone, but Sandra slammed my car door and all that was left was eerie silence. Snow coated her hair and clung to her eyelashes, but it did nothing to disguise the fanatical light in her eyes.

She stared down at me like a terrifying angel and recited, "Your task is to single-mindedly serve Christ. Do that and you'll kill two birds with one stone: pleasing the God above you and proving your worth to the people around you."

"I doubt Christ approves of lighting people on fire," I muttered, then snapped my mouth shut when she lifted her hand again.

"You're both sinners. You both have to be purified."

Now that she wasn't posing as a harmless shopper, I knew she wouldn't get the drop on Milo again if she went after him after—well, whatever she was planning now. Besides, Rob was with him and the police would be here soon. I'd just try to keep her talking, even if it meant listening to her twisting lines from the Bible for her own purposes.

Then a ball of dread settled in my stomach. "Where's Eve?"

"Lost."

My head jerked and I asked, "What do you mean, lost?"

This woman might have taken a few too many things literally regarding purification by fire, but I hoped like hell she meant the kid was *lost* in a religious sense, not out wandering in the snowstorm.

Sandra started to pace in front of me, shaking her head back and forth. A tiny avalanche of snow tumbled down onto her shoulders with the movement. I didn't see any weapons on her, but she was wearing a dark, oversized coat that could have hidden a rifle or a baseball bat, for all I knew.

"The girl has lost her way. I tried to keep her on the path. Mary, too. It's too late for them both. They left me, they left the path."

"Where is Mary now?" I asked.

Behind her, I saw a faint flash of light against the snow in the distance. Either the storm was about to kick it up a notch into thundersnow or the police were headed our way.

"Sandra, Eve is a good kid. She's not lost," I said, climbing slowly to my feet. "Is your sister involved in this with you?"

The woman continued muttering, but she didn't rush toward me as I rose. My knees ached and a hot trickle of blood burned against my frozen skin as it oozed from the scrapes. I didn't dare take my eyes off Sandra to check my palms, but I knew from the sting that they were probably shredded, too.

In light of Eve's arrival during the self-defense seminar, most of Arnaud's newest lessons from that night had been forced out of my mind. It was hard to forget the elbow and palm strikes I'd learned in my classes, though. I was no match for a weapon, and Sandra's fervor might lend her more strength than I could contend with, but I thought I could hold my own against her until the police arrived.

Assuming they were as close as I hoped, anyway.

"Pastor Baumgartner is worried about you," I lied. Then again, he seemed like a nice guy, so maybe he *was* worried about her.

Sandra spun to face me. "He doesn't know."

I frowned and asked, "Doesn't know what?"

"He can't know," she replied. "He'd never forgive me."

"For stealing the car and the collection plate money, you mean? Or for trying to kill Milo?"

An odd cackle of laughter burst from her lips. "None of that matters. None of anything matters now. Once you're both dead, my penance will be paid."

"Penance for what?"

"Stop talking!" she shrieked.

I shut my mouth, positioning myself so she wouldn't see the driveway leading from the street to the warehouse. My hands and feet were starting to feel like lumps of ice—cute ballet flats might be more comfortable in the shop than heels, but they were worthless in the snow. My teeth started chattering as the cold worked its way through my limbs.

"You took that store from the Baranskis," she muttered. "They would have served the Lord. I thought it was only the man corrupting innocent lives, but it was you, too."

"Milo hasn't corrupted anyone," I replied sharply.

"Leads them astray. You're leading them all astray. I knew when I saw you through the window that I'd have to deliver vengeance on you both."

Careful not to make any sudden movements, I said, "Did you throw the brick? Who was in the car with you?"

"Shut up!" She swiveled and leveled a finger in my direction, reciting something beneath her breath.

When I spotted two dark shapes coming up the driveway, I forced my gaze back to Sandra and silently debated my options. I could go on the offensive, try to take her down and hope she didn't have a weapon hidden under that coat, but I wasn't confident that would work out in my favor. I could try to run, but between my aching knees, frozen feet, and flimsy shoes, I suspected I wouldn't get far. Keeping her talking no longer seemed like a viable possibility, given how she'd screamed at me a moment ago.

That left waiting for her to make a move—or for the police or Milo to arrive—and preparing to defend myself.

The snow and wind had kicked up enough to obscure my view of the driveway when I tried to subtly glance over her shoulder. Even Sandra was now barely visible just a few feet away from me. In the distance, I heard a rumble that could have been thunder or an engine.

Either way, I braced.

Sandra heard it, too, and she lunged toward me. The momentum almost sent us both to the ground—the topic of Arnaud's next seminar at Garden of Delights, which was no help to me now—but I managed to keep my feet under me as she wrapped an arm around my throat to position me in front of her.

From out of the white veil before us emerged several figures in dark blue uniforms, guns raised. Sandra's arm went tight enough to cut off my breath. For a second, I yanked at her coat, trying to drag it away, then Arnaud's instructions filtered through the fog settling before my eyes.

I let go and jabbed my elbow hard into her stomach, twice in quick succession. As soon as her grip loosened, I grabbed her wrist, spun around to face her, and drove the heel of my hand into the base of her throat.

Unfortunately, when she gagged and staggered backwards into the grasp of a police officer I didn't recognize, I stepped on a patch of ice and my legs went straight out from under me. I landed hard on my back, the impact forcing all the air from my lungs.

From my place on the pavement, I stared up at the falling snow, blinking a flake out of my eye as I struggled to suck in enough oxygen to fill my lungs again. A harsh wheeze whistled from my lips, but over it, I heard the sweet sound of Milo's voice calling my name, layered with an officer reciting Sandra Billings' rights as he placed her under arrest.

Milo was safe. I closed my eyes and let the sweet relief of that knowledge seep through my frozen limbs.

It was finally over.

Chapter Thirty-Nine

MILO

I FELL TO MY knees beside her, clasping her frigid hands between both of my own while an officer assessed if she needed an ambulance. Eden looked terribly still, illuminated by the scattered headlights around us, and even though I was watching closely, I could barely see the rise and fall of her chest.

"Come on, beautiful," I coaxed gently, unable to look away. "I need you to breathe for me, Eden. Did she hurt you? Are you injured?"

Snowflakes dotted her cheeks, pink and chapped from the cold, as her eyelids fluttered open so she could blink up at me. We'd pulled into the deserted parking lot behind the string of police cars—just as Sandra Billings yanked Eden in front of her like a shield.

My heart still felt like it was going to pound out of my chest.

I stroked her hair back from her face, murmuring encouragement until she managed a series of tiny, broken breaths. Her fingers tightened around mine, though she flinched like the movement pained her.

With a frown, I turned her hands over and saw the rough scrapes across each palm. "Shit, I'm sorry. Can you tell me where else it hurts?"

"Everywhere." The word escaped on a breathless whimper that broke my heart.

"Okay," I soothed, keeping hold of her as I ran my other hand along her cold limbs. "Do you think anything is broken?"

For a beat or two, she stared up at me, still trying to catch her breath, then she rasped, "Only my street cred."

Her voice was hoarse, the words interrupted by her gasping breaths, but I sat back on my heels, threw back my head, and laughed. Though I wasn't convinced she was completely unharmed after a landing like that, she was the only woman I knew who'd crack jokes while flat on her back on the snowy pavement.

"Believe me, that wipeout can't negate just how badass you looked punching her in the throat. I've never seen anything like it."

A tiny smile curved her lips. "I'll have to thank Arnaud for teaching me those moves."

"I'll thank him, too."

Rob appeared at my side with a blanket. "Hey, cuz. Think you can sit up?"

I eased one arm around her to help her into a sitting position and Rob wrapped the plaid fleece around her. The black tights she wore under her dress were shredded at the knees, the skin underneath torn and bloody. Beneath my hands, her entire body trembled with the cold.

"Do we need to call for paramedics? I'm afraid it'll take longer for them to get out here than it would to get you back to town," Rose said, crouching on Eden's other side. "But if you're injured, we'll call them in."

"No," Eden replied. "I'm okay. Just cold. Eve—is Eve safe? She kept saying Eve was lost."

Rose smiled. "Safe and sound at home with her parents. Do you think you could answer a couple questions?"

I opened my mouth to protest, but Eden winced and beat me to it. "I'd really like to get away from this place."

To my relief, Rose nodded and stood. "Then we can have an officer drive your car back to town," she said to Eden, but her eyes were on me.

"That'd be great," I replied quietly. "Thank you, Rose."

"Let's get out of here. You're taking her to the clinic?"

I nodded. "Yes. Better safe than sorry."

"Good. We'll get your statement there, Eden. Drive safe. We'll be right behind you."

Eden breathed a sigh of relief, then leaned heavily against me as she tried to get her feet under her. Between the three of us, we got her upright and tucked into the warm cab of Rob's truck with a second blanket spread over her lap.

Once the doors were closed behind us, I wrapped my arm around her and Eden dropped her head to my shoulder. The shivering slowly faded, but every few minutes, a new tremor shuddered through her entire frame.

"You're safe now," I murmured into her hair.

"So are you," she whispered.

Every other possible outcome of this afternoon thudded through me as we made the slow commute back to Spruce Hill, each image more gruesome than the last. It wasn't until we turned onto Main Street that my pulse finally slowed to a normal pace.

"I don't really need a doctor," Eden protested when Rob pulled up outside the clinic.

"Eden, baby, I saw how hard you fell," I replied gently. "It's not just a doctor, it's Libby. You're family now. You have to know there's no chance in hell she'd let you go home without being checked over."

Rob jogged around to the passenger side to help me get her blanket-bundled self out of the truck and winked at her. "Remember that time we were playing hide and seek and I tried to do a backflip off the neighbor's porch wall?"

"And you blacked out when you landed flat on your back? Yes. Addie was convinced she killed you and we were all going to prison," Eden replied, grinning weakly.

"Yeah, well, you might not have attempted a flip, but you caught some serious air. At least I landed on grass. You hit the asphalt."

She scowled at both of us but stopped arguing as I slipped my arm around her waist to help her into the clinic. Rob planted a loud, smacking kiss on Eden's cheek when we reached the door, then left to go relay the afternoon's events to his sister.

Libby met us just inside the lobby to take Eden directly to an exam room. I started to follow, but Rose came through behind us and crooked her finger at me.

"Go ahead. I'll be fine," Eden said quietly.

Gently, I cupped my hand around the back of her neck so I could pull her forehead to my lips. "Damn right, you will."

Even with Rose waiting to speak to me, I watched until Libby and Eden disappeared around the corner. Anxiety kicked my pulse up again, but at least it wasn't the dizzy pounding I'd experienced in our rush to get to Eden.

I didn't have much of a statement for Rose, so we spoke only briefly in the corner of the deserted waiting room.

"Remember when I said not to do anything stupid?" she asked, arching a brow.

I grimaced. "I didn't know how long it would take you guys to get there. I wasn't going to let her face down that woman alone."

"Uh huh. Well, we were contacted by Simon Baumgartner, the one who'd reported the burnt car stolen. After he spoke to Eden, he found some things Sandra left for him in his office, flyers about repentance and journals full of ranting passages from the tangles of her own mind."

"About role-playing games opening the gates of hell for innocent teenagers?" I asked.

Rose grimaced as she nodded. "You guessed it. Turns out Martha Baranski is Sandra and Mary's second cousin. Word got around that they were looking for a space to open the store, and after they lost out on it, Sandra saw one of your new ads. I guess she put two and two together and placed the blame on you. She didn't know Eden was related to her brother-in-law until after the fire."

I blew out a breath. "I'm glad. Eden's been hurt enough as it is."

"Baumgartner said he was extremely concerned she was planning to do something reckless after she called him, especially once he realized Sandra had gone off the rails."

"Reckless," I mused, staring at the nondescript artwork hanging on the wall across from me. "She was trying to protect me."

"Maybe next time she'll let us do our jobs," Rose said, but she smirked at me just before Libby waved for her to go in to take Eden's statement.

My sister-in-law sat in the chair Rose had vacated and grabbed my hand. "Hanging in there?"

"Trying. Is Eden really okay?"

"Yes, though I'd like her to take it easy for a few days. Nothing's broken, but she'll probably have some serious bruises. You two are quite a pair."

"A match made in paradise," I murmured.

Libby squeezed my hand, then we sat in silence until Rose and Eden emerged from the exam room. I caught a glimpse of the bandages on her knees, but she had shed the blankets and otherwise looked blessedly whole, even if she was moving a bit stiffly.

"Will you still love me if I start wearing combat boots?" she asked as she walked straight into my arms.

"Hell yeah, combat boots are hot. Please tell me you're not already planning for your next tussle with a would-be murderer, though?"

Her silence was answer enough. I rolled my eyes heavenward as Libby's laughter rang out behind me. A faint giggle, muffled against my shirt, shook Eden's shoulders when I growled against the top of her head.

Oh, yeah. A match made in paradise, for sure. Everything I'd ever wanted was right here in my arms.

Chapter Forty

MILO

EDEN WAS NO MORE good-natured a patient than she was a caregiver when I was hurt. It took threatening to tie her to my bed to get her to grudgingly agree to relax and let me look after her—and even then, I was certain she only caved because she was too sore to make better use of my threat.

On the morning of her birthday, she woke up to breakfast in bed—coffee and the custom cake I ordered from her favorite food truck baker, decorated to look like the Garden of Eden.

"Milo," she breathed, blinking sleepily at the gorgeous design.

I had given the baker full creative freedom and she had come through beautifully. A tiny, shiny apple adorned one corner, and a golden snake was hidden among the leaves in another.

"Happy birthday, my love."

She pivoted and threw herself into my arms. "Thank you. I've never…"

I waited for her to continue, then drew back just enough to study her expression, but I couldn't interpret the mixture of joy and sorrow. "Please don't cry on your birthday," I begged her, peppering kisses across her cheekbones.

With a shaky breath, she said, "I've never had a birthday party before. Addie and I have gone out to dinner or whatever, but I never had a cake. Not like this."

"Then we'll make a toast." I handed her a coffee mug, made just the way she liked it, and tapped my own gently against it. "To new beginnings."

The smile that spread slowly across her face was the most beautiful thing I'd ever seen. "To new beginnings."

To my surprise, she insisted we still go over to my parents' house for dinner, but we spent the morning eating cake, drinking coffee, and watching Jiji chase after balled up wrapping paper as Eden opened her gifts.

I'd decided to swap out the dragon statue she'd admired, though I had it hidden away in case I was able to feel her out about it in the future—it was a work of art, and I didn't want her to hold one woman's violence against the sweet little dragon, but it definitely felt too soon to appreciate the sculpted pewter.

Instead, I'd found her an old-fashioned filigree locket and added tiny portraits Carter had painted of the two of us.

Inscribed on the back of it were the words, *Welcome to Paradise.*

Eden threw herself across the couch and into my arms, where she cried into the crook of my neck until I thought my heart would break.

"Baby, please," I whispered. "This is a joyful day. Please don't cry."

"I love you. I love you, and I need time, but I want it. I want it all."

I stared at her in confusion. "You want what?"

"Everything. Marriage, babies, employees to watch the store while we're on vacation. I want all of it."

My grin grew so big, it was hard to kiss her, but I managed it. Several minutes later, I was still kissing her, soaking in the beauty of all that was my sweet Eden, when her phone rang in the kitchen.

"I'll get it," I told her, planting one last kiss on the side of her neck before jogging to grab the phone from the counter. Even if she insisted she was fine, I knew she was sore from yesterday, and I needed those moments of taking care of her after the entire ordeal—to remind myself we'd all survived and to show her the depth of my appreciation for how she'd gone to battle for me.

For us. For our future.

"Who is it?" she asked as I returned to her side.

I frowned down at the screen and passed it to her. "It's your brother."

For a moment, she just stared at the device in her hand like it might jump up and bite her, then she hit the button to accept the call and put it on speaker. "Isaiah? Is everything okay?"

"Hey, Eden. Happy birthday. Everything is fine, I just...I wanted to call and see how you are. Simon was in a panic yesterday when he called. I've been worried sick about you."

She lifted her eyes to mine, shock and uncertainty shimmering in the golden swirls. "Oh. Thank you. It—a lot happened, but I'm okay."

"Would you tell me if you weren't?" he asked, his voice gentle.

Shit, he sounded just like my own brothers would after something bad happened, that same warm thread of concern edging the words. I lowered myself back down to the couch beside Eden and tugged her onto my lap, wishing I could magically smooth things over for her sake, if not her brother's.

"I'm not sure," she admitted. "I...this feels weird."

"That's my fault, Eden, and I'm hoping to make it up to you, if you'll let me." The words rang with sincerity, and Eden's eyes glistened as she cleared her throat.

"I'd like that."

"I dropped the ball years ago and should have made more of an effort to pick it back up again. That's why I called you, back when Mom and Dad were leaving. I hoped I might be able to mend some of what they'd broken."

A shaky breath slipped past her lips. "I'm sorry I didn't give you that chance."

"I should have fought harder for you, Eden, then and now, and I'm sorry I let you down." He paused, then added, "The police will probably be in touch with you again, but Sandra's accomplice has been arrested."

My body jolted as Eden gasped, "What?"

"Mary was up half the night doing some digging. She feels responsible for not recognizing what Sandra was planning. We both do. Anyway, she found Sandra's phone and went through it before we turned it over for evidence this morning. There was a...a boyfriend, I suppose. A man she was involved with. He confessed to letting the air out of your tires, Eden, because they believed the car was Milo's—something about a parking spot everyone knew was his?"

"Fucking hell," I muttered, and Eden shot me a warning look.

"He also confessed to throwing the brick through that window," Isaiah went on.

"Oh, what a relief. I was afraid she'd made Eve do it," Eden whispered.

He gave a soft laugh. "Eve would no more hurl a brick through a window than she would set that store on fire. She reminds me so much of you, Eden. Fierce and determined and full of love. She's been asking about you."

Eden's lips curved upward. "She has? Is she okay?"

"She's fine. Asking when we can come out to see you, so she can be properly introduced. Eden, I'm so sorry. The wedding, Eve's birth. I wanted to tell you, but Dad—"

"It's okay," Eden said, and miraculously, it was clear that she meant it. "It's okay. I'd just really like to get to know her. And you."

"We'd like that, too. This was our fault, all that happened to you."

Eden started shaking her head even before he finished speaking. "No, it's not."

"Eve used to spend an evening each week with Sandra," Isaiah said quietly. "They'd have dinner together, that kind of thing, while we went out on a date. Eventually, as Eve got older, she wanted to be with her friends instead. They started playing Dungeons & Dragons and when Sandra found out that's why Eve wasn't spending time with her, she lost it. I should have realized it was going to lead to something like this."

"You didn't know," Eden insisted. "And if you had known, you would've stepped in. This isn't your fault."

"I think it will take some time before I'm able to accept that."

"You'll get there. I didn't get you back in my life just to lose you because you're feeling guilty over something out of your control."

"You've grown wise," Isaiah said, his voice teasing in a gentle sort of way. "I can't wait for Eve to get to know you, Eden. She needs another strong woman in her life."

I stroked her hair as she and her brother discussed plans for a visit once the weather improved, listened as a piece of her heart clicked back into place, and wondered—not for the first time since meeting Eden at Comic Con—about the hand of fate in everything that had happened.

By the time the siblings hung up, Eden was glowing, though she blinked back a sheen of tears as she dropped her head to the cushion behind her.

"You doing okay?" I asked, brushing my thumb over her knuckles.

"Definitely, but what do you say to a normal couple of weeks? Maybe we should take up knitting or cribbage or something."

I snorted a laugh. "Normal is overrated, but I wouldn't turn down some rest and relaxation with my girl."

Her eyes twinkled at me. "Your girl, huh?"

"My rockabilly goddess," I growled, catching her at the waist and rubbing her neck with my beard. "My temptation and my paradise."

She sighed and wound her arms around my shoulders. "Rest and relaxation sounds perfect."

"Doesn't it? What do you say we go relax in the bedroom until it's time to head to my parents' house?"

"I think I could be convinced."

Before releasing her, I dropped my head and kissed her, savoring the sweetness of frosting still gracing her lips. Whatever residual soreness plagued her muscles after that fall last night seemed to melt away under the power of that kiss, and when I cupped her ass with my hands, I was startled when she hopped up without flinching, wrapping her legs around my waist.

"Paradise," I whispered against her mouth.

From the contented sigh that slipped from her lips, I knew she agreed.

WHEN WE GOT TO my parents' house that evening, my mom immediately sent us both out of the kitchen to relax on the couch. Eden, wearing soft black pants and that blouse with the floppy bow at the neckline, the pink daisy clipped into her hair, nestled into my side like she was meant to be there.

And she absolutely was.

Carter joined us and, for the first time since Eden's escapade yesterday, she laughed outright when he slipped us each a cookie he'd tucked into his sleeve.

"Now, that is my favorite kind of magician," she told him.

Carter grinned. "Uncle Milo got me a magic kit for my birthday one year. He helped me learn all the tricks."

"You've got a couple pretty cool uncles, I guess."

"And aunts," Carter added.

I watched a soft smile bloom across Eden's face at that. "I've never had a nephew before, so you'll have to let me know if I'm doing okay."

"I will. But you know, I still don't have any cousins," Carter said.

It sounded offhand, but I caught the sidelong glance he sent me. "Nope, no cousins yet," I replied, widening my eyes at him over Eden's head.

"Sure wish I had some," he mused. "Cousins, I mean."

"When my brother comes to visit this spring, you can meet my niece, Eve," Eden offered. "You guys are kind of like cousins."

Carter hummed, sounding impressively dejected despite the impish light in his gray eyes. "I really wish I had some baby cousins, though."

Eden looked first to him, assessing his attempt at innocence, then to me, eyebrows raised. "Babies, huh?"

"Yeah," he sighed. "I love babies."

"Is this some kind of ambush?" she asked.

"No!" I protested.

"Yes!"

I dropped my head to the back of the couch with a groan as Carter's shouted affirmative drowned out my response, but Eden burst out laughing. For a second, we both watched her, Carter looking both relieved and hopeful—the exact combination of emotions tangling in my chest. That full-throated laughter was too much for us to resist, however, so we both ended up laughing alongside her.

Eden slumped against my chest, still giggling, when my mom poked her head into the room. The smile that moved across her face was so sweet it made my chest ache, but she lifted a finger to her lips so as to not interrupt the moment.

When Eden finally caught her breath, she tipped her head to look up at me, the joy still dancing in her eyes. I couldn't help myself—I leaned down to kiss her, ignoring Carter's exaggerated gagging sounds from the other end of the couch.

"Consider the subject under advisement, kid," Eden said.

"Don't encourage him."

She cupped my cheek in her hand, ruffling her thumb through my beard. "I love you."

I nuzzled her jaw and murmured, "I love you back."

Out of the corner of my eye, I saw Carter sneaking back into the kitchen, so I kissed her more thoroughly while I had the chance. We were still locked together when Maverick came in to announce it was time for dinner, heaving his own disgusted groan.

"Is this what life is going to be like now? Couples making out all around me?"

"Yes," Eden said primly.

I threw back my head and laughed, tucking her against my chest. "What the lady wants, the lady gets."

Maverick just shook his head as he turned toward the dining room and muttered, "Welcome to the family."

Also by

Rachel Fitzjames

Keep in touch! Sign up for Rachel's newsletter at https://rac helfitzjames.com/ for FREE bonus content, sneak peeks, sales, and news about upcoming releases!

Spruce Hill Series

Unpacking Secrets

A Lonely Road

Canvas of Lies

Crumbling Truth

Playing for Paradise

Sinister Returns

Treasured Legacy

Lucky Save

Wrenching Hearts

Flash of Danger

Acknowledgements

First, to anyone in WNY who knows enough about the local comic cons to spot the inconsistencies in this book—thank you for overlooking my fast-and-loose details regarding the time of year and venue in order for Milo and Eden to meet. Sometimes, creative license is necessary!

To my husband and kids for answering every DND-related question I had, for coming up with comic book heroes and nerdy sayings, and for inserting Jiji into this book, you guys are the best. I took this idea and ran with it, but you guys are the ones who made it actually work out in the end.

Melissa Rotert—as always—thank you, I love you, and I'm sorry for making you edit the smuttier parts of the series. Without you, none of these books would exist, and even the ones that might have eventually seen the light of day would be in much crappier shape without your eyes on them. Your sacrifices do not go unnoticed, and I definitely owe you a margarita after this one. And the next...and...

My trusty CPs, Christie Curry, Briana Newstead, and Christina Brennan, thank you for always being there to bounce ideas off of, even during my fastest of fast-drafting periods.

Tobie Carter, Lindsay Barrett, Sia Williams, Tara Ryan, Christina Brennan, and Anne Knight—you guys honed this book in so many ways and I am eternally grateful for your insights! And to each one of you who asked when Maverick is getting a book, well...you'll just have to wait for the final book of the series!

About the author

Rachel Fitzjames is the author of a contemporary romantic suspense series set in the fictional town of Spruce Hill, NY. She started writing on her brother's ancient computer back in the early 90s and never looked back, though her first short story about an underground cat thievery ring was sadly lost. With a degree in geography inspired by wanderlust, Rachel has a keen appreciation for the escape that the romance genre allows. She is a lifelong resident of Western NY and created Spruce Hill in order to give a little bit of home to all of her characters.

Connect with Rachel at https://rachelfitzjames.com/ or on Instagram/Threads at @rachelfitzjames.